SOMETHING MORE

SOMETHING MORE

BY JILLIAN SZWEDA

SOMETHING MORE

This is a work of fiction. All of the characters, names, incidents, organizations, and dialogue in this novel are either the products of the author's imagination or are used fictitiously.

iUniverse books may be ordered through booksellers or by contacting:

iUniverse
1663 Liberty Drive
Bloomington, IN 47403
www.iuniverse.com
1-800-Authors (1-800-288-4677)

Because of the dynamic nature of the Internet, any web addresses or links contained in this book may have changed since publication and may no longer be valid. The views expressed in this work are solely those of the author and do not necessarily reflect the views of the publisher, and the publisher hereby disclaims any responsibility for them.

Any people depicted in stock imagery provided by Thinkstock are models, and such images are being used for illustrative purposes only. Certain stock imagery © Thinkstock.

ISBN: 978-1-5320-2767-3 (sc)
ISBN: 978-1-5320-2766-6 (e)

Library of Congress Control Number: 2017912334

Print information available on the last page.

iUniverse rev. date: 08/01/2018

Acknowledgements

This story is a culmination of inspiration from so many people, places, songs, movies, and books. Above all else, it is inspired by real-life accounts of children of addicted parents and survivors of sexual assult, in all degrees. I'd like to thank all those who suffer with the consequences in the form of depression, anxiety, and suicidal thoughts who were brave enough to tell their story. Hearing your story helped so many not only survive, but to thrive. Without their courage I would not have been able to properly tell Alex's story.

Many thanks to my friends who encouraged me to write and publish this story. It's not near enough to repay you for all you have done for me. Even as I write this, mere thanks seems inadequate. Olivia, Alli, Katy, Reagan, and Hannah – how do I sum up our friendship with just a few sentences? Olivia, we've been best friends since we were little. There are so many times you helped me. I hope I can bring a fraction of joy to your life that you have brought to mine. You could tackle and conquer the world with your eyes closed if you wanted to. Reagan, you are truly one of the best people the world has been blessed with. Your kindness, generosity, and humor will go on to change countless lives the same way it has changed mine. I love you all, thank you for being my best friends.

I would be absolutely nothing in life if not for my family. Mom, I love you beyond words. You have been my #1 fan since the day I was born. I couldn't ask for a better role model. From instilling in me such good taste in music to wiping away the tears some stupid boy caused…you've been right there. Thank you for helping me turn my dream into a plan. But most of all, thank you for your gift of unconditional love. Craig, thank you for stepping into that role and for being our rock. You have been a parent to me in every way that counts. Joe, thank you for always making me laugh and for being the best brother a girl could ask for. Rachel, thank you for your sisterly love. You have encouraged me to put aside my doubts and publish this despite everything. Grandma Charlotte, thank you for never ceasing to laugh at my jokes and instilling principles of never-ending love and spunk into me. To Grandpa Jim, Grandma Jan and my extended family – Uncle Jimmy, Aunt Dee, Aunt Kristi, Uncle Neil, and all my weird and funny cousins Heather, Kyle, Kaydence, Josh, Jake, Max, Maddie, Luna and Lucy…you all mean so much to me. Your steadfast love and support has given me the light, love, and laughter that I drew upon for inspiration in this book and in my life. Thank you.

To A.D. – I'm so grateful that you were my makeshift editor, even though I kinda forced that role upon you. Nevertheless, you have stayed my friend through every possible sign that you should run the other direction. You made me believe in myself enough to bring this story to life. You were instrumental in bringing this story into the hands and hearts of others. No matter what life brings I will never ever forget that.

Thanks to iUniverse Publishing for helping me every step of the way. From writing to editing and marketing your personalized attention was amazing. I couldn't ask for more.

Finally, I'd like to thank my hometown community. This book would not have been possible without the support of my school and community. Thanks to the teachers, students, friends, and neighbors who helped me raise funds to publish and market this book. A shout-out to those two brave teachers, Mr. NcNeeley and Mr. Buss who got "stuck for a buck". A special thanks to Kara Kaser who fostered my love of books into something deeper. I will always remember and give back to the LOL club. My little town may be small but we are strong. Time and time again I have seen what it means when one of us needs help and we all come together. The experience of growing up here has given me a compass for what is right and good in this world. Thank you JGSC family.

For reasons far too personal to mention here, I can't express all my feelings for my father, so I will just say thank you.

As I journey through life, my hope is that I will always have the courage to do two things: pursue my dreams and be someone who helps others pursue theirs. If I can do that, I will already be a success.

For Mom

after

This world will surprise you more than you expect. People you trust will betray you. People you love will abandon you. You will endure pain until hurt is all you can see, until you think you can't survive another day. You live.

I thought I had more time.

Above all else, there is warmth. It is to the point where sweat beads begin forming on my temples and in my knee pits, but I am not uncomfortable. I flex my fingers and feel nothing. My senses come back to me one by one. I open my eyes, and there is darkness. I should feel claustrophobic with the darkness and heat, but I don't. In real life, I would panic and hyperventilate. But, here, as soon as those thoughts start creeping in, an overwhelming tranquility washes over me. It reminds me of morphine, almost.

There is a rhythmic noise vibrating where I lay in this cocoon, like a heartbeat. It does not come from within me. Inside my own body, I feel no heartbeat.

I start thinking about where I am, and wonder if this is death. I don't remember how I got here. Maybe this is just a screwed up dream, and in a few minutes my mother will wake me for breakfast.

Did I have a mother?

The pain starts in my toenails, as tingling. It resembles the feeling of when your foot falls asleep. Before I realize it, the burn snakes its way up my legs and into my intestines and up my esophagus and through my skull. I am bending, breaking, trying to get this poison out of my naked body. My blood boils; my bones screech; I scream and scream and scream. No one ever comes to my rescue. My body itself is buzzing like a bee. I don't know how long it all lasts. I don't know if time exists in hell.

Choking. Choking. I am choking.

I cough everything up, trying to clear my lungs. I roll over onto my stomach and retch until nothing is blocking my airway any longer. I curl up into the fetal position and dig my dirty fingernails into the ground beneath me. Sand.

Slowly, I look around. The sky is overcast and fierce wind blows around me. The air smells like a thunderstorm. Waves are crashing four feet away from me, and wet sand is beneath me. Dirty seashells dig into my hips. I am no longer naked; a tattered T-shirt and wet jeans cling to my wet body. A big wave comes onto the sand, soaking the tips of my toes again. I scoot away from the water and reach up to feel my wet, tangled hair.

The memory hits me like a boulder. I used to have long, beautiful hair that almost reached my waist. When I close my eyes, I can hear the *snip* of the sharp scissors and see the long locks hitting the floor. My hair now rests sadly at my shoulders. I don't know why I cut it.

New sounds come from the weathered cliffs surrounding the small beach above me. My eyes snap to their attention, but they don't notice me. Two men dressed in police uniforms are walking toward the edge, and I notice caution tape set up around where they're walking. At least a dozen cop cars' lights are flickering in the distance, stationed in the small parking lot a few yards away. Past that is only forestation, and it looks so foreboding that it sends a chill down my spine.

The officers still don't notice me, but I can hear bits of them talking despite their distance from me.

I hear, "Sinclair—" I strain to hear more, but it's getting harder to focus. *Sinclair.* Darkness takes over once more.

My eyes bolt open and I take in a sharp breath of air as I sit upright from my slumber. A completely different setting surrounds me, and I'm no longer drenched from the ocean. A slight breeze blows, allowing the meadow's flowers to breathe. The wildflowers reach up to my knees and I can't help but smile at the familiarity of it all. It is dusk, and I should be completely confused, but I'm not. I know exactly where I am. I'm home.

There's flat ground to east for as far as I can see, and a sloping hill toward the west and the setting sun. Surrounding the meadow is a dense forest, but this one doesn't scare me. I know this place like the back of my hand, and nothing's changed. I turn around in a full circle, smiling in disbelief. Tears form in the corners of my eyes, and slowly I return to face the sun again.

He stands in view of the sunset. Streaks of light peak underneath his armpits and around his head, creating an angelic halo of light. How ironic. I don't remember anything else, but I know that face instantly.

"Daniel," I whisper, and it's the first time I've heard my voice since I woke up. The name feels so familiar, yet so strange escaping my lips.

Daniel smiles and walks toward me, closing the distance between us. He cups my cheek, and his hands are so warm that I feel it flood through the rest of my body. I close my eyes and sag with relief at his touch, then immediately open them back up to make sure he's still here. He is. Daniel's smirk grows in the face-splitting, dimpled grin that I fell in love with. Instinctively, I grin back.

He leans in close, his hand still on my cheek, and I feel his lips against my ear. His breath tickles my neck and makes the hair on my arms stand up. When he speaks, the tone doesn't match up with the kind expression I saw just a few seconds earlier. His voice is frantic, rushes, almost scared.

"You need to remember, Alex. *Remember.*"

I open my eyes. He's gone.

Alex—my name. Alexandria. Alexandria Sinclair. I'm 18 years old. I am dead. This is death.

I remember my parents. They were like night and day; my mother had long, thin hair and dark eyes. My father had thick, blonde hair and baby blue eyes. My brother inherited our mother's beauty. I looked too much like my father, with my crooked nose and bright eyes.

My brother. Luke. *Luke.* My best friend. Carlie.

Daniel.

before

Six Years Old – Summer

We'd been going to the meadow ever since I was a small baby. It was close enough to my house that Luke and I could walk to it by ourselves and play around for hours. We lived in a safe neighborhood, a tight-knit community, so my mother always trusted us to be home for dinner. We always were.

Dad packed a picnic for us. This was his absolute favorite place. While we eat, Mom tells us the story of how he took her here for their first date and wooed her with his knowledge of astronomy. Mom was a big scrap-booker, so she was constantly taking pictures of everything. They give Luke and I sticky popsicles that coat our lips and run down our forearms. I smiled a big, toothless grin as Mom snapped another picture.

We stay after it grows dark and lay on a quilt as a family, staring up at the stars. Luke was younger than me, so he fell asleep on Mom's chest, but I stayed awake. Dad wooed me with his knowledge of astronomy. The stars blinked and winked at us. It was the happiest memory I can recall.

before

Seven Years Old – Summer

A thunderstorm rages outside, waking me in the middle of the night. My bedroom is pitch black, but slowly my eyes adjust to the darkness. Every so often, the room is illuminated by a flash of lightning and a crackle of thunder. I pull my covers up around my chin, already beginning to quiver with fear. The chair in the corner of my room covered with toys and dolls is shapeshifting into something sinister, and before long, I can't stand it any longer.

My small feet frantically search for the floor from my high white bed, making sure to grab the safety blanket I was clutching before making my escape. I run down the hallway and staircase as fast as I can, my bare feet pattering against the carpet and then hardwood. Above the thunder, I hear soft music creeping from our living room. As I round the corner, I see my parents standing in the middle of the room pressed against each other. Mom's arm is around Dad's shoulders, and their hands are interlocked. They're slow dancing.

"Mommy," my frail voice squeaks out. Her head raises gracefully from Dad's shoulder and her eyes meet mine. They stop dancing, but their hands stay interlocked. "I'm scared."

"You're scared?" Mom replies and smiles at me.

"What are you scared of?" Dad asks, not unkindly.

"There's a monster in my room."

"A *monster?*" Mom questions incredulously. She lets go of Dad's hand and walks toward me, replacing his hand with mine. "Well, let's go check it out."

As she opens my bedroom door, I hover around the threshold. She switches on my bedside table lamp; shadows fall across my room from the sole bulb and lampshade. Then, she bends over to check under my bed, moving my comforter up with a flourish.

"All clear. The bed is safe." I run from the doorway and climb up to my bed. I pile the blankets on top of myself while she crosses my floor to check in my closet. Again, she slides my closet doors against the wall with a flourish, and scoots the clothes hanging apart.

"Closet is clear." She moves onto the chair covered in toys and an assortment of clothes in the corner of my room that was scaring me the most. Quickly and mechanically, like any mother, she grabs the toys and puts them in the toy box next to the chair. She hangs up the few shirts that were sitting there, then comes to sit by me on my bed.

"Wait," I say as she reaches toward my lamp. "It's too dark."

Mom sighs, then reaches into my bedside table's first drawer, pulling out a night light I used when I was younger. There's a plug in the far corner of my room, where she plugs it in and shuts off my light. "Better?"

"I guess."

"Good," she sits next to me again and pulls the covers tight up to my chin. "Now, try to go to sleep."

"Mom?"

"Yeah, honey?"

"How come you and Daddy were dancing?"

7

She smiles. "Because that was our song."

"What does that mean? 'Your song'?"

"That means that the song has special meaning to us. It was playing when we met for the very first time."

"Will I have a 'song'?"

"Maybe with someone really special when you're older. Then, you'll always dance with them."

"I'm not a very good dancer."

She smiles. "Neither is Dad." I laugh quietly. "Try to get some sleep, Ally. I love you."

after

Of all things to remember, I remember the perfume my mother wore. Or, rather, the way she smelled. It came in this little bottle with flowers fastened to the cap. As a child, I was fascinated by this. She told me she'd used it her entire life. Even when she didn't spritz it onto her wrists, or behind her ears, she smelled like those perfume flowers. I was thoroughly convinced that she'd used it for so long that it had fermented itself into her skin permanently.

My point is, the strangest things in our lives are the most necessary comforts. We don't realize how badly we need them until we can't have them.

before

Nine Years Old – Winter

Only a few days after my ninth birthday, our distant
grandmother on my father's side passed away. After their youngest
child moved out, before I was born, my grandparents divorced and
my grandmother moved down south, toward her family and away
from ours. Dad only occasionally spoke to her, and I had only met
her once during one of our summer trips to the coast where she
met us halfway. Nevertheless, Dad drove down there a few days
before the funeral to make the arrangements.

Her death didn't have any large impact on my life, only because
I never knew her very well. She was a small woman, the kind of
grandmother who always had four-year-old butterscotches in the
bottom of her purse. It was common knowledge that Dad and
his siblings were abused during their childhoods, and I'd heard
snippets of things before like, "He still blames her." And, "He
didn't want anything to do with his family." But I neither knew nor
cared about any of that at my age. We had our little family, and I
had my school friends, and that was enough for me.

The day he left to go help prepare funeral arrangements, after
Luke and I had hugged him and said our goodbyes, Mom stood

next to his running car talking to him through the rolled down window. As we sat on the porch shivering in our winter boots waiting for her, we tried not to eavesdrop, but it was impossible to resist. Mom's eyebrows were furrowed together, and she looked angry. We couldn't hear anything Dad said.

"We can hire a babysitter..." Mom started, but he interrupted her with muffled words. "You shouldn't have to go alone, Charlie..." Another response we couldn't make out. "I don't feel comfortable letting you..."

"I'll be *fine*, Renee!" We finally heard Dad explode. Luke and I shared a worried look. There was more shouting, but we didn't bother to listen to their words. Our parents had never shouted at each other before – not in front of us. Just seconds after the mutual shouting began, Dad screeched out of our driveway and Mom stood there with her arms crossed, scowling after his truck.

Mom turned around and smiled at us, but her reaction was far too delayed to ever be legitimate. Luke, being younger than I am, shrugged it off and let it go, but somehow I knew better. She made us hot chocolate, and she put on a good show, but I watched her face when she thought we weren't paying attention to her. She looked sad.

Three days later, Mom drove us down the coast to the funeral. I was wearing a black dress, and somehow Mom wrangled Luke into a shirt and tie. As we drove, I watched the ocean waves crash against each other with the howling wind. The sky looked sad and the water looked angry.

Dad met us at the funeral home with dark circles under his eyes and a wrinkled dress shirt. Mom's anger toward him had been culminating in the few days he'd been gone, and reached a boiling point somewhere along the way. But when she laid her eyes on him, all the anger she'd pent up dissipates. She got out of the car, leaving us. When she reached him, he opened his mouth to say something, but she stopped him. Straightening his crooked tie, I heard her sniffling from inside the car. Then, slowly, they both began crying. It's the first time I'd ever seen my father shed a tear.

"Ally," Luke whispered to me and grabbed my hand. "Dad's crying." I watched them wrap their arms around each other; I watched my mother hold this crumbling man.

I didn't say anything to Luke, but I didn't let go of his hand, either. Eventually Mom pulled back from him to tell him something we couldn't hear, and he nodded and visibly pulled himself together. They walked toward the car, hand-in-hand, and I jumped out before they reach us to hug my father.

He knelt down to my height and wiped a tear off my cheek with his thumb. "Why the long face?"

I didn't say anything, but he grabbed me and lifted me up to carry. Burying my head in his neck, we walked over to the car and he opened the door for Luke to get out. Mom took a hold of his hand and we walked in to the funeral home together.

The funeral itself was filled with dozens of mourning old people I'd never met before. They shook my father's hand and told them how sorry they were for his loss. On the other side of the room were my aunts and uncles; Dad made it blatantly obvious he didn't want anything to do with them, even at my grandmother's funeral. My grandfather, her ex-husband, my dad's father, never showed.

after

My eyes shoot open, and air fills my lungs too quickly. I roll over onto my stomach and cough so hard that my body convulses. I can't breathe. I can't breathe. Saltwater trickles past my lips and something stuck in my throat dislodges. Water fills my nostrils. I'm choking on my own breath.

The ocean swallows me whole and doesn't spit me back out.

Every memory hits me so hard that I relive it, rather than watch it happen.

before

Ten Years Old – Summer

The air crackles with humidity that only breaks as the scorching sun begins to set. Mom douses Luke and me with bug spray, and tells us to stay in the backyard since it's getting dark. Our neighborhood friends have already gone back to their respective homes and backyards.

Luke is building a fort of blankets and large sticks. I'm lying down in the grass a few feet away, hands behind my head and ankles crossed, staring up at the sky as it changes colors. Stars begin peeking out from the veil of orange and blue. The moon is full and on the rise. Soon I'll be able to see the constellations.

Halfway through Luke's construction, as it begins to get really dark, we see Dad's truck headlights pulling into the driveway. Mom is cooking dinner and hasn't called us in yet, so we both stay put. After a few more minutes, when she still hasn't called for us, I let Luke stay outside while I go in.

As I approach, I hear angry voices, and I don't let the back screen door swing shut loudly like I normally do. They're yelling at each other around the kitchen table. They don't hear or see me as I creep closer around the corner to listen better.

"Are you *kidding* me, Charlie?" Mom yells. "This is the last thing we needed right now. We can barely afford to keep food on the table. We're going to have to take out a damn second mortgage!"

"Would you keep your voice down? The kids are going to hear you." He sounds significantly less concerned than she does.

"Yeah, so what! I'll have to tell them I won't be able to buy them new school supplies anyway. I can't believe you lost your job."

"I already feel terrible enough about it. You don't need to make me feel worse!" He yells back.

Frightened and angry, I retreat back outside and slump down on the last step of the back porch. Inside, their voices reach a new crescendo, but I don't focus on what they're saying anymore. Luke stops what he's doing in the middle of the yard and comes to sit next to me.

"What are they doing?" He asks quietly.

"Fighting."

"Why?"

"How am I supposed to know, Luke?" I snap at him. The screaming match continues. I flinch as the front door slams.

The inside of the house is silent. Luke and I share a look. After a few minutes, we walk in the house together quietly. I'm in front and still taller than him, so I'm the first to see Mom hunched over the table, crying into her hands. I freeze in my spot behind the corner, unknowingly shielding Luke from seeing. He pinches my arm to see around me, and I snap out of my reverie and whip around to yell at him, startling Mom. She pulls herself together and wipes the running mascara from under her eyes. Luke stands by my side, as shell-shocked as I am by the sight of our mother crying.

"Hey, guys," she sniffles and wipes her hands on her jeans before going over to the stove. "Dinner's ready, if you're hungry." She sets plates out for us and leaves, climbing the stairs up to her bedroom and closing the door.

"Ally," Luke says after a few seconds of us staying in the same spot.

"Yeah?"

"Does this mean we get to watch TV while we eat dinner?"

Luke and I eat silently on the couch as we watch our TV show. Dad still hasn't come back home, and Mom still hasn't come out of her bedroom. Luke is a messy eater; I have to tell him repeatedly to keep his head over his plate.

"Ally," Luke starts. "Does this mean Mom and Dad are getting a divorce?"

"No, Luke. They're not getting a divorce."

He continues noisily eating. "What were they fighting about?"

"Money, I think." I pause. "I think Dad lost his job."

Luke is quiet for a few seconds. "How come he always leaves the house when they fight?"

"I don't know. Maybe he doesn't want to say something he'll regret."

"Adults are weird." And that's the last of our conversation.

before

Ten Years Old – Fall

It is the week before Halloween, my favorite holiday. Boys are starting to become slightly less icky and my love for the sky is ever-growing. That morning, my family had taken a long-awaited trip to the pumpkin patch. I pick out the biggest possible pumpkin, and Mom and Dad help carry Luke's. He's only eight.

"Which princess do you want to be this year, Ally?" Mom asks from the passenger seat of the car, craning her neck to look at me.

"I don't want to be a princess. I want to be an astronaut." I saw Dad looking at me through the rearview mirror. When I make eye contact, he looks back at the road.

"An astronaut? Why do you want to be an astronaut?"

I'm perplexed by her question. "Why not?"

Mom waits a few beats before she responds, wearing a funny expression. "How about being a princess instead?"

I start to grow frustrated. "I don't want to be a princess. I want to be an astronaut."

"Ally, don't be difficult." Mom says in her adult-voice, and I know I'll be in trouble if I continue arguing, but her comments infuriate me. *What's wrong with being an astronaut?*

Dad pipes up cautiously. "Renee, she wants to be an astronaut. Let her be an astronaut."

Mom scoffs. "Right, of course. Let *me* be the bad guy."

Dad stays silent.

I look over at Luke, and he has his nose shoved in the iPad. My gaze fades over, out the window. I stare at the red, orange, and gold leaves blurring together as we drive past. In the front seat, Dad reaches toward Mom's hand on the middle compartment. She pulls away and crosses her arms and legs. I look back out the window, ignoring it. The sound of the car's motor lulls me to sleep.

Halloween night, the princess dress is too tight and itchy, and I tell my mother so, but she only yells at me. Realistically, I'm being more difficult than usual because I didn't want to be a princess in the first place. Dad peaks his head into my bedroom, where Mom is making adjustments to the dress, trying to make it more comfortable for me.

"How do you like it, Ally?" He asks innocently.

"I hate it." I respond, sulking.

Dad grins at my bemusement. "I think you look beautiful. You make a wonderful princess."

"I would've made an even better astronaut."

"Alexandria, quit being such a brat. All I do is provide for you and baby you and I get no goddamn appreciation." Mom snaps loudly, abruptly standing. Effectively scolded, my eyes widen as I watch her leave the room. "I'm the only goddamn adult in this house!"

"Renee..." Dad tries to say as she shoves past him, but to no avail. He walks after her without looking at me.

Mom's outburst toward me has soured my mood even more, and I'm depressed as I carefully adjust my costume in a fruitless attempt to make it more comfortable. I walk over to the full-length mirror leaning against my bedroom wall. Mom put my hair in curlers the night before, something she usually never does. She applied a little blush to my cheeks. I look girly, and I hate it. Desperately, I want to change into shorts and a tank top, rub the blush off, and put my hair in a ponytail, but I know that will only get me in more trouble and I don't want to miss out on the Halloween candy.

After I think the dust has settled, I slowly make my way downstairs for dinner. I hear rustling around in the dining room as Mom sets the table. Stealthily, I peak my head around the corner to watch her. I see Dad walk over to Mom and put his hand on her arm. She pulls away, almost flinching at his touch. They share a silent look, and I realize that I'm witnessing the first time my parents have ever looked at each other and not loved who they saw.

It's nighttime. The street is alit with porch lights and the sound of children's laughter. I can practically smell the sugary sweet candy in the air. Luke and I run down the street, our parents walking along behind us. Every once in a while, they stop and catch up with other parents or coworkers, and we share awkward glances with these strangers' children.

I spot my best friend, Carlie, dressed as a green fairy and shout her name. She turns toward me and grins, then tugs on her mother's coat to get her attention. Mom talks with Carlie's mom, and Dad talks with Carlie's dad. Carlie is an only child, so Luke twiddles his thumbs, waiting for the conversation to be done with.

We stand in a circle, discussing costumes and candy collection. After a few minutes, we're itching to get back to trick-or-treating. The adults say their goodbyes.

"Alex, we're going back to the car for a few minutes," Mom announces to me. "Stay with your brother until we get back. If anything happens, come to the car."

I nod and take Luke's hand as they walk away from us. House to house, we go together and collect our candy, putting on our Nice and Polite faces, bearing through a few pinches to our cheeks. After about ten minutes of this, we start to grow anxious as to where our parents were. Surely, they'd never leave us. Perhaps something happened to them…? No, that's ridiculous. Bad things like that don't happen in towns like these. Only on television.

"Ally, where are they?" Luke asks me. He just lost his front tooth, so he looks like a silly cartoon.

"They're at the car, Luke," I scold in a condescending tone. He immediately quiets.

As we're walking along a crooked sidewalk, skipping to avoid the cracks, I hear Luke crash, a loud *crunch* sounding behind me. He had tripped on one of the uneven patches of concrete, falling face forward onto the sidewalk. Blood gushes from his nose as he wails and wails. Quickly, the whole upper half of his costume is covered in blood, as are his hands and face. I pick him up and start running towards the direction of where we parked the car, totally abandoning our candy buckets.

Carrying my baby brother whilst he is bleeding profusely, all over himself and me, is not an easy task. I see the car in the distance, and I see Mom and Dad. Mom is still sitting half-way in the car, with the door open. Dad is standing in front of her with his head bent. I see them in a tense conversation, and I'm confused. *Why are they fighting?* I don't have time to worry about that now.

"Mom!" I shout. Her attention snaps to me, her eyes widening. She pushes past Dad and runs to me. As soon as Dad turns around with a scowl on his face and sees me, the scowl disappears and he starts running too.

"What happened?" She asks in a frenzy, taking Luke from my arms and rushing to the car.

"I don't know, we were just walking along the sidewalk and I guess he tripped and fell." All the words were coming out in a rush and I start crying, just because I'm young and overwhelmed and that's what children do.

Mom rushes into the passenger seat and Dad starts the car, with barely enough time for me to get in the back seat. We speed away towards Quincy Jones Medical Hospital.

I sit in the waiting room, like the good little girl that I was. Mom is with Luke and the other doctors; Dad's gone home to get me a change of clothes. I do everything I can to keep myself busy, keep myself from worrying about my brother, keep myself from wondering why my parents were engaged in an argument that looked more serious than the others when I found them. Eventually, my princess costume becomes too much to handle and I find a bathroom to destroy it.

Staring at myself in the mirror, I see that my cheeks are stiff from dried tears, and there is still blood on the front of my formerly pink dress, staining it a gross-looking brown. I look down at my white knuckles and tried to pray that Luke was okay. In a bout of rage, I rip off the itchy sleeves on each side and tear at the hem of the tulle skirt away until it reaches my previously-scabbed knees. I run my fingers through my tangled hair, pushing it behind my ears. Turning on the faucet at ice cold, I splash the cool water over my hot face. I throw the pink scraps of material in the trash as I exit the bathroom.

Blood is still smudged on my neck and my hair is still a mess, but I feel slightly better having destroyed something. Feeling satisfied, I plop back into the waiting room chairs and wait.

A few minutes later, a boy enters and sits across from me, around my age. He isn't wearing a costume, or the tattered remains of one, like I am. I frown, wondering why, but quickly look away.

21

Despite sitting in the waiting room of an E.R., he looks eerily at home. Maybe he isn't closely related to anyone here. After getting a quick look at him, it's all I can do not to stare. He has floppy, dark hair that gets in his eyes. *Doesn't that bother him – the way his hair is always in his face like that?* He looks utterly bored as his dazzling blue eyes sweep across the entirety of the room, inevitably landing on me. Embarrassed and having just been caught staring, I look back down at my hands.

"Nice costume," he says. I look around the room; we're the only ones in here. I look back up at him through my eyelashes and see that he's got a smirk on his face. He's making fun of me.

I ignore him.

"Whose blood is it?"

I stare back up at him, wondering why he's talking to me. "My brother's."

"Ah," he says, then looks back around the room. "How old is he?"

"Why are you talking to me?" I snap.

"Do you see anyone else to talk to?"

I look back down and grit my teeth. "Eight. He's eight."

The boy is quiet for a few minutes, then digs through the front pocket of his dark jeans. After a few seconds of rummaging, he holds out something across the aisle to me. I look at his hand but don't take what he's offering me.

"For your brother," he explains. In his hand is a brand new, wrapped, cherry sucker. "I'm sure he'll be mad about all the candy he's missing out on tonight."

Staring up at him with wide eyes, I still don't take the sucker. I hear the automatic doors open down the hallway. *This boy doesn't even know me.*

"Why do you care?" I ask quietly. He opens his mouth to speak, but someone steps in front of my view. I look up and see

Dad standing there, his eyebrows knit together. There are wrinkles etched in his face from worry.

"Let's go see your mom and brother." He grabs my hand and pulls me up.

As we walk together towards the elevator, I look over my shoulder at the boy, who is now staring at the floor. I squeeze my fingers tightly around the cherry sucker and face forward.

"Well, the worst of it is that Luke broke his nose. He'll have some scary-looking bruises for the next couple weeks." Luke's doctor says in a soothing voice, trying to calm my mother. I hold tightly to Dad's hand as I take in the bruises on my brother's face. One of his eyes have swelled shut. Despite his nose being totally covered in gauze, I can see purple and yellow bruises sticking out.

"I wouldn't worry too much, Mrs. Sinclair. He'll be all better in good time. In the meantime, I want you to come back in a few days so I can look it over once more," he looks at Luke, whose eyelids are drooping. "You're going to have one impressive scar when this is all healed up."

That perks Luke up instantly, and he gives the doctor a huge grin. I smile and let go of Dad's hand. He puts his arm around Mom, and she doesn't shrug it away this time. That only makes me smile more.

In a few minutes, Luke is discharged with pain pills and an order to not fall asleep for the next 24 hours in case of a concussion. When we walk back through the waiting room towards the exit, Sucker Boy is gone.

"Stay awake," I snap in front of Luke's face, and he perks up instantly, then groans and closes his eyes. "Mom, can I hit him?"

"No," she calls from the kitchen.

23

I sigh and keep clapping in front of his face. Finally, his eyes open and he stares at me with clear disdain. "I *am* awake, dipstick."

"Don't call your sister a dipstick, Luke."

"Yeah, don't call your sister a dipstick, Luke." I repeat in a high falsetto and he sticks his tongue out at me.

I laugh and run up the stairs to my bedroom. In the hallway, I pass the bathroom Luke and I share, stopping in my tracks. Dad's in there, rummaging around in our medicine cabinet. I see him pull out the prescription bottle, filled with Luke's pain medication. He sets down the beer bottle that was in his hand as he tries to open the cap.

"Dad?" I query. He startles at my voice, nearly dropping the pill bottle. "Those are Luke's."

"What?" He asks, distracted. He looks sweaty and tired. "Oh, yeah. Luke. I know – I was getting these for him." Dad smiles, but I don't smile back. He shakes a few pills out, then puts the bottle back. Grabbing the beer bottle and kissing my head on his way out, he leaves. I don't move from my spot, expecting him to go downstairs to give them to Luke, but he doesn't. He goes to his room and shuts the door.

after

I wish I could make it stop. My family... they were everything
I needed. *Why did I leave them?*

My father played the piano. He tried to teach me how, but I
couldn't wrap my head around all the different notes. He got mad
at me for not learning; "You're not trying hard enough," he told
me. "You're thinking too much. Just let the music flow through,
Alexandria."

But I didn't know how. I knew how to write a haiku and solve
algebra, but I couldn't play "Twinkle, Twinkle Little Star." I felt
so disappointed in myself, and my father never told me that it
was okay. He never told me it didn't matter if I couldn't play the
stupid piano. He just got up from the bench in anger, mumbling
something not nice.

"I'm sorry I couldn't learn how to play, Mom," I told her after
Dad still wouldn't talk to me.

She smiled at me. "Your father loves you, Alex. He's just angry
right now."

"Because of me?"

"No, honey. Not because of you. We make your father very
happy."

"Then why is he sad?"

"Oh, lots of reasons. Grown up stuff," she kissed me on the forehead. "Nothing for you to worry about. Go to sleep."

But that night, I couldn't sleep. I wondered what it felt like to be sad about grown up things, and if I would ever know what it meant.

I wake up in the soft grass. It feels as if I've been in a deep sleep, and I'm just now coming out of it. A breeze blows my hair around my head and rustles the trees around me. Slowly, I open my eyes and see the sun poking through a tree above me.

I'm in my high school courtyard. There is no usual commotion of students bustling to get to class. Instead, it's quiet except for the occasional bird song and breeze.

before

Ten Years Old – Winter

On account of blizzard warnings for our area, school is released early, forcing Mom to come pick us up earlier than normal. Luke and I are ecstatic. Mom's mood mirrors ours when she picks us up, something abnormal for her in recent months.

In the car ride home, the snow is already beginning to pound down. The snowflakes are bigger than I've ever seen before, despite living on the east coast my entire life. Music is coming quietly through the speakers as I watch the oversized snowflakes land on her windshield before slowly being wiped away.

Mom asks us how our day was before we left school. She tells us she had been out buying Christmas presents all day when she got the call that school was ending early. Luke enthusiastically replies, but I stay silent, lost in my own thoughts. Once home, Mom rushes us inside the house so we don't stay out in the freezing cold for too long. Mom is fumbling around with Luke's coat and boots as I walk through the foyer and into the living room.

At first, I'm confused by what I see lying on the couch. I don't recognize this person, and he scares me. Empty beer bottles, and other hard liquor I don't recognize, are scattered around him. He's

27

slumped over himself, practically drooling. Pain medication is in a disarray on the coffee table. *Who is this stranger?*

The dust clears from my mind and my eyes focus, and I recognize the shirt on this man: *World's Best Dad*. Luke and I made it for him on last year's Father's Day. I almost laugh in shock and disgust.

I hear Mom's unknowing footsteps behind me, but I don't have the strength to stop her from seeing him; I don't have the strength to do anything. I think she says, "Oh my god," before beginning to shout at him. She tries to push me back, tries to shield Luke and me from what we're seeing, but I don't move. Dad's eyes shoot open—albeit sloppily—and he sits up as best he can. She is screaming at him to get out, get out, and he stands up and says things back. He isn't shouting. He's crying.

Luke is crying too. So is Mom. Everyone is crying but me. I feel Luke press into my back and cover his face with my shirt. I should comfort him, but I can't. I don't feel anything.

Mom turns to us and shouts something, but I don't hear her. Luke grabs my hand and pulls me. That snaps me out of my reverie. She shouts, "Go to your rooms!" Dad cries and says no but she stops him.

Luke runs us to my room and slams the door shut behind him. Numbly, I sit down on my bed and stare at the floor.

"Ally," Luke says quietly, still standing across from me. I don't answer. "Alex. *Alex!*"

I look up at him and see that he has tears in his eyes. Luke doesn't know many things about the adult world, but he knows enough to understand what state Dad was in. Still, he asks, "What was that, Ally?"

"I…" I'm stammering, searching for an answer. "I don't know." My voice cracks on the last word.

Luke comes over and sits next to me on the bed. "What do you think Mom is gonna do?"

"I don't know."

"Do you think they're gonna get a divorce?"

For the first time in my entire life, I'm not sure that the answer isn't "yes." Instead of lying to Luke, I say nothing at all. I hear a truck pull into our driveway and I run to my bedroom window with Luke trailing behind me. It's an unfamiliar vehicle, with an unfamiliar driver. I see Dad trek from our front door, on his way to the revving car. He has a bag in his right hand. He's leaving.

"No," I whisper. I bound away from the window and down the staircase. Finally, all the emotions that had been building up inside of me burst over the dam and tears streak down my face as I try to reach him before he leaves us. Mom is standing at the window, watching him leave, and turns to see me sprint out the front door.

"Daddy!" I cry, and he turns around. Mom unexpectedly catches up to me and grabs me before my foot ever touches the snow lining our walkup. The pain on his face is blurred by own tears getting caught in my eyes. I try to squirm out of Mom's grip, but it only tightens.

"Get out of here, Charlie." She says, and it only fuels my anger.

"No!" I scream and fight even harder to get her away from me. Painstakingly, he turns around, gets in the truck, and drives off. When he does, I turn on Mom and push her away from me. "I hate you! I hate you! I hate you!" I punch my little fists into her stomach, but she doesn't flinch. I run back inside past Luke, into my bedroom, and slam the door. I bury my head in my pillow and cry myself to sleep.

I awake to the sound of timid knocking on my bedroom door. My curtains on the windows are still open, and it's pitch black outside. I turn over, ignoring my mother's knocks, and go back to

29

sleep. The ache of missing Dad is almost strong enough to keep me awake. Almost.

"Alex? Come on, honey, you can't stay in there forever." It's daylight now. I've been awake for nearly two hours, staying in my bedroom. Outside, the snow still pours down. There's got to be at least a foot and a half of it now.

"That's it. I'm coming in." Mom opens the door and steps into my room, then shuts it behind her. I only look at her for a brief second before turning over in my bed and looking the other way. She's carrying a tray of food.

"I know you're upset with me, honey. But you need to eat."

I don't say anything.

"Alex, your dad—"

"Get out." I say it stone-faced and dead of emotion. I want to hurt her, more than how much she's hurt me.

She doesn't say anything for a few seconds, so I roll around to look at her. Her mouth is open, and she's already put the plate of food down. "I said get out."

Mom opens her mouth to say something, but decides against it. I look away again and close my eyes, trying to feel exhausted instead of hungry.

Boredom eventually takes over, and two days after my father initially leaves, I emerge from my bedroom. Mom hasn't tried to talk to me again, but has put meals on a tray by my door twice a day. Luke is sitting on the couch, watching TV and stares at me as I sit down next to him. I fidget under his gaze. The living room has since been cleared of all prescription pills and alcoholic beverages since the last I've seen it.

Clearing my throat, I say, "Where's Mom?"

"Welcome back, Alex." Mom says as she walks in front of the TV, shutting it off. She sits on the coffee table across from us, right where the pills were. I shudder and close my eyes, pushing the memory out of my mind. Quickly, I reopen them.

"I know what happened a few days ago must've been scary for you guys. I know it's hard to cope with." She acquiesces, pointedly at me. "I understand all of that. It's hard for me, too." Long pause. "Listen, guys. Your dad, he… he's not going to be around for a while. He's getting… some help."

"Is he going to come back?" Luke asks.

"I don't know, Luke," She answers patiently. "I hope so."

"Do you still love him?"

She looks like she doesn't quite know how to answer it. I stare at her, waiting for her to say, "Of course I do." Instead, she swallows thickly and says, "We have to wait a while before we see him. We have to wait until he gets healthy again. Even if he does end up moving back in with us, things are going to be changing around here. I'll have to start working, which means you'll be spending some time with a babysitter." She grabs our individual hands. Mine lays limply in hers. "And no matter what happens, you guys have to know that I will always love you, and I will always care for you."

Luke gives her a hug, but I don't move. I never forget the fact that she didn't answer his question. *Do you still love him?*

after

In death, it's hard to decipher where time ends and I begin. I pinch myself, and it *feels* real. There's no way I can be dead. This is some sick dream. It has to be.

I try to keep my mind on my family. They're the anchor that keeps me from going insane. My brother, and his contagious humor. My mother, and her radiant smile. My best friend – *Carlie*.

Daniel. My Daniel. *Especially* him.

It's terrifying, being this alone. In life, I was surrounded by people and couldn't feel more alone. In death, I truly have no one. I don't know which is lonelier. But this is worse; this is much, much worse. I wish I would've let someone help me, or care about me. Plenty of people tried.

I once saw an interview with a man who tried to commit suicide off the Golden Gate Bridge and survived. He said, "About two-thirds of the way down, I realized that every single problem that led me to jump had a solution. And I regretted it." And I thought, *Not me*. If I was going to commit suicide, I was going to be sure and I was going to have no regrets. I never understood why he would regret it if he felt bad enough to do it in the first place.

I understand what he meant now.

before

Eleven Years Old – Spring

Carlie is braiding my hair. We're sitting on the pavement in the middle of recess, and she just learned how to French braid a few days ago. She's been going around braiding everyone's hair, showing off her new skill.

A group of girls are in my peripheral vision. They stare in my direction, and I hear them whispering. I squirm under their gaze and pretend not to notice them. Carlie is too enthralled with my hair; she doesn't see at first.

"Did you hear about her dad?" One girl, presumably the pack leader, says. A bunch of the others chime in all at once.

"No—"

"My mom said he was a bad dude—"

"Yeah, my mom told me to stay away from that whole family—"

The first girl speaks again. *"My mom told me he left them. Just got up and walked out."*

"Why'd he do that?"

She speaks again, feeding off of their attention and my pain. *"My mom said he's a criminal."*

I've heard enough. I yank away from Carlie, who hadn't fastened by braid with a rubber band yet. I stomp over to those girls, their faces shocked that I'm approaching them. Secretly terrified, they recoil only slightly as I approach them.

"My father is not a criminal, you idiotic brat."

As an eleven-year-old, this was the worst insult I could come up with. I speak to the pack leader directly, Kate Fieldsman. She's a whole four inches taller than me, and burlier too. She's already developed breasts, and is therefore the most lusted after girl in our grade. By now, a decent-sized crowd has surrounded us. Carlie pushes through to the front, staring at the spectacle in awe like everyone else. This is the first schoolyard fight of the year, and between two girls no less.

"Yes he is. My mom said he—"

"Your mom is a moron."

Her mean-girl eyes brighten with passion and anger. She sets her jaw and prepares to ruin my life. "Yeah, well, your dad *left* you. Looking at you, we can see why." Kate looks back at her posse for approval, and they snicker.

I have no response to her hurtful words digging their claws through my heart. I can only react physically. I lunge at her and knock her down, then begin throwing punches. My peers' reaction around us is a mixture of "ooh's" and "ah's." I grab a fistful of her hair and pull, and she shrieks. The sound is music to my ears.

Kate scratches my face with her long fingernails, but that only fuels the fire. I punch her over and over again. I feel hands wrap around my arms, and I keep punching and kicking, but my attacks are no longer meeting flesh. I'm being dragged away from Kate; I open my eyes and see two teachers carrying me away. Another is tending to her, and two more are ushering the kids away. I see Kate and stop thrashing immediately. She's bleeding profusely from the face, and crying for her mother. Her eyebrow is split open. Bruises are already forming.

The teachers carrying me away are a man and a woman. The man teaches first grade; he was Carlie's old teacher. His wife died two years ago from cancer, and I remember our mothers taking baked goods over. Back then, the news barely fazed me, other than the fact that he didn't come to school for two weeks straight. When he finally came back, he was different in a way my child mind could never put a finger on.

The woman was a sixth grade teacher – Ms. Rodden. She was young, only a few years into teaching, unmarried, and pretty. She was the first crush of many boys my age, and older. She was known for her unorthodox teaching methods and fun field trips. I heard she has a tarantula in her room as a class pet.

They take me directly to the principal's office. The principal calls my mother and shames me for a few minutes before sending me back outside his office to wait for Mom to arrive in one of the uncomfortable chairs. As I close his door behind me, I see Ms. Rodden waiting for me. She's sitting in one of the chairs I'm supposed to be in with her legs crossed, looking slightly bored and flawless without much effort.

I don't say anything as I sit next to her. She looks over at me. I think she's going to shame me like everybody else, but she doesn't. Her voice is kind. "Your face is bleeding."

I reach up to my cheek, where Kate scratched me. My fingers touch the cut and it stings. Sure enough, when I bring my hand back, it has blood on it.

"Let me clean that up," Ms. Rodden stands. Before I can protest, she's already brought back a first aid kit. Ms. Rodden kneels in front of me and opens the kit. When she dabs cortisone on the cut, it stings, and I suck in a deep breath of air.

"I know," She soothes. "Almost done."

Ms. Rodden prepares a wet paper towel to wipe away the dried blood already smeared on my cheek from before. While she's cleaning me up, I look up. Across the room, and through windows, I can see the school nurse tending to Kate's face. It looks even worse than before. I try to feel bad, but the remorse won't come.

Ms. Rodden places a Band-Aid on my cheek and looks up to see what I'm staring at. When she looks back at me, I'm already looking down at my hands. She sighs, gets off her knees, and cleans up the mess. She comes over to sit next to me again.

"What's the verdict, kid?"

"Suspension, and he called my mom."

She ooh's, as if that's painful. "Rough."

I don't say anything, and we're silent for a while.

"What'd she do?"

Surprised and frowning, I look up at her. I don't understand her question, and apparently she can read my expression, because she speaks again.

"You're not the type of kid to just attack someone for no reason. So, what'd she do?"

It's a few seconds before I speak. Ms. Rodden is the first to ask what provoked it, instead of just blaming me. "She said bad things about my family."

"Yeah?" She cocks her eyebrow.

"Yeah." Ms. Rodden only waits for me to elaborate, so I do. "She said my dad was a criminal. She said he left us because of me."

"Why'd she say that?"

I shrug and look back at my fidgeting hands.

"Well, just between you and me, it sounds like she deserved it." Despite everything, I smile to myself and she smiles too. A few seconds later, Mom walks through the door and takes me away from Ms. Rodden.

The punishment for suspension is a grounding under the house, and taking everyone else's chores for a week. She gives me a lecture about how it's okay to stand up for myself, but violence is never the answer. I try, desperately, to withhold eye-rolling. I am unsuccessful, and get another week of chores.

"Kate hasn't been back to school," Carlie whispers into the phone, long after lights-out. I'm not supposed to have the phone, so I'm hiding under my covers and whispering.

"Really?"

"Yeah. I heard some of her friends talking; they think she has a concussion."

I roll my eyes. "She didn't even hit her head. You know how they talk."

"Still, though. You never know."

We're silent for a few seconds. I talk first. "Do you think they're going to be mean to me if I go back?"

"Oh, I think it should be blown over by then." The hesitation in her voice betrays her reassuring words.

When my suspension is up and I go back, Kate's group shoots me looks that could kill. I ignore them and keep my head down as best as I can, even when they shove into me in the hallway and all my books and papers go crashing to the floor.

Ms. Rodden yells at them for it and sends them to the principal's office, but nothing happens. She even helps me pick up my things from the floor. Trying to avoid more ridicule for being a teacher's pet, I ignore her and hurry away after all my things are collected. I don't even thank her.

Kate is back at school, and I live in fear of what she'll do to me. After carefully avoiding her since my arrival back, I turn the corner and run into her. She stares at me like a deer in headlights, and there are still traces of bruising and cuts on her cheekbones.

Her friends are stock-still behind her, looking awkwardly from her to me, waiting for her to do something. Even *I* cringe a bit, bracing myself for a physical attack of some sort. Much to my surprise, she never touches me. She averts my gaze and walks around me, taking her following of hyenas with her. After that, they never bother me again.

after

Before I could be a student in Ms. Rodden's class, she moved away to Vermont and became *Mrs.* Gable. Two years later, she was pregnant. I heard she had a miscarriage and switched from teaching to counseling.

I wonder how she found out about my death. Maybe she ran into one of the old teachers who moved to Vermont to get away from our small town just like she did, and that person told her. Maybe she would've had to swallow down the bile that rose in her throat and express pity for our family that didn't fully express the grief because nothing ever could, and run to the bathroom to throw up after saying goodbye with promises of "getting together soon" to her old friend. Maybe she would've seen it in the newspaper, if she still checked our local one; maybe her husband would've had to console her.

Maybe she didn't feel anything at all; only the itch of slight grievance for the child she used to know.

before

Eleven Years Old – Summer

It's the last day of school, and Luke and I get off the school bus for the last time of the year excitedly. However, upon walking along the sidewalk up to our house, something seems to have shifted. Mom's car is in the driveway, not our babysitter's, even though she should still be at work.

As we get closer, we see that the car parked in front of Mom's, nearest to the garage, is Dad's truck. We share a look and sprint up to the house, pushing open the door as quickly as we can. I see Mom first, facing Dad, and then Dad turns around to look at us.

It's *him*. It's my dad, the one I'd grown up with, idolized, and loved. His hair is clean and smooth, he's wearing a nice shirt, and he's freshly shaven. *He's back.* No longer is he the stranger growing in the place of my dad.

I run into his arms, and he kneels down to hug Luke and I at the same time. His big arms wrap around us, and he kisses both of us on the forehead.

"I missed you guys so much," He says, his voice muffled by our hair. After too short of a time frame, he releases us and stands up to look at Mom.

She stares at him painfully, with her arms folded across her chest. He steps toward her slowly and puts his arms around her. I see him whisper something in her ear, though I can't hear it, and kiss her temple. She closes her eyes and wraps her arms around his neck. Softly, she cries.

That night, we eat dinner as a real family for the first time in a very long time. Nobody talks about when or why Dad left, or where he'd gone, and I'm glad. I want nothing more than to return to my old life, when both of my parents were always here and Mom wasn't always working.

By bedtime, though, I can stand it no longer. Dad tucks me into bed securely, kissing my forehead and reaching toward my bedside lamp.

"Wait," I tentatively speak. His hand freezes, hovering over my bedside table, and looks back at me. "Where were you, Daddy?"

It seems like a century passes before he speaks. "I was getting help, honey."

I frown. "Help for what?"

"I was sick." Dad swallows thickly. "I was sad and I didn't know how to get better. I'm better now."

"Will you have to leave again?" I can't keep the sadness out of my voice.

"No, Ally." He sounds so sure of himself, no question in his voice at all, that I smile and believe him. "I'm going to be around for a long, long time. Try to get some sleep."

With that, he turns off the lights and I quickly fall asleep.

after

He lied.

before

Twelve Years Old – Summer

Mom doesn't want to put us through the heartbreak we faced when he left the first time. That's why she lets him stay around, I think. I listen in on their "private conversations," even though I'm not supposed to, even though they're not conversations, they are arguments, and they're not really private either.

I hear that Dad can't find a job. Or, rather, can't keep one. Mom becomes the sole provider for the family. She tells him she can't do it on her own, not in this house, not with his "binges." I don't know what that means.

She threatens him, and he'll sober up for a week. He used to come to Luke's baseball games, used to come to my soccer games – but now, whenever he does, I see the parents whisper among themselves. Carlie's parents no longer want to come over to our house, and I don't know why because Carlie and I are still friends. Mom pretends it doesn't bother her, but Dad can't pretend. I wish he would.

My entire world is squeezed, picked up, then shattered on the concrete when my parents break the news that we have to move out of our beautiful house. Our *home* – the home I'd grown up in for the past 12 years.

Mom and Dad no longer sleep in the same bed. Sometimes I hear her crying, only on the nights when Dad is really tired. He spends a lot of time in the guest bedroom, or in the garage.

"The economy is really bad right now," Mom tells us. "Daddy can't get a job, and my salary can't pay all the bills. That's why we have to move."

My mother, who didn't need to have a job for all my life until Dad first left, was suddenly working two of them.

When I was a kid, I became obsessed with the sky. The sunsets, sunrises, the stars, the planets – it was all so fascinating to me. I saw everything in a bold explosion of color, and the breathtaking nebulas that matched my imagination only fueled the fire. After we moved and my parents' fighting got worse, that bold explosion of color quickly simmered out. Instead of studying the stars, I studied "signs of an addict." Instead of chasing my little brother around our expansive backyard, I held him tightly as we fell asleep in my locked bedroom when you couldn't drown out the sound of objects being thrown around the house and Dad's shouting.

Our new house was uglier than sin and smaller than my bedroom at our old house. It was in the bad part of the neighborhood where teenagers smoked weed and children's hair was always greasy. I didn't know where Dad was, but Mom was making us help unload the boxes from the moving truck. We had to sell most of our stuff to fit into the new house.

Luke gets distracted by the stuff from his bedroom, but I keep helping Mom until all the boxes are gone and inside the house somewhere. Afterwards, she smooths my hair back from my face and kisses my forehead. For some reason, I think this was important to her. I grab the last box of my things and start carrying it toward the house when something to the right catches my eye. Looking over at our neighbor's house, I see the curtain pulled back just barely an inch. When I look at it, the curtain falls back. The house is dark inside.

Shaking that weird experience from my brain, I trudge up the concrete walkway to the house and into my new bedroom. It's completely empty, and it obliterates my false cheery mood. I put the box down and collapse on the carpet in a huff. My old room had hardwood floors; this carpet is itchy and I immediately detest it. Despite how desperately I want to fall apart, I have to keep a good face for my brother and my mom. They need me now.

Mom's footsteps approach and she looks around my room, sighing. "Don't worry, Alex. Once we get some paint and all your things in here, it'll look just like your old room, or maybe you can change it up a bit."

I nod, not having the strength to say anything. She sits down beside me. "I'm sorry things have been so bad lately, Alex. The last thing we'd ever want to do is hurt you and Luke."

Taking a deep breath, I try to push it all back. "I'm fine, Mom. Really. Luke's too young to care." I smile weakly. "It's a new adventure."

Mom smiles back and kisses my temple. "My little trooper."

I look away just as we hear Dad's truck pulling up the short driveway. Mom stands up and walks out, presumably towards the kitchen. I close my eyes and lay my head back against the wall. The front door opens, and I hear every one of his movements.

Taking off his jacket. Dropping his keys on the table next to the door. Taking off his shoes. Walking into the kitchen, opening the fridge, grabbing a beer, kissing a solemn wife on the cheek, opening said beer. Walking into the living room and plopping down on the couch.

In that moment, I hate him. I hate him for not being able to get a job. I hate him for changing from my favorite person in the world to someone I hardly even recognize.

Before I can start crying, I stop listening to his movements and open my eyes. Directly in front of my bedroom window is the neighbor's treehouse. The thought that they might have children around my age perks me up instantly. Quickly, I get up and run to the window. I see movement in the treehouse. Rushing out, I run into Luke—who was on his way to my room—and push him out of the way. I don't even have enough time to put shoes on, I just run out. Once in another family's backyard, I call up to the treehouse.

"Hello!" I call. "We just moved in next door! My name's Alex."

A dark-haired boy sticks his head out from the haphazardly carved window and my friendly smile immediately dissipates.

"Hey, I remember you!" The boy shouts. I turn around on my heel and speed-walk away. "Wait up!"

"Leave me alone, Sucker Boy!"

"Sucker Boy? I have a name, you know!" He chases after me, and I run towards the house. I grab the door handle of my front door, but it's no longer there. I look back at the boy and run right into Dad.

"What on earth…?"

"Dad!" I say, exasperated.

"Sir," The boy says, breathing just as heavily as me. He sticks his right hand out to shake. "I'm Daniel. Your daughter's new friend."

Dad looks at me questioningly. "Alex?"

I look at Daniel, scowling. He smiles at us, feigning ignorance. "We're not friends."

Dad smiles and claps Daniel on the back, much to my dismay. "Don't be rude, Alex. New friends are always important."

Our conversation is interrupted by Daniel's front door opening and a skittish-looking woman poking her head out. Her hair is pulled back in a greasy, messy ponytail and her face has acne scars and scabs on it. She's wearing ratty pajamas and dirty, old bunny slippers. At first I'm confused when she looks over here at Daniel, but as I watch his face I know this must be his mother. Her lifeless, bland eyes flicker from Daniel to my father. Despite her ghoulish color and sunken cheeks, I can imagine she was beautiful once. I imagine her eyes once were a bright, brilliant shade of blue like Daniel's instead of the glazed-over grey they are now.

I ignore the woman and watch Dad and Daniel instead. His cheeks flush – I think he's embarrassed, and I understand why. I try to imagine if my mother dressed like that, looked like that. Dad stares at her, transfixed. She meets his gaze and I can visibly see her flush.

"Sorry," Daniel says abruptly and bounds off the porch. "I have to go."

The encounter is over in just a few seconds as Daniel reaches his house and his mother ushers him in, slamming the door behind them and my father does the same. But I don't forget the look in my dad's eyes. It's the same way he used to look at Mom.

after

Daniel.

before

Twelve Years Old – Summer

Quickly, the summer reaches its hottest peak and I hear the adults whining about the mosquitoes as if their life depended upon it. This summer, Luke has become obsessed with all things involving a flame, thus our predicament with the neighborhood about the constant offset of fireworks.

On the 4th of July, the formidable arguing between my parents' ceases and they seem to indulge Luke's playfulness just for the sake of a distraction. The neighborhood, despite its overall lousiness, clung together on the life raft of familiarity during holidays. Most of the households in the area had no other family to visit, no fun summer plans. The ones who could afford it lit up a grill in their front yard, conversed with their neighbors, and told their children not to run with sparklers in their hand.

It's nearly midnight when Mom and Dad finally take us back home. Mom is adamant about us going to bed right away because it's so late; exhaustion takes over and I don't fight her. Just as I've settled into my bed, though, and the house has gone quiet with sleep, I hear the floor creak with the weight of someone tip-toeing down the hallway, from my parents' bedroom.

My ears perk up at the sound and I'm instantly awake. I wait for a few seconds, then hear the front door open, scowling and grouchy from fatigue. Suddenly, I feel an overwhelming sense of dread; something is telling me to get out of bed and go look out my only window – the window that faces Daniel's house.

And so I do, of course. Quietly, so as not to disturb Mom through the thin walls. When I reach the window, it's hard to see anything through the darkness. The lone streetlight at the end of our cul-de-sac is the only source of light.

I see my father appear underneath the streetlight, shoving his hands into his pockets, walking swiftly... toward Daniel's house. *What is he doing?*

Peering through the darkness, it's hard to see him entirely. But I know he bounds up the steps of their front porch and timidly knocks on the door. Their front door swings open, and I think I see those bunny slippers shuffle out just a tad before my father enters their home and the door closes behind him.

When I wake up the next morning, Dad is at the breakfast table. He behaves as if nothing is wrong, and asks me if I'm feeling alright when I stare at him weirdly. Maybe I just dreamt him going to Daniel's house and being greeted by his mom last night.

Nevertheless, when Daniel comes knocking at my door, I readily go with him despite my sour mood. Daniel has become increasingly annoying over the short weeks I've known him. Every day, he comes to the door, says hello to whichever parent of mine is home at the time, and asks if I'd like to join him to "discover the summer's possibilities."

Our shabby little neighborhood is tucked away in the corner of our otherwise picture-perfect small town. The elementary school, junior high, and high school are all located together in the center of town on a large campus. I'm two years older than Luke, but I'll be able to walk over to his grade-specific courtyard at lunchtime when I'm old enough. Our town only has one small, private beach; rather, we have high, jagged cliffs. We would get lots of tourists here during the summers, being a coastal town, if we weren't surrounded by dense forest and had more of a beach.

My old house was right in the town square, across from the school and nearby all the local ice cream parlor, boutiques, and diner. But our new house is at the very edge of the low-rent houses, next to Daniel's, in front of where the forest really begins. Our chain-link fence is the only barrier between us and miles of unexplored territory.

"You know, 'discovering the summer's possibilities' is an awfully cliché line." I point out to him snobbishly as we hop over my backyard fence, entering the forest.

"It worked, didn't it?" He says over his shoulder, oozing cockiness.

I huff and continue maneuvering myself through the thick brush. After a few minutes of walking, the thickness clears and I can smell the clear, mossy scent of water, can almost hear the bubbling creek.

"Where are we going, anyway? It stinks out here," I sniff, taking it in.

"You know, you do a lot of complaining for a girl who lives in the ghetto."

I stop in my tracks and look at him; he looks over his shoulder at me. "We don't live in the ghetto, Daniel." I don't quite believe it, but I don't want to accept the possibility of him being right.

He scoffs and faces forward again. "Whatever you say, princess."

Daniel starts walking again. Out of pure spite, I still don't follow him. I'm staring after him in dismay, wondering about who he is and what happened to make him so cynical. "How come you never stay for dinner, Daniel?"

"Huh?" He calls, moving a fairly large tree limb out of the way of our path. The sound of rushing water gets louder.

I move forward a few steps. "How come you never stay for dinner? My mother asks every night, and you always say no."

Quietly, he looks me up and down and goes back to clearing brush. Then, he shrugs. "Guess I just know you don't want me there."

"I do want you there."

He cracks a grin, and I know our serious conversation is over. "Why? You got a crush on me or something?"

I scowl at him and cross my arms over my chest. "Of course not."

"I knew you wouldn't be able to resist my charm." Still grinning – all I want to do is smack that sly smirk off his face.

I out-right laugh in his face. "Please. You smell terrible. Your clothes are always dirty. Your so-called 'charm' is more 'being in love with yourself' than anything. Your mother is a freak, and—"

Daniel doesn't let me finish. He slams down the tree branch he had picked up and was using to trace circles in the dirt, and crosses the few short feet to me, getting right up in my face.

"Yeah? Well at least my dad isn't a drug-addicted prick."

That snaps my self-control. I reach my small, child-sized fist back and push it forward to punch him in the jaw. With cat-like reflexes, he catches my fist in his one hand. His face is inches from mine, and as he catches my fist, I'm utterly stunned. His expression turns into stone. I can see freckles I hadn't gotten close enough to notice before dotted along his cheeks, right under those blue eyes.

Daniel was the kind of kid who always got away with saying "prick" at such a young age, and people admired him for it. He carried a pocketknife, but it was more for protection than show. He knew about magical places like the one we stood in right now, and no one knew how. I guess he just had too much free time on his hands. He refused to accept pity, apology, or charity from anyone; he wouldn't take a friendly meal from us, even though I could hear his stomach grumbling most days. The teachers let him sit in the back and not participate in class, because everyone felt sorry for him; felt sorry because of his mom. I *knew* his mother was like my dad. I didn't understand it all, but I knew enough to not ever talk about. I knew enough to feel sorry for him. And I just threw it all back in his face.

"Don't you *ever* talk about my mother again." He whispers with menace. He still clutches my squeezed fist. "And next time you try to pick a fight, make sure it's with someone you can beat."

With that, he lets go of my fist, turns on his heel, and walks away at a brisk pace.

"Daniel, I—"

Already a great distance away, he calls without turning around, "Go home, Alex."

Solemnly, I make the trek home. As the seconds progress and I'm left alone with just my thoughts, I can't help but keep feeling more and more stupid. How could I have been so insensitive to Daniel and his situation? All I ever do around Daniel is complain, and yet he still shows up every afternoon at my door like clockwork, taking me on another quest.

When I get home, it's around dinnertime. I smell Dad's famous chili and my mood instantly brightens. Walking through the door, I expect things to be just like old times. I'm even expecting the interior of our old house. Dad might be playing the piano, or blasting The Rolling Stones or AC/DC a little too loud (but still not loud enough) on the speakers. Mom will be bopping her head slightly to whatever music choice he makes, and Luke will come along and do something silly like he always does, and everyone will laugh. But that is not the case.

The house is silent, and empty. Looking out the front window, I see that both Mom and Dad's cars are missing and there's no note as to where they went, but I shrug it off. My stomach growls and I get myself a bowl of chili, then sit down to watch some TV.

After a few hours of radio silence and being home alone, I start to get nervous. It starts to get dark outside. I check the house one more time for a note, but find nothing. I decide to go next door and start asking questions.

After knocking on Daniel's door, I hear a rustling inside and then the sliding of locks on the door. It opens just a crack and I see Mrs. Walker's deer-in-headlights ghost face.

"Ma'am, did you see my family leave?" I question. She looks at me with scatter-brained eyes and doesn't say a word.

Then, she says, "Daniel isn't home," and begins to close the door. I put my foot in the threshold, stopping the door. Her eyes widen impossibly, and I think she's scared of me.

"Mrs. Walker, I know that you and my dad are... friends. If you know something, please tell me. I'm home alone.

She clears her throat, and looks around the neighborhood, opening the door an inch wider. "He went to the other side of town... to run some errands for me. He took your brother with him. He'd been gone a while, and I think your mama went after him." Then, sort of as an afterthought, she adds, "I'm sorry."

My blood runs cold, and I don't thank her before walking back over to my house. When I finally open my front door, the phone is ringing through the silent house. I rush over to pick it up.

I answer frantically. "Hello?"

"Alex?" Mom is on the other line, and her voice sounds even more frantic than mine.

"Mom—"

"Honey, there's been... a situation. I've been at the police station with your brother."

"Mrs. Walker said Dad—"

"Alex, if your father comes to the house, don't let him inside. The cops are looking for him. I'll be home in a few minutes."

There's a *click* and the line goes dead. I clutch the phone to my chest and pace around the living room. This makes no sense. What was Dad doing? By now, it's fully dark outside and I hear crickets chirping in the quiet. When Mom's headlights flood the front windows, I take a deep sigh of relief.

They walk in the front door quietly, and when I see Luke, he's got his arms wrapped around himself. Mom makes eye contact with me and shakes her head. It happens quickly and unexpectedly, but soon there is the sound of someone skidding to a stop in our driveway. Mom is on alert and pushes Luke toward me gently.

"Alex, call the police."

"What?"

Dad stumbles in and laughs at himself. His eyes are half-closed when I see him. The phone is still in my phone, and I dial 911 like Mom told me to. The look on his face reminds me of how I saw him when I was young, and he was surrounded by pills and booze.

"Hey," Dad's voice booms. He opens his arms wide. "What's with the long faces?"

"911, what is your emergency?"

"My father is under the influence. I am scared for our safety."

He looks at me in disbelief. A mask of anger overtakes his expression. "What are you doing? Get off the phone." Dad takes a step toward me, but Mom gets in the way. I stay on the phone with the operator and answer her questions. "Get off the fucking phone!"

I'm shocked by his outburst of harsh language. My father has never cussed at me. My parents erupt in a shouting match, like they always do. I put myself in front of my brother, then hear sirens in the distance. Mom lets them in when they pound on our door. I'm trembling.

"Whoa, whoa, whoa," he says, stunned, as the policemen surround him. "What's this?"

I blow up in an instant. "Are you freaking *insane?* I don't know what you were thinking, taking my brother on one of your drug runs. What is *wrong* with you?"

Dad narrows his eyes at me. "You have no right to speak to me that way. Stay out of it."

"No! You need to start paying the consequences for your decisions. I'm sick of you getting away with everything, like you aren't ruining our lives!"

"Sit down, you spoiled little shit."

His words are like a slap in the face. My father has never, ever said something mean to me or about me. This person standing in front of me isn't the father I idolized as a child. This man, this trespasser, this alien, doesn't belong in my home anymore.

Mom speaks, clear and calm. "Charlie, you need to leave now."

"Fuck you, I'm not leaving. This is my home."

She flinches at his words.

"Sir," one of the cops says, grabbing Dad's arm. "We're gonna take you outside now and search your truck."

"Get your damn hands off me!" He pushes the cop away. The other police officer grabs Dad's arm and twists it behind his back. Dad resists even more, jerking his whole body to get out of the officers' hold. I hear the tell-tale sound of cuffs being smacked down on his wrists. I can hear him sputtering out a string of cuss words as he tries to wrangle his way free, but it doesn't work. I hear threats, and I close my eyes to the sound of it. Luke is grabbing around my thigh, searching for my hand, and I grab his.

My little brother buries his head in my back, and wraps his arms around himself, clutching in pieces of my shirt. As we listen to our own father screaming and cussing at his children at a sound level that would wake up the whole neighborhood, all I could focus on was the sound of our own hearts breaking.

After one of the police cruisers take him away, the neighbors go back in their house and the neighborhood is reduced to an eerie silence. There are still a few cops here, but Luke and I ignore them. Luke falls asleep on my shoulder.

"Ma'am?" A police officer approaches and looks between Luke and I on the couch awkwardly. *We don't want your pity.* "Could I speak with you in the kitchen, please? Privately?"

"Of course," she says, still a bit dazed. She stands and leads him into the kitchen. Their voices are hushed, but I hear the words "paraphernalia" and "locked away." I close my eyes and let my pent-up tears slip out. Luke stirs against my side, and I immediately put my wall back up.

Who knows what could've happened to him today? I should've been here to protect him, and instead I was out making Daniel feel terrible about himself. Softly, I crane my neck to kiss him on top of his head. I start to gently rouse him. He sniffs and opens his eyes sleepily at me.

"Come on, Luke. Let's go to bed."

"Alex?" Luke whispers as I tuck him into bed a few minutes later.

"Yeah?"

"Do you think we'll ever be able to see Dad again?" His voice is quiet as mouse, and he looks younger than he actually is tucked in like that.

I furrow my eyebrows together, and answer with the truth. "I don't know, Luke."

"I'm sorry I scared you guys,"

"You didn't scare us, Luke. He did." I cradle his head and make him look me in the eye. "None of this is your fault."

"Will you stay with me?"

Nodding, I say, "Scoot over," and crawl in beside him. He makes room in his bed for me to slip in. We face each other, and I tell him to close his eyes. He does as I say, sighing. I wait for him to stop fluttering his eyelids and the sound of his deep, serene breathing until I allow myself to fall asleep.

Mom tells us they're getting a divorce, and he's not allowed to see us anymore. Privately, Mom tells me he was released from jail on bail but he'll probably be in and out. Luke cries and cries and cries, and I'm the only one to comfort him. What do you say to a child whose heart is breaking? Daniel knocks on our door every afternoon, but no one answers. Mom goes back to work right away, trying to keep it as normal as possible for us. I stay in my room, coming out every few hours to make sure Luke's still alive. He was always an adventurous child, deeply influenced by our father, but now he stays in the living room, staring at the floor. He entertains himself by playing with matchbox cars or watching TV, but he doesn't disappear for hours outside anymore. Neither do I.

After the first week, the mail has piled up too much to be left out there anymore. I take a deep breath before opening the door to go out. I hear Daniel rummaging around in his treehouse, and pray that he doesn't notice me. Calmly, I walk to the mailbox, retrieve the mail, and walk back to the house. Out of my peripheral vision, something catches my eye.

Hanging from the window of Daniel's treehouse is a huge, hand-painted sign. In big, sloppy letters are the words, "Come back." Daniel is leaning out the window, tacking the last corner up. It faces my bedroom window; the only person it could be for is me. His head is down, staring at his work, and this would be my chance to ignore this and calmly walk back into my own misery. But I can't – I can't walk back in. Something has glued me to this very spot on my walk-up, staring at Daniel's grand gesture. The thick bulk of mail quivers in my hand, and tears begin to slip out of the corners of my eyes.

My vision blurs just as Daniel notices me. I feel like I'm about to drop the mail, but I don't have the strength to move. My eyes hurt and my legs hurt and my brain hurts and I'm so, so tired of being alive. I just want to be able to let go; I just want things to go back to normal. *I just want to be normal.*

"Alex?" His voice sounds underwater. "Are you okay?"

I open my eyes and my senses come back to me; I feel the cold wetness of tears streaming down my cheeks – big, fat alligator tears plopping on the starch whiteness of the bills. I don't have the energy to talk; I can only shake my head. He snakes his arm around my shoulders and guides me toward his open backyard, underneath the shade of the treehouse. I drop the bills on the grass and plop down next to them. He gingerly sits next to me.

After most of the crying subsides and I'm not a blubbering, snotty mess anymore, Daniel acquires the confidence to speak.

"I heard about your dad." He says.

I sniffle, and can't look him in the eye.

Quiet as a mouse, he continues. "I'm so sorry, Alex."

All I could do was look up at him and try to keep from hyperventilating in a puddle of my own snot.

"I know how hard it is," Daniel pauses. "I know that you'll get through it."

"How?" I squeak out, my voice hoarse. "How could you possibly know that?"

Daniel gives me a small smile. "I just do."

"Where's your dad, Daniel?"

Simply, he says with a shrug, "I don't know."

"What's it like? Living with her and nobody else?"

"It's... hard. But you won't have to worry about that."

"Why not?"

"Because you have your mom, and your family. We don't have any other family. It's just me and my mom." Daniel stares up at his house. "Sometimes I wonder what'd happen if she just died – who I'd go with. That night I saw you in the hospital, I was in there because my mom accidentally overdosed. It was on her pain pills, and she made up some good story to say she didn't know that she shouldn't have mixed it with these other pills she was taking, or whatever."

I don't say anything, staring at the grass I'm plucking from the ground, and Daniel turns his head to look at me.

"Do you blame me?"

I look up at him, perplexed. "For what?"

"Introducing myself to your dad. My mom..."

I shake my head profusely. "No. He was sneaking pills before then. It would've happened on its own." Now it's my turn to search for words. "I'm sorry what I said about your mom the other day."

He takes a deep breath. "It's okay. Sometimes you just have a knack for being an asshole." I breathe out a laugh, and he grins.

"Yeah, well, you're certainly no better."

"Come on, now. You could've seriously hurt your hand, trying to punch me!"

This actually makes me laugh, and Daniel laughs along with me. Somehow, we don't have to say much else. It's comforting, being able to just sit there in perfect silence with someone. There's a cool summer breeze that blows the wild grass behind us, on the edge of the neighborhood. Eventually, Daniel gets some more laughs out of me, distracting me in the only way he knows how.

In my peripheral vision, I think I see our babysitter come out on the porch, looking around for me. She watches us for a few minutes, then goes back inside. I don't know what we'll do now, as a family. I don't know how to cope with this loss. But as I watch Daniel laugh along with me, I almost feel okay again. Almost.

after

911, what is your emergency?
Has he harmed you?
Where are you right now?
Uh-huh. Has he ever hit you or your family before?
Do you know if he's been drinking or taken something, sweetie?
Alright. Stay on the line until the police arrive.
They're almost there.
Alright, hang up now, okay?

Come back.

before

Thirteen Years Old – Fall

I had almost gotten used to the teasing at school. Everyone knows that my father is a heroin addict, but the worst part of it all is when they start teasing Daniel. They say terrible things, things like, "Wow, can you imagine if *your* dad banged my mom, and then went to jail? *So* crazy." Daniel said it didn't bother him, but I always saw the way his jaw clenched and his knuckles turned white from clenching his fists so hard.

Luke is immune to it all, making friends in the most unlikely of circumstances. Today the bullies decided that Luke isn't going to be immune to it anymore. Kids from my grade are surrounding Luke when I turn down his hallway to walk him home. Daniel had already left, saying he needed to take care of something at home. I slow my pace in an attempt to figure out what they were doing, and then they shove him up against a locker.

Sprinting towards the group, I call out to him. The bullies—there were about four of them, all boys—turn their heads and I practically see them lick their lips in anticipation of tearing us apart.

"What the hell do you think you're doing?" I shout at them, pushing them away from Luke.

"None of your business, skank," The ringleader says and stalks forward, towards Luke.

"Oh, *how original.* Call me when you learn a new insult, troglodyte."

"I'm not afraid to hit a girl." He gets close to my face and talks real slow, enunciating every syllable, as if I was the one who couldn't keep up.

Smiling, I say, "Yeah? Me either."

Before he can respond, I make the first move. I punch him right across the jaw, doubling him over. White hot pain explodes in my fist, but I ignore it. I get a chance to give him a good kick to the balls before the other boys grab me and slam me against the locker; I must've hit just the right spot at the back of my head, because my vision blurs for a few seconds. My hand and head are throbbing, but it doesn't matter, because one of them punches me in the gut. I hear someone approaching down the hallway. The boys drop me to the floor, scrambling to run away in fear of a teacher catching them.

It's a false alarm. No one comes down the hallway. Luke scoots over to me as I'm groaning in pain and clutching my gut. They only knocked the air out of me, but I try not to throw up. After getting myself relatively under control, I look up at Luke to see he's terrified. Despite everything, I try to give him a reassuring smile.

"I'm fine, bud."

"You're not fine. They just beat you up."

"Nah," I groan and use Luke as a crutch to stand up. "They hit like a bunch of pansies. Are you alright?"

Luke gives me a *"Really?"* look and lets me drape an arm around him to walk. He carries my backpack home for me.

We walk past Daniel's house on the way to ours. Like always, it's dark inside, even though the sun is starting to disappear outside. In the backyard, there's a light emitting from his old treehouse, presumably from a flashlight set up to project light around the room.

"Go ahead, Luke." I tell him and remove my arm from around his shoulders, limping toward the treehouse. "Tell Mom I'll be inside in just a second."

He goes in without protest.

When I reach the treehouse, I grab ahold of the knotted rope we use and swiftly climb up, just like I've done a thousand times before. Daniel is sitting with his back resting against the unfinished pine wall. His long legs are splayed out in front of him, and he's slouched over staring at the floor. His eyes are red and puffy, as if he's been crying.

If I were any other girl, or if he were any other boy, he might've frantically wiped the wetness underneath his eyes away and took on a macho façade, and I might've looked away awkwardly and fidgeted. But we were Alex and Daniel, and that's not how we rolled.

"What's wrong?" I ask him tentatively as I sit next to him.

"My mom left again." His voice is scratchy and raw, and I can tell he's been crying for a while.

Daniel doesn't say anything more, and he doesn't have to, because I understood. Every once in a while, Loretta Walker would leave her 13-year-old son alone in their house to go on a binge of drugs and partying. She'd be gone for a few weeks at a time, only to come back with withdrawals, promises she won't keep, and empty apologies. In the weeks, or even months, following the binge she'd try her best to be present in Daniel's life, and he'd fall into the trap of being hopeful. *Maybe this time it'll stick.*

But it never did. And every time she left again, it was like ripping open the stitches of a knife wound.

68

Daniel would never admit it, but I think he finds solace when she left. At least when she was gone, she couldn't do anything new to hurt him.

"I don't know why she keeps leaving. She gets better, and then she leaves. She doesn't care about me at all." Daniel lifts up his legs to rest his elbows on his knees and fists his hair in his hands.

I rest my hand on his shoulder. I should be trying to tell him that's not true, that she loves him, that she cares about him, but there's no way he'd believe me. And, really, what evidence do I have to back it up?

Daniel turns his head to look at me, still inconsolable. "You and Luke and Carlie are all I have, Al."

"It'll be okay, Daniel."

Suddenly, Daniel is leaning toward me. I'm too stunned to move when his tear-stained lips softly press against my dry, chapped ones. Daniel's eyes are closed but mine are wide open. I blink quickly a few times. *This is my first kiss.* There are no fireworks, or bells and whistles. There's just his lips pressed against mine, the warmth and comfort of it, and the background fear of the smell of my breath. It feels different than how I imagined it. Softer, almost. He is gentle, like he's afraid if he makes any sudden movements the moment might disappear forever. Daniel pulls back slowly and sees my stunned face.

He interprets my silence as a negative reaction. Without saying anything, he scurries out of the treehouse and across his backyard, slamming his back door behind him. I sit in the same position, star-struck, and touch my freshly-kissed lips tentatively, smiling a little.

Eventually, I have to leave the treehouse. I walk in the house dazed. Mom tells me dinner is ready, but all I can think about is how I just got my first kiss, and nobody knows it. Somehow, this becomes a playfully dangerous secret I'm determined to keep between Daniel and I. I smile to myself as I eat my dinner.

That night at bedtime, I visit Luke in his room to tell him goodnight. I sit next to him on his bed, preparing to talk to him about the bully incident that happened earlier today.

"Ally, you don't have to protect me so much." Luke says, before I can start. "I can take care of myself."

Lately, Luke has started maturing in the face and growing taller. At school, he probably could protect himself if he really needed to. Yet, looking at him like this, with his cornflower-blue quilt pulled up to his chin, he looks like my baby brother again. Just the thought of Luke even *needing* to protect himself against bullies hurts my heart.

"Luke, I'm not going to let anything happen to you. No matter how big and tough you get, you're always going to be my little brother."

"And you're always going to be my big sister," He says it as if that proves his point. "I don't want anyone to hurt you."

I smile. "Well, I'm a big girl. I can take care of myself, too. Those kids were bigger than you; it was four to one. There was no way I was just going to stand by and watch you get your ass beat."

Luke chuckles, then gradually stops. "Are you okay, though?"

I think back to Daniel's kiss; the kiss that made all the pain in my abdomen and head disappear. "Yeah, I'm okay."

"Good. Goodnight, Ally."

"Goodnight, Luke."

Daniel usually knocks on our door in the morning, picking us up to walk to school. I feel giddy as I wait for his arrival, but it never comes. Luke and I walk together, alone.

When we arrive at school, I turn to him before he scampers off toward his friends.

"Luke, if anyone in my grade starts messing with you like they did yesterday, I want you to yell as loud as you can or run as fast you can. I don't care if people call you a snitch, or if people look at you weird. I want you to protect yourself today, okay? Can you do that for me?"

Luke nods seriously, recognizing my tone of voice.

"Good. Thank you. Have a good day at school."

I watch Luke run off toward his friends, and smile to myself. I look up, away, toward the school. Near the door, waiting for the bell to ring, is the group that attacked Luke yesterday. With confidence and my head held high, I walk past them – even as they mutter "trailer trash" under their breath.

The rest of the day crawls by. When the lunch bell finally rings, I rejoice when I see Carlie putting her books away at her locker. The news of my first kiss has been bouncing around inside me all day, waiting for me to tell my best friend. Daniel hasn't come to school yet.

"Where have you *been?*" I mutter to Carlie between clenched teeth as I approach our lockers.

"Uh, class. Because, you know, that's what one does at school." She replies sarcastically.

"Daniel kissed me." The news rushes out in a hushed whisper.

"*What?*" Carlie exclaims loudly, turning a few heads and nearly dropping the remaining books in her hands.

"Keep your voice *down!*" I look around at the few turned heads, which quickly go back to their own lives.

"Daniel *kissed* you?!" Her voice is incredulous and, though quieter, still too loud for my liking.

"*Shh!* I'd prefer to keep this out of public knowledge, if that's alright with you."

She ignores me and we begin to walk toward the lunchroom together. "When? How? What was it like?"

71

"What do you want, a play-by-play? He did it last night, in his treehouse, and now I'm pretty sure he's avoiding me. I don't even know if he's at school or not."

"He's here. He was in my English class."

"Great, so he *is* avoiding me."

"I'm sure he's just... waiting for the right time."

"Well, he sort of ran out on me last night."

"What happened?"

We walk through the lunch line, preparing our trays. Our peers around us are oblivious to our conversation, and we're oblivious to theirs. The lunchroom buzzes with activity, conversation, and laughter.

"He kissed me, out of nowhere, and I was surprised, obviously. But he must've thought that meant I didn't like it, and he—"

"Did you?"

We walk together to the nearest empty table, sit down, and begin eating.

"Did I what?"

"Like it?"

Just then, Daniel walks up with his lunch tray and sits down next to me. This is not uncommon; he has lunch with us every day, and sits next to whomever he's closest to. But with our kiss still on my mind and fresh on Carlie's, our table is silent with awkwardness. Daniel is ignorant to it, or maybe just chooses to ignore it.

"Hey," He greets, to no one in particular.

"Hi," Carlie and I respond in unison, still looking at him in shock.

Daniel swallows his food and looks at us. "Why are you staring at me?" He looks at me, and my heart falters with self-consciousness.

"What?" I stutter briefly, then regain my sanity. "Oh, nothing. I just... haven't seen you all day."

"I've been in class." He takes a drink out of his water bottle and looks away from me.

"That's what I told her." Carlie says, breaking her silence and smiling cautiously.

Carlie tries to distract us by talking with Daniel, but I stay silent for the entirety of our lunch hour. I eat quickly and stand up to dump my lunch tray, walking forward just a few feet before I feel someone's foot collide with my ankle and I go crashing down to the hard cafeteria floor. What little remained of my food is now all over the front of my white shirt. Students' heads turn, and my face turns scarlet red. Slowly and shamefully, I look up to see the main bully bothering Luke yesterday – the one I kicked in the nuts.

"Whore," He mutters before turning back to his laughing table of friends. Before I have time to respond, or even pull myself up off the floor, Daniel has him by the collar of his shirt and sucker-punches him straight across the jaw. He falls back against the table momentarily, and the girl sitting next to him screams. Vaguely, I am aware of the principal shouting at Daniel from across the room, but I don't hear what he's saying. Carlie comes to my side with napkins to help me up. I strain my ears to listen to what Daniel says next.

"If you ever touch, talk to, or even *think* about Alex or her brother, I will personally ensure you never walk again." His words sound like snake venom, and I'm shocked at their intensity.

Before I can say anything, Daniel is whisked away by the principal. He goes willingly, without one look in my direction.

The rest of the day, there are stares and whispers thrown all around me, but that's as far as it goes. No one says anything to me or touches me; maybe they're afraid to. I hear rumors that Daniel was suspended, but I don't know what to believe anymore. His seat behind me in science class remains empty.

Luke and I walk home alone once more. He asks where Daniel is, but I don't respond, keeping my head down. We walk in silence, and I keep my gaze fixed on the sidewalk in front of me until we pass Daniel's house. His bedroom is the only light in the house that's on.

When we get home, Mom is frazzled, running around the house trying to get ready for the night shift. Her blue uniform isn't tucked in properly, and I tell her so. She smiles at me and kisses the top of my head, tucking it in. Luke drops his backpack on the floor by the door and goes into the kitchen in search of food. She's been working constantly, even more so since Dad left.

"I think there's frozen pizza in the fridge, and there's macaroni. Don't forget to tell Luke to do his homework. Oh, and Alex... Daniel called about an hour ago asking for you. He didn't say what he wanted. Where are my keys? Bye, guys!" she talks a mile a minute, and in five seconds, she's out the door.

Ignoring Mom's information about Daniel calling, I take a deep breath and sit down on the couch, opening my backpack and pulling out my homework. We don't have Wi-Fi or cable TV, so the only thing left to do is homework. Luke retreats to his room with arms full of food; I should tell him not to eat it all so quickly, but I know he won't listen. He doesn't think about the future like I do. I breeze through my English comprehension, then breeze through Algebra.

After I finish my schoolwork, I clean up the house a little bit, just to keep my hands busy. The silence is deafening – so deafening that it feels as if my head might explode. I try to breathe deeply, but the air won't work properly in my lungs. The walls feel like they're closing in on me. Deciding I just need some air, I walk out the back door and drop my butt on the concrete steps leading to our backyard.

I shove my palms into my eye sockets, trying to calm down. After a while, I get my breathing under control and look up at the sky. The stars are already twinkling in half the sky, even though the sun has just begun to set. Purple and blue blends with red and orange, the sun and moon stuck on opposing ends of the field.

Inside, the phone rings for a few seconds. I hear Luke rush out of his bedroom to answer it. There's muffled talking, and then I hear his footsteps toward the back door. Quickly, I try to pull myself together. Luke comes crashing through the back door, stopping in his tracks when he sees me in this state.

"What's wrong?" He asks tentatively, the phone frozen in his hand.

"Nothing," I give him a weak smile and rub my palms against my thighs. "What's up?" I look at the phone in his hands.

"It's Carlie," He says after a while, handing over the phone. "She wants to talk to you."

I put the phone to my ear and he goes back inside slowly, still watching me like I'm a deer in the middle of the road. I take a deep breath.

"Hello?"

"Hey. You okay?" *Why is everyone suddenly so worried about me?*

"Yeah, I'm fine. Why?"

"Well, with everything that happened today... I just thought I'd check on you." I'm so silent that I can hear her breathing on the other end. "Daniel called me after school. He got suspended for two days."

I grunt in response.

"He wanted me to ask how you are." Again, I stay silent. Absentmindedly I pick at a loose thread at the ankle of my jeans. "Alex?" Carlie says again.

"I'm fine. How is he?"

Carlie is quiet for a few beats. When she speaks again, her tone is softer and more serious. "Alex, you can talk to me. I won't judge you."

"I'm okay, Carlie. That kid today, he's just a dick. I don't think I have to worry about him anymore." I scoff and roll my eyes.

"Okay," She sounds unconvinced, but doesn't push it. "I just want you to know that you don't have to be all alone in this – in whatever you're going through. Me and Daniel care about you."

Anxiety and embarrassment bloom in my chest. I want to tell my best friend how hard it is to be alive right now, that I miss my dad so much it hurts, but I don't know where to begin. She wouldn't know what to say anyway. People care about me, sure, but nobody wants to hear my sob story or join in on a pity party for Alex.

"Thanks, Carlie. But I'm okay."

"I think you should talk to Daniel."

"I don't know. I just kind of want to forget all about it."

"Even the kiss?"

"*Especially* the kiss."

We talk for a few more minutes, until finally Carlie says she has to go do homework. We say our goodbyes and I hug myself against the dark autumn cold. There is an urge inside me to cry, to shout, to scream, but my limbs won't move. It seems I've used up all my tears.

after

I don't remember anything. Why can't I remember? I try to remember his face, his laugh, but there's nothing. Only empty space that should be filled with him.

I try to conjure up images of my father. He was the best person, the best dad, and then he wasn't. I miss him. I miss him so much. *Why did he do this to me? THIS IS YOUR FAULT.* Something is coming back to me. A memory? No, a picture. A video.

A conversation. Tears. *"Why did you choose..."* It fades away, and I ache for it to come back. I scream for the memories. I scream to be *me* again. I scream to be alive.

"It wasn't supposed to be like this, Alex..." It fades away again. *"I'm so sorry..."*

So many apologies. I can hear them ringing in my ear, so many different voices. *Why did you leave me, Dad?*

before

Fourteen Years Old – Winter

Today is my birthday – a Saturday. Mom lets me sleep in, and has breakfast ready when I wake up. I used to love my birthday, but as I've gotten older, it just depresses me. I used to get all kinds of presents and have wonderful parties where Dad would perform on the piano for just me, and now that's all gone. Mom can't afford to shower me with gifts anymore, or get me a fancy cake from my favorite bakery. Dad is no longer here to serenade us.

Mom bakes a small cake and manages to fit fourteen candles on it. Carlie, Daniel, Luke, Mom, and I all crowd around our small breakfast bar as they sing me happy birthday. I look up at Daniel across my candles, our kiss forgotten many weeks ago. Carlie grins at me, still singing to me. There are bags under his eyes, but Daniel smiles at me anyway. I still wonder, from time to time, what would've happened if I had kissed him back all those weeks ago.

As "Happy Birthday" reaches its close, I think of what I want to wish for. I think back to all my old birthdays, all my meaningless wishes, and suddenly I know. Swiftly, I blow the candles out and they all clap. I can't help but smile shyly at them.

After we eat cake, Mom lets me open presents. Carlie got me some clothes and gift card; Mom bought flower seed packets to plant; Luke made me a dream catcher to hang up on my bed post. The only present left is Daniel's, and it's a small rectangle in black wrapping paper. Almost hungrily, I unwrap it.

Inside is a picture I don't even remember taking. We – Daniel, Carlie, Luke, me – are all arm-in-arm in the meadow. Before my dad got really bad, my parents would frequently take us there for picnics. My hair is long and wispy in the picture, and I wear a broad smile marred only by braces. Tan lines from a bikini top show above my camisole. Daniel's hair is much longer than it is now, covering the tops of his eyes, and he'd only just begun to lose his baby fat. His smile matches mine, and his hand is frozen ruffling Luke's hair. His free arm rests innocently around my shoulder, and mine on his waist. Carlie's lips are wide in a captured laugh, and she's wearing one of the flower crowns I used to always weave for her. Luke is still just a small child, scrunched even more in an attempt to get away from Daniel's assaults. There is a glint from the sun behind us in the photograph, making everything feel more nostalgic. Despite being taken only a year or so ago, it feels like an entire lifetime has passed between then and now. I don't even recognize my own laughing face staring back at me.

The picture is surrounded by a minimalistic, metallic silver frame. Immediately, tears form in my eyes. I pick up the picture frame, hugging it to my chest, and a small note falls out and flutters to the ground. I pick it up, recognizing Daniel's chicken-scratch handwriting.

Alex,

> *You've been my closest friend, my only friend, ever*
> *since I can remember. It's been an honor to upgrade*
> *from "Sucker Boy." Happy birthday.*
>
> *Danny*

Daniel fidgets, waiting for my response. Without saying a word, I quickly stand up and walk the few feet to him. He stands up and I wrap my arms around him, nestling my face in his neck. Stunned, he slowly puts his arms around my waist.

"Thank you," I whisper into his neck. He nods and holds me tighter.

I blink away tears as I pull back from him. Mom reads his card and smiles at him, saying what a nice present that was. *You did good, Sucker Boy.*

Later in the evening, I drift into the kitchen to be alone with my own thoughts. I watch my mom, my brother, my friends... they're all so at ease with each other, so comfortable. This is the only family I've ever known. Suddenly, I feel nothing but overwhelming love for them. I wonder how I ever got so lucky to have these few people in my life who'd do anything for me.

after

I wished for that moment to last forever.
It didn't.

before

Fourteen Years Old – Spring

Luke squeezes my hand under the dinner table, visibly tense. I look over at him for a few seconds and squeeze back.

"Everything is fine, guys. Don't worry," Mom says as she sits across from us, her hands folded in front of her. Luke relaxes fractionally, but his hand stays tightly coiled around mine.

"Your dad..." Mom starts, then trails off. My heart is palpitating in my ribcage; I can feel it beating through my shirt. "He went to rehab. He has a job."

My mouth goes slack and I focus on my breathing.

"He wants to see you guys."

Breathe.

"He's staying with your grandfather."

In.

"I saw him a few days ago."

Out.

"He seems a lot... healthier than he was. I really think he's turned over a new leaf."

In.

"We won't be getting back together, but you can see him whenever you like, if that's what you want. Alex?"

Out.

"Alex, are you alright?"

"I'd like to see him," Luke says quietly, snapping me out of my trance. I nearly break my neck from how fast my head turns to look at him.

"Are you sure that's what you want, Luke?" He nods, and Mom looks over at me. "What about you, Alex?"

"I..." I can't let Luke go over there by himself, not again. I don't trust Dad. "Okay."

"Okay?" Mom searches my eyes for something, but she won't find anything. I'm empty.

"I'll go." I repeat.

"The visits will all be at your grandfather's house, and they'll be supervised for a while. You'll be safe." *I don't believe that for a second.*

Luke holds tightly to my hand as we ring my grandfather's doorbell. Mom has to work right after this, but stayed long enough to introduce herself to the social worker who would be surveying us. Mom said she was sorry, but I couldn't hear it; all I could think about was how alone we were now.

"Are you ready for this?" I whisper, looking over at him sideways. Luke doesn't say anything, only nods and stares straight ahead. I take a deep breath and ring the doorbell again.

The door opens, and I prepare myself for the absolute worst. But the man standing behind the threshold of my grandfather's home is exactly who I needed most – the person I've been missing ever since I was twelve years old. It's my *dad.*

His skin color has returned to its normal shade, no longer yellow or pale; his cheeks are rosy and his eyes are alit with joy. I rush into his open arms and wrap my arms around his neck. Tears immediately spring to my eyes. Dad kneels down on our level and Luke rushes to the other half of his embrace.

"I missed you guys so much," He says, tears springing to his eyes. He showers kisses on Luke and me. "I'm so sorry, Luke. Alex. I love you both so much."

"Dad," I sob, and hold tightly to him.

"I'm so sorry, baby," he says to me, tears streaking down his face. "I'm so sorry."

We stay there for a while, like that, being what we were always meant to be – a family.

after

That summer, Dad was everything he used to be. He didn't have much money, and regretted all of the life choices he'd made in the past couple years, but he never let us see how stressed and worried he was. He was all smiles and love around us. Frequently, he told us that we were everything in the world to him.

But, still, Mom didn't take him back. After the months passed, I started to believe maybe she never would. I could tell Dad was lonely. All my life, with the exception of the last few months, I had seen them together as an impenetrable team. Before, I felt proud in the fact that I got to brag to anyone who'd listen that my parents were still madly in love. And now, Mom wouldn't even give him a second chance. I had a lot of bitterness in my heart, making me susceptible to anger, making me susceptible to hate.

Dad loved us, that was undeniable. But he never passed up on the opportunity to interrogate us on how *she* was doing, how she was holding up, if she was dating anyone new. At first, his questions remained harmless. Then, as the weeks progressed, it was like he became frenzied with impatience in the amount of time she needed to heal before she took him back. I wanted to tell him, wanted to scream at him, *"She doesn't love you anymore! She doesn't even know who you are now!"* But it would break his heart, almost as much as it broke my own.

I knew he was lonely, and I felt sorry for him. I loved him as much as any girl could love her father. Maybe that's why I didn't stop him when he cuddled me, or told me he loved me so much that it began making me uncomfortable. Maybe that's why I didn't listen to the warning bells sounding in my head when he told me I was all he had.

He's lonely. He's sad. You're reading too much into this. He's lonely. He's sad. You're reading too much into this. He's lonely he's sad you're reading too much into this he's lonely he loves us please stop you're reading too much into this please stop he's lonely he's sad please stop stop please stop.

I wake up in a dark room with only the sound of my own rapid breathing to fill the empty space. Slowly, my eyes adjust to the darkness, but I can't make out any specific shape. My senses don't have much time to recuperate before I feel hands gripping me on both sides.

"What—" I squeal and try to shimmy away from the hands, but soon more pairs of hands are gripping me from behind. I scream and go forward again, where the other pair of hands meet at my stomach. "Stop it! Stop! Please stop!" I scream at the top of my lungs, but my words only bounce back at me against the dark walls. It feels as if more and more people are coming to touch me, to grab me, to pull at me. I'm being pulled in all different directions. Some hands are stroking my hair, some stroking my stomach, some squeezing my wrists and arms. I scream again and again, and soon whispers begin to form among the hands.

I can't make out any decipherable words, only terrifying whispers being passed around. I keep screaming as the hands quickly grow more assertive and begin hurting me; squeezing my arms and legs too hard, pulling my hair. I've become so horrified by their assaults that I haven't noticed my feet left the ground until it's too late. All at once the hands reach a climax of assault and lift me up an inch higher before slamming me back down on the hard floor.

After that, they vanish.

before

Fourteen Years Old – Fall

We sit around the dinner table at my Grandpa's house, picking at the cheap plastic covering from the '50s. It's orange. The walls are stained with cigarette smoke, and there's a very sad film of dust encasing the top rim of the kitchen cupboards. Even if I had all these months to get used to the house, how much dirtier and older it got each time still astonishes me.

There is an uncarved pumpkin in front of me, and one in front of my brother, and one in front of my father's empty chair. He was bustling around the kitchen, grabbing the proper knives and paper stencils. There is a horror movie playing in the living room; I can hear the theme music.

"Alright, guys," Dad says, walking in and setting the carving knife down on the table.

We continue together, Dad making us laugh, a comforting buzz overtaking the uncomfortable silence. We're engaged in a heated debate about the existence of aliens when we hear the garage door open. Dad pauses, hand filled with pumpkin guts frozen in mid-air.

"Dad?" I say, wondering why he's so upset at the sound of Grandpa's car engine turning off and his door opening.

"Shh," He hushes, then puts his head down and continues removing the inside of the pumpkin. "Don't say anything to your grandfather, no matter what he says to you."

The door opens quickly and Grandpa stumbles in, a stench of cheap booze and stale cologne following him. The screen door slams shut behind him, and I can't help but look up and meet his gaze, then quickly look back down. I clench my jaw and feel Luke pull at the hem of my skirt underneath the table. Briefly, I meet Luke's gaze and give him a small smile, trying to ease his nerves.

"Well, ain't this *sweet,*" Grandpa says, his words slurring a little. His eyes travel slowly over each individual person. None of us say anything. "Aren't y'all gonna answer me?"

"What do you want?" My father asks, still not looking up at him. Luke and I are frozen in our seats, watching the train wreck unfold. Dad keeps working.

Grandpa steps back, ready for a fight. He chuckles, shaking his head. "Boy, you got alotta nerve, talking to me like that. I lend out my generous hand to you and your mutts, and all you give back is debt and a smart mouth. Ungrateful, little bastard."

"Please do not use that kind of language around my children." The muscles in Dad's jaw tense. I can see him visibly trying to restrain himself so as not to scare us, or to do something he'll regret.

"Oh, yeah, cause you're such a saint father yourself." He walks over to the fridge, his face illuminated in the stark white light inside it. He bends down and retrieves a beer, then closes it back up.

"You know, kids, I remember when your dad used to be all scared and pussy-like, just like y'all." Grandpa walks over to Dad, sipping on his beer, and claps his hand down on Dad's shoulder. I watch Dad flinch. "But I made him into a man. Didn't I, Charlie boy?" My father doesn't respond, and Grandpa grabs a handful of his hair and pulls it back, *hard*. Dad flinches again but makes no other sound. I audibly gasp and Luke clutches my hand, his eyes wide in fear.

"What?" Grandpa starts, looking over at us. "Cat got your tongue?" He laughs maniacally and releases Dad's hair, shoving him into the table. The metal legs screech against the linoleum floor.

No. I will not cower to you.

"Stop it right now." I command him. "You think you're tough, trying to scare your son's children right in front of him. But we're not scared."

Grandpa laughs, and Dad gives me a pleading look to shut up. But I don't – I can't. "Oh, really?"

I nod, oozing confidence I didn't know I possessed. "Because we know that you're just a frail old man trying to feel big by making others feel small. It's pathetic, actually."

"Wow. You've got quite a mouth on you. Didn't anybody ever teach you it's rude to talk to your elders that way?"

"Didn't anybody ever teach you it's despicable to beat your children?"

The room crackles with tension. This seems to be what Daniel would call a "pissing contest."

"We'll see how far that smart mouth gets you." Grandpa mutters, slurping his beer loudly. He walks back into the living room, plops down on his chair, and turns on some old TV show no one but him cares about. I can hear him muttering about what would happen to me if I was *his* daughter with that mouth.

I look over at Dad, who is sitting in the chair that's older than me. He looks sunken in – deflated. He's breathing heavily; probably the first time he'd taken a breath in the past ten minutes.

I realize then that I'm angry at him; he didn't defend us, when he should have. He cowered like a scared little boy, and I had to protect my brother and myself. It should've been him. Dad meets my gaze, then quickly looks back down again. With that look, I know he's thinking the same thing.

before

Fourteen/Fifteen Years Old – Winter

My birthday is just a few days away. We are at Mom's, listening to the TV and the light snowfall against the roof. My legs are dangling off the arm-rest of the couch, and Luke is lying on the floor, throwing a rubber ball up in the air and catching it. We've been on Christmas break for a few days, and are bored out of our absolute minds. There's a knock on the door; I spring up, exclaiming, "I'll get it!"

I fling open the door and see Daniel standing there, shaking melting snow out of his dark hair. The tips of his hair are curlier than usual and wet. His blue eyes are bright and wide, having been exposed to the sun. Daniel's cheeks are pink from the cold. I don't answer the door with my normal witty remark; for a brief moment, I'm silenced by his appearance. He looks like an angel.

He gives me a funny expression. "What?"

I shake my head, picking up my chin from the floor. "Nothing. What are you doing here?"

Daniel grins at me. "Is Luke here?"

"Yeah," I open the door wider. "Do you want to come in?"

He shakes his head again. "Nah."

"Alright..." I say, turning back to Luke and beginning to close the door.

A ball of compacted ice hits my stomach, and I gasp at how cold it feels through my thin cotton shirt. It falls down to my feet, breaking apart and soaking through the tips of my fuzzy socks. I look up at Daniel and see that he's grinning like the Cheshire cat. A lock of dark, curly hair falls into his eyes, but he doesn't push it back.

"Oh, this is war," Luke says behind me, slipping into his boots and coat. He runs toward Daniel, laughing, and knocks him into the fluffy snow. I laugh as well and grab my coat, already yanking on my boots. The door slams behind me and I bend down to make a snowball, but another one hits me right in the middle of my back before I get the chance. I turn around slowly and see Daniel and Luke, pointing at each other.

I scowl at them, trying to mask my smile. Hiding the snowball behind me, I wait until the right moment as Daniel approaches me with his hands above his head. I take the open shot to his gut and run around the house, away from him. His legs are longer than mine, though. He quickly catches up to me and grabs me from behind around the waist, spinning me around to face Luke.

"Get her, Luke!" Daniel exclaims and Luke grabs a handful of snow and dumps it on my head. I squeal and try to wiggle out of Daniel's grasp, but he's holding me too tight. I keep kicking and laughing and yelling until we all fall down, me on top of Daniel and Luke right next to us.

Daniel looks me directly in the eye, a beautiful smile alive on his face. Snowflakes have lodged themselves between his thick, long eyelashes. His lips are blue, his cheeks rosy. He's my best friend, but all I can think about is how much I want to kiss him. He doesn't say anything, but pretty soon his smile falters a little bit and he looks down at my lips. My heart is beating rapidly as I scramble off of him, suddenly remembering who I am and what we are, *where* we are. Daniel lifts his head from the ground to look at me, his eyes wide from I don't know what.

"Um," I start to say, but Luke is already talking a mile a minute.

"Let's build a snowman!" He yells. Daniel and I look over at him, already packing in snow. He smiles at me and shrugs, then stands up and brushes off snow.

"You okay?" Daniel asks, quietly, as we walk toward Luke. I look up at him and smile whole-heartedly, nodding. *I'm more than okay, Danny. I'm perfectly happy.*

We congregate in the kitchen, drinking hot chocolate and trying to nurse our frostbitten fingers and toes. The sun had started to go down, and I'm standing by the window looking out at our snowmen. A little one for Luke, a bigger one for me, and an overly large one for Daniel. Our snowmen hold onto each other's stick hands.

"Whatcha staring at?" Daniel asks, startling me. I smile and shake my head. "How are you doing, Alex? We haven't really gotten a chance to talk about everything..."

"I'm fine." I answer quickly, reassuring him. "Don't worry about me. How are you?"

Daniel looks out the window, avoiding my gaze. "I'm okay."

"How's your mom?"

"She's... same as always." He looks at me quickly, then looks away again. "She asks about your dad a lot."

My good mood evaporates. "Yeah?"

"Yeah. I think she misses him."

I swallow. "My mom misses him too."

"How do you know?"

Because I can hear her crying herself to sleep every few nights. I see her tired eyes and her weary smile. I see the way she perks up every time the front door opens, then deflates when it isn't him. She still sleeps on his side of the bed, even though his scent must be long gone. It's like she's waiting for him to come home any second and take care of us again.

I look over at Daniel. "I just do."

I'd never had to have two separate birthdays before now. Dad still hasn't found a permanent job because of his record – only part-time jobs here and there. All he can afford is a birthday card and a ten-dollar bill. He looks sad as I open it, and I try my best to hide the disappointment in my face. Grandpa is a horse's ass, as always, and he throws birthday money at me as I pass. He hasn't been drinking very much today, but that's only made him crankier. I throw his money back at him in a bout of rebelliousness a few minutes later.

We spend the night at Dad's. He's lying on the couch in the basement, watching a Christmas movie with Luke. His eyes are glazed over, his mouth hanging open. His head is on one end of the couch and mine is on the other; I wish I could watch the movie, but all I can do is stare at him.

"Dad?" I ask. He doesn't answer. "Dad," I try again. Sluggishly, his eyes move over to me and he grunts. "Are you okay?" He grunts again and turns back to the TV. I clench my jaw and, after a few minutes, look at the television. But I can't pay attention. Every few seconds, I glance back at him.

After ten minutes, I can't stand it anymore. I get up off the couch and walk towards the bathroom. Dad closes his eyes and falls asleep as I pass him. On the way to the bathroom, I pull out my small, clunker cell phone and dial Daniel's phone number. I close the door behind me and lean my back against it as the phone rings.

"Hey, birthday girl." He answers in a cheery tone. His voice is warm and it reminds me of home. I try to not get choked up at the thought.

"Please tell me you're having just as miserable of a time as I am."

He laughs deeply. "That bad, huh?"

"Worse. All he got me was a card for my birthday."

"You poor girl." He retorts sarcastically, but there's a mean undercurrent.

I roll my eyes. "I'm not saying that because I expected some big present. He didn't even have to get me anything; I should be happy he got to spend my birthday with me at all."

"So what's the problem?"

I sigh. "I don't know. I should be happy I'm just with him, but I'm not. It's not enough."

"Why not?"

"He's just… not the same. He's not the same person I grew up with."

I look towards the toilet paper holder; it's empty. Sighing, I open the bathroom closet doors and pull out the package of toilet paper. Daniel is now talking, but something in a small basket, shoved behind random knick-knacks and a stack of wash cloths, catches my eye. I kneel down, pulling the basket out, and my breath catches in my throat. I jump back, my back hitting against the sink cabinet.

Needles. Three of them, just sitting there in that wicker basket. Bile rises in my throat and I cover my mouth to keep it from coming up.

"Alex?" Daniel asks, worry laced in his tone. "You okay?"

It takes me a few seconds to get my breathing under control. Slowly, I sink to the floor and drop the phone next to me. The needles are right in my line of vision, sitting there, mocking me. I put my head in my hands and stare at them, feeling a panic attack quickly coming on. After a beat, I pick up the phone again. I can hear Daniel saying my name through the receiver.

"Danny?" My voice cracks on the last syllable of his name.

"Alex, what's wrong? You're scaring me."

My voice is deadly silent. "He's using again."

Daniel is quiet for the longest time, and when he finally speaks, his voice comes out as a squeak. "What?"

"He's using again. There are needles in the bathroom closet. There are..." A sob escapes my throat and I cover my mouth to hide it. "There are fucking needles in his closet."

"Needles?" He sounds panicked, frenzied. "Why would he just have needles lying around? Maybe they're for something else."

I laugh maniacally. "Yeah, you're right. It's just his EpiPen. Just lying around."

He ignores my snide remark. "I'm calling your mom."

I scramble, sitting upright. "No! You can't do that."

"Why not?"

"Because then Luke will know and we'll never get to see him again."

There, that's a reason. Luke can't know that he has these here. *Jesus.*

"Daniel, what do I do with these?"

"Don't touch them!" He shouts frantically. "You have to leave them. You can't touch them."

"What if Luke comes in here and sees them?"

Daniel is silent. "Ally, I have to call your mom. If he's using, you can't stay there tonight. What if he tries to hurt you guys?"

Dark images flicker through my mind, but I push them back and swallow thickly. "You know he's not like that." I say it, but I don't quite believe it, and my voice betrays me. "We're going home tomorrow. I'll... figure out something to do before we come back."

He stays quiet, and I can practically hear the gears in his brain working. "You have to promise me you won't call my mom, or the cops. Okay?" He's still deceptively quiet. "*Okay,* Daniel?" I say more forcefully.

"Alex..."

"I'll never talk to you again if you do. I'll never forgive you."

After a few beats, he acquiesces. "Okay."

"Promise me."

"I promise." I don't say anything. "Stay safe, Alex."

before

Fifteen Years Old – Winter

The next morning, I wake up next to Luke like I always do when we stay with Dad. Bright winter sunshine is flooding in from the window, coating the pillow and half of Luke's face. I watch him sleep for a few minutes as the previous night's discovery of the needles floods back to me. He's nearly 13 years old now, but when he sleeps, he looks so young. He looks like my baby brother again. Nothing is more important to me than protecting him.

I remember what I promised Daniel about going home. But when Dad wakes up, he's so cheery and he tells us he has fun plans for us today. Warily, I watch him drive to my aunt's house.

"Alex, you're acting weird." Dad says, looking at me sideways, and switches lanes. "What's up?"

"Huh?" I stutter, then avert my eyes. "Nothing. I'm fine."

"You sure?"

I fake a smile and take a deep breath. "Uh-huh."

My aunt fawns over "how much we've grown" and "how beautiful we are," kissing both Luke and I on the cheek. We go to a family friend's house, and there's more astonishment at how much we've grown from them, more hugging, more loud laughter.

I keep a watchful eye on my father. I watch what he drinks, how much he's drinking. The family has children, and I used to be close to some of them, but we're galaxies apart now. It's awkward being thrust upon one another while our parents get drunk in the kitchen.

We stay long into the night. Luke falls asleep on the couch next to me, but I try my best to stay alert. I hear Dad's raucous and drunk laughter flood over from the kitchen as I check my cell phone.

New text message from: Danny
I thought u were coming home today???

New text message from: Danny
Hope ur okay. Txt me soon.

New text message from: Danny
Ally, I'm starting to get worried. Call me.

Looking over my shoulder to make sure no one is reading these, I quickly type a response.
Composing text message to: Danny
Everything's fine. I'll explain tomorrow.
Right after hitting the "send" button, I'm disturbed by noise from the kitchen. I look up to see Dad holding his car keys and saying goodbye to the family.

"Charlie, you can't drive." The woman looks worried, but I know they're all just as drunk as him.

"Please, stay here. It's really no trouble." Her husband joins in.

He ignores them all, saying he's fine to drive. Luke stirs awake at their loud protests and Dad's rising voice. Scared, I stand up and their heads turn to me.

"Dad, I can drive." I say quietly.

He laughs unnecessarily. "You're a kid."

The room is silent.

"Why is everyone freaking out about this? I'm *fine*. Let's go." His voice is at a yelling-level on the last word.

He storms out of the house. I can hear the engine revving in the driveway, and he honks the horn. We all put our boots and coats on, but our aunt is still trying to get him out of the truck. He's yelling at her as Luke and I approach. Luke is still half-asleep, but he's aware of his surroundings. I keep my arm around him as we approach the truck.

My entire body is quaking with fear. I put my seatbelt on and ensure Luke does too. It's all a blur, but I know that he skids out of the driveway with our aunt in the passenger seat. He swerves along the road, sliding on the icy patches. There had been a snow storm the week before, and there were towering piles of snow beside the roads to remind us. My aunt screams at him to pull over, and he screams back.

It all happens like a dream. I look over at my brother, trying not to be afraid.

I grab Luke's hand and just as I hear my father say, "I should be teaching these kids to quit being such pussies. Dad taught us."

"Yeah, and look where we ended up, Charlie!" My aunt screams at him.

He ignores her and I see the muscles in his jaw clench. As if in slow motion, I see my father jerk the steering wheel to the side, and my aunt's screams reach a new crescendo. But her voice is underwater. Everything is underwater. All I can focus on is Luke, my brother; named after a Star Wars character, back at a time when my parents cared about things like that.

Glass shatters around us and my head slams into the window at my side. I feel a sharp pain in my temple, then a cold rush of air from the outside. The car rolls and spins my whole world upside down. My eyes close upon impact. Earth-shattering pain laces through my body after a few seconds, overbearing all my senses. I have no time to scream. All I remember is the fear.

There is an oxygen mask over my face. There are unfamiliar faces crowding around me, telling me to be strong and keep breathing. I don't understand – I feel fine; like I'm floating, even. My eyelids feel too heavy to keep open, and I'm so, so tired…

I wake slowly, and pain is the thing I feel first. My temple is pulsing and there's a sharp pain in my left side whenever I slightly move. I try to open my eyes, but there's a bright white light in front of me. It burns my brain. After a few seconds of slow adjustment, I try to open my eyes again.

"Honey, it's okay," Mom says in a soothing voice, rushing to my bedside. I look around slowly, my head still clearing. I try to adjust – a slice of pain shoots through me and I wince. "Oh, honey, you should stay still."

"Water," I manage to choke out.

"Of course." She whispers and runs over to the counter by the window to grab me a glass of water. Tentatively, I sip it, and she sets it back down. Looking around the room, I see we're the only ones in here.

There's a scattering of cheery flowers and "get well" cards in the corner, resting on the air vent. Blinding sunlight is shining in on them through the open curtain. The walls are baby blue. There's a very uncomfortable-looking leather armchair next to my bed with blankets strewn over it, and I immediately know that's where my mother has been sleeping since I've been out.

"Where's..." I say slowly, still testing my voice. "Luke?"

"He's okay, Ally." Mom smiles. "A lot better than you are. He's at home."

"Yes, Alex, your brother is fine." A doctor says, strolling in with a clipboard. "I'm Dr. Levitz. I'm treating you and your brother." I regard coolly, precariously, then look back at Mom. She looks away quickly.

"Mom?" I look at her, but both of them ignore me.

"Do you remember the accident, Alex?" Dr. Levitz asks.

"I..." stuttering, "I think so. I remember bits and pieces."

"Your father was intoxicated. He crashed the car on purpose." I nod. "His custodial rights have been permanently removed."

"What does that mean?" I ask, my nerves standing on edge. My brain hurts trying to process all this information.

Mom speaks up, squeezing my hand. "It means that he won't be able to have any part of your lives for... the foreseeable future."

They have me connected to a heart monitor, which rapidly speeds up when they break that news. *I still don't understand.* Dr. Levitz places his hand on my shoulder, gently telling me to calm down. I would like to gently tell him to shove it up his ass.

"Does Luke know?"

Mom nods sadly. "Yes."

My brain switches into auto-pilot. They're waiting for me to blow up, so I have to show them that I won't. They're waiting for me to cry or scream, so I have to show them I feel nothing. "What happened to him?"

The doctor assumes I mean about my brother, and I let him assume that, but I was talking about my father. "He only suffered from a concussion and fractured rib, along with the need of stitches in his head. We only kept him overnight, about a week ago." I'm shell-shocked, so he continues.

"Your head injuries were a bit more severe, and your brain began swelling. We had to induce a coma. You also needed stitches, more than he did. Your right arm, unfortunately, is broken, as you can tell." He gestures to my arm in its cast. "You have some intense bruising on your broken arm and right side. Your brain swelling has gone down considerably, and you should make a full recovery. You are a very lucky girl, Alex."

I don't feel like it.

Things are quiet for a few minutes. Dr. Levitz breaks the silence first. "How are you feeling?"

"I'm..." My brain is still throbbing and my side is still in wretched pain. "In pain."

"That's understandable. Your side will give you the most trouble, but I will increase your pain medication to make you as comfortable as possible. We want to keep an eye on your brain, to make sure the swelling doesn't flare up again. If you keep healing like you have, you should be out of the hospital in a few days."

As Dr. Levitz checks my eyes, my reflexes, my vitals and such, I use the time to ask questions.

"What about Dad's injuries? My aunt?"

The doctor shifts uncomfortably, and looks at Mom. "Your aunt is remarkably fine. She is the one who called the ambulance. She had minor cuts and bruises, but other than that, she's alright." I sigh with relief, a little bit. *At least someone made it out okay.* "I am not his doctor, but I can tell you your father suffered from a severe neck injury due to his seatbelt and is in the ICU like you. He had to undergo an emergency surgery last night due to internal bleeding, but he is still alive. He's in police custody."

My heart rate spikes again. "Why?"

"He crashed the car on purpose, Alex. He endangered you and Luke. Not to mention he was driving while intoxicated." Mom says it like I'm stupid.

Sensing how touchy this subject is, I dutifully change the topic. "Do Daniel and Carlie know?"

Visibly relaxing, she nods and smiles. "Carlie and her mom dropped off some flowers at the house, and I brought them here." I look over Mom's shoulder at a vase full of fresh daisies. "Daniel hasn't been allowed up, but he's been going crazy in the waiting room. He hasn't left since he found out."

This news relieves me. All I want to do is see him, hug him, and hear him tell me that everything is okay.

"Can I see them?"

Mom shares a look with Dr. Levitz. "I don't think so, Ally. Not yet, anyway."

Tears spring to my eyes. "Mom..."

"I know, honey. But you just aren't healthy enough to see them yet. I'll tell Daniel you're awake and fine, and try to convince him to go home—"

"You know he won't leave until he's seen me."

Dr. Levitz interrupts us. "Alex, I've got to go finish up my rounds. I'll increase your pain medication, but in the meantime, I want you to try to eat something and get some rest."

I ignore him and stare down at my pale, folded hands. He exits the room, leaving my mother and me alone in awkward silence. The rest of the day passes by in a blur; nurses hovering around me, Dr. Levitz coming in every once in a while checking my vitals, stitches, and head. Sometime during the day, a nurse brings in food, but I have no appetite. I try to rest, but every time I close my eyes, I hear the sound of shattering glass and feel nauseous as the car rolls around me. Mom doesn't leave until night falls, and she's teary-eyed even to go home to be with Luke.

After she leaves, I call in a nurse to take me to the bathroom, embarrassingly. She wraps a steady arm underneath my armpits. My legs feel like Jell-O and I have to lean on her heavily. We reach the ajar bathroom door, and she doesn't go away, even after I've gotten a good grip on the long, metal handicap bar and am hovering above the toilet.

"You can go." I instruct, perhaps a bit too harshly, but the fact that everyone is treating me like a porcelain doll grates my gears.

If the nurse notices my snotty tone, she doesn't let on. I'm sure she's dealt with her fair share of sick, bratty teenagers. In that instant, I feel sorry for her.

"Are you sure?" She questions kindly.

Bemused and biting my tongue, I nod. Hair falls around my face as she leaves the bathroom, but the door stays cracked open. After doing my best to pee as quietly as I can due to embarrassment. When the nurse hears me finish and flush the toilet, she comes in and hands me a walker.

I look up at her, bashful. "Thank you."

The nurse smiles at me and exits.

It takes great effort to walk to the sink, and I lean heavily on the walker. When I finally reach my destination, I audibly gasp at my reflection in the mirror. My face is pale, like I've just seen a ghost. My collarbones are jutting out in the sliver of skin that peeks away from my large hospital gown. There are stitches along my hairline, as well as yellowing bruises.

I don't recognize the girl in the mirror. This isn't Alex Sinclair. This is a stranger. *It must be. It has to be.* Terrified, I turn away from the mirror and rush out of the bathroom.

The room is dark and silent as evening falls. My side is now just a dull ache, no longer pulsating with pain. I close my eyes and let my head rest against my pillow just as I hear the door softly open and someone creep in. My eyes spring open and I whip my head towards the door. Daniel stands there, creeping slowly in, and puts his index finger against his lips. He closes the heavy door behind him and tip-toes towards me. I watch him warily, but he just pulls up a chair and grabs my hand. He's wearing a dark sweatshirt that's worn down from too much washing, and his hair is a tousled mess.

"I'd hug you, but I'm scared I'll hurt you." He whispers, sitting down at my bedside.

I don't say anything for a few seconds. Even though his hair is wet from a shower, there are still dark bags under his eyes and his knuckles are bruised. "You look like shit."

Emptily, he chuckles. "You don't look much better yourself."

"Well, I *was* in a car accident. What's your excuse?"

There are a few seconds of awkward silence, and I regret my harsh comment. Instantly, he clenches his jaw, wincing, and releases my hand. "I didn't know if you were going to be alive by the time I got here, Alex. I was so scared that I'd walk through that door and see your mom sobbing, and I'd know you didn't make it."

I look away. "I'm sorry. I didn't—"

He won't look at me. I stop talking, afraid I'll only make it worse.

I change the subject. "How's Luke?"

"Scared. You know. He'll be okay. Carlie's out of her mind, though – been calling me all day, asking if there's anything new. Your mom called her mom."

"Yeah."

Daniel's eyes flicker up to mine momentarily. He hangs his head and runs his fingers through his hair, slicking his curls back for an instant before they drop back down over his eyes. There's only a small light from the bathroom coming in, and it makes him look haunted and jaded, but he's still my Daniel.

"Danny—" I start, but he interrupts me.

"I was so scared, Alex." If I had to pick a word to describe him, it would be *broken*. "Nobody would tell me anything, and I tried asking your mom, but they wouldn't tell her anything either. I thought you were going to die. After that call..." he trails off, and I swallow thickly as I remember what he's talking about. What I found. "I felt so guilty for not telling anyone about the needles. I kept thinking, 'This is my fault.'

"I kept thinking, you know," he says again. "What I would say to you if I did get to see you again. I actually prayed, Ally. I prayed I would just get to see you one last time. Can you believe it?" Daniel scoffs, shaking his head. "I went through all these different scenarios in my head, about *this* moment. But now..."

"What? Now what?"

He meets my gaze and chooses his words carefully. "I never understood people who said they'd kill for somebody they... care about. But after I found out what your dad did, I get it now. I want to kill him, Ally." I tentatively open my mouth to say something, but a nurse opens the door and scolds Daniel.

"What are you doing in here, young man?" She scolds, her voice high-pitched. It's a different one than the lady who helped me earlier. "I thought we told you to go home. How did you get in here? Family only!"

I want to kill her.

"I'm going." Daniel stands and squeezes my hand one last time before being escorted out by other nurses that had gathered around the door. When the door finally closes again, I can't help but want to run after him, however physically impossible that may be. The gaping hole that felt full when he was around was now empty once more.

The nurse who helped me reach the bathroom slowly enters, the other nurse passing her while escorting Daniel out.

"That boy was pretty determined to get in here to see you." She comments gently, checking my clipboard. "Is he your boyfriend?"

"No," I respond. "Just a friend."

She raises her eyebrows. "He doesn't seem to look at you like he's just a friend."

I give her a polite smile and pray that she goes away soon. Thankfully, after I don't respond and she finishes her work, she retreats and closes the door again. I close my eyes and let my thoughts wander. *What if Luke had died?* I can't stomach the thought. The glass, my aunt's screams... my dad and his cruel words. He did it on purpose. He was trying to kill us. No, not kill us, but scare us. Scare us into being tough, just like his father had with him. Well, I am tough. And I'm not scared anymore.

before

Fifteen Years Old – Winter

"How much of the accident do you remember, Alexandria?" The social worker questions, pen wielded in her left hand and a notepad file in her other. *Hmm... a lefty.* I fidget, adjusting myself in order not to bother my bruises. The hospital bed sheets crinkle underneath me.

I look up from her hand to her eyes. She reminds me of my mother. "It's Alex."

"Alex, then." She smiles kindly and I cringe. *Why is she being so nice?*

"He was fighting with my aunt." I sigh, resigned, and try my best to look bored.

"Alright." She says with no particular judgement, scribbling something down on the notepad. "Do you know what they were fighting about?"

"I wasn't listening to them. I was too focused on my brother." She waits for me to continue, and I soften a little bit. "He was saying something about teaching us to be strong, or something."

"I understand that your father had an abusive father himself. I know this is hard to talk about, and take as much time as you need, okay?" I nod. "Did your father ever beat you, harm you in any way, or threaten physical violence on you or brother?"

A memory pokes at the corner of my mind, but I push it out of reach. *Not now. That has nothing to do with this. Dad wasn't doing anything wrong.* "No." The word cracks as it leaves my mouth and my voice sounds unsure. I clear my throat and repeat it.

"Good, that's very good. Did he ever verbally abuse you or your brother?"

"No," I shake my head. "Not that I can remember, at least. Nothing besides the car accident."

"Your father has a history of drug abuse." She states it, doesn't ask it.

"Yes."

"Has he been showing any… odd characteristics or symptoms lately? Behavior that would be typically out of character to someone sober."

I calculate my answer. This is it – fight or flight. I can expose what I know, or I can keep it hidden away, at the possible expense of Luke or myself. No matter what I choose, someone will get hurt. *How many people have to suffer before he's out of our lives for good?*

"I found needles in his bathroom the day before the accident. They were hidden in the back of the bathroom closet. Luke didn't see them."

"I see. Did you touch or move the needles in any way?"

"No."

"That was very smart of you. I'm glad you didn't touch them. Did you tell anyone else about this incident, Alex?"

I think about Daniel. "I called one of my friends, but I made him promise not to tell anyone."

"Why did you make him promise that?" The question should sound condescending, but somehow she makes it compassionate. I thaw a little bit.

"I didn't want my brother to find out. I thought I was protecting him."

The social worker pauses for a bit. Her eyes are a warm chocolate brown. She's young, but she looks like she could be somebody's mom. Maybe her children, if she has any, are younger than Luke – maybe they're toddlers, or maybe she has a newborn. I wonder if she has a husband. Her hair is shiny and pretty, but her nails aren't manicured, and I see a hint of a small tattoo poking past the bottom of her sleeve. Idly, I wonder what kind of life she'll be going home to.

"Alex, I think you are very, very brave for telling me this. This is going to help us a lot. I think you are an incredibly strong young woman, and I commend you for wanting to protect your brother like you do." I furrow my eyebrows together at her compliments. *You're a stranger; how could you possibly know enough to say such nice things about me? I'm not brave.* "Alex, would you be willing to testify against your father saying that you saw these needles?"

My blood runs cold. "What?"

"At this point, your father is unfit to be a part of you and your brother's lives. We need more evidence against him in order to remove custody, and this is a perfect example of that. You'd never have to see him, or even be in the same building as him at the same time. We just need a recorded statement, discussing all the details."

"I..." I stutter. "I don't know if I'd be able to do that."

"Alex," She puts her hand over mine and I tense up immediately, but she doesn't remove her hand. "I know that you care about your brother, and you want to protect him. This is the only sure way of being able to do that. It's hard, and it's scary. But I'll be there, and your mom will be there. You'll never be alone in it."

Somehow, I had a feeling she was very wrong about that.

I'm released from the hospital and close to getting the cast off my broken arm by the time I have to give my statement. When the cops show up in the enclosed courtroom, everything feels normal. I've been around policemen enough to know that they aren't the biggest threat in the room. In order to make me more compliant, the CPS worker and the judge say will be an extra force of policemen in the building in case my father does show up, however unlikely. We are at a long, dark, thick oak table in the middle of what looks like a poorly-decorated and dusty conference room. My mom sits to my left, the CPS worker to my right. A court-appointed lawyer settles himself into a chair next to the judge. Judge Burns sits across from me, leaning back in the leather swivel chair that is identical to all the others around the table.

"Alex, I'm George Stephens." The lawyer introduces and sticks his hand out. Shyly, I shake his hand and nod at him. "I'm just going to be asking you a few questions about your experiences with your father, Charles Sinclair. It will be recorded right here." He points to the voice recorder in the middle of the table. "And I will be taking some notes. Some of the questions may be pretty hard to answer, but you take as much time as you need and be as detailed as possible. Is that all right with you?" I nod again, and he presses the "record" button on the voice recorder.

"Please state your name and age." Judge Burns requests.

"Alexandria Sinclair, age 15."

"And on the night of January third, where were you?"

"I was with my father, my aunt, and my brother at a friend of the family's party."

"What happened on that night?"

"Uh, it was snowing pretty badly. Our friends were trying to take away my dad's keys, and were insisting that we stay the night, since both my aunt and father were too drunk to drive. He wouldn't let them. We got into the car and he was swerving all over, and my aunt was screaming at him to pull over but he wouldn't. I was crying and stuff and he kept ranting about how he needs to make us tough. And, uh, I watched him jerk the steering wheel all the way over, and then we got in the accident."

"How old were you when your parents separated?"

"They divorced when he went to jail the first time. I was 12."

"And you knew of your father's drug addiction then?"

"I connected the dots." I pause. "But my mother never specifically confirmed it." The lawyer stares at me, waiting for me to continue talking – waiting for me to confess. If I do it now, it will be over with. Everything will be over with, and I won't have to kill myself worrying about Luke every time he goes out with my father. If I do it now, it will be over. So I do.

"The night before the accident," I start, clearing my throat. "My father was falling asleep randomly. He couldn't keep his eyes open. And normally, you can't get him to fall asleep. He's a night owl. But lately he had been excessively tired, or just acting strange. I went into the bathroom to get toilet paper, and I was digging around for it, and…"

The room's walls seem to be growing smaller and smaller. My lungs seem to closing in on me, my own body betraying me. My mother puts her arm around my shoulder, but her touch is too much and all I want her to do is *get away from me*. Everything is suddenly too close. My throat itches and my skin crawls with claustrophobia. I can't breathe, I can't breathe, *I can't breathe*.

"I…" I stop, trying to catch my breath. "Can I please be excused for a moment?"

The adults share a look amongst themselves and don't say anything, but I don't give them time to. I spring up from the leather chair, sending it rolling back. I run out of the room, not even bothering to close the door behind me. The public restroom is right there, and I try my best not to run into it. Once inside a stall,

I collapse on my knees and retch into the toilet. When I'm done, I sit back up and scoot along the floor to the side, leaning the back of my head against the cold, tiled wall. I close my eyes.

This isn't how I want to live, God. I can't do this anymore. Please let me die, God. Please. That's all I want. I can't do this anymore...

before

Fifteen Years Old – Summer

Summer. The smell of freshly cut grass and cherry Popsicles permeates the air and I wiggle my toes deeper into the soft, long grass of the meadow. Carlie sits next to me, hastily licking up the drippy stickiness of her Popsicle.

"Are you going to Eric's party tonight? I heard from some kid that he likes you." She wiggles her eyebrows at me and I laugh, clear as the summer breeze.

I shake my head and look down at my bare feet. I was twisting a flower crown together from the weeds. "Probably not, and I doubt he likes me."

Carlie scowls. "Come on, you're a total babe. Why wouldn't he like you?"

I give her a close-lipped smile and place the flower crown on top of her head, matching my own. "I wasn't talking about *him,* Carlie. I was talking about the party. But, the last thing I need right now is a boyfriend."

"Alex, just because your dad—"

"Don't," I interrupt her. "Just… don't."

"I'm just saying. You don't have to spend your entire life looking out for your brother."

I think of Daniel. "I'm not. I have you and Daniel."

"Another one who's pining after you!"

"Oh, stop it. Daniel is like my brother."

"Yeah, maybe when we were in sixth grade. But you're all grown up now, kid, and he's got those hormones a-ragin'." I laugh and shake my head, wondering if what she said has any truth to it at all.

I walk through the door with a smile on my face, having just been dropped off by Carlie. I promised to *consider* going to Eric's party, even if only for a few hours.

That all changes when I walk through the door. Luke is sitting at the breakfast bar with his head hanging low; Mom is standing across from him, a worried expression on her face.

"Alex, honey."

"What's happened now?" I ask without much emotion.

These "meetings" had become so frequent, often involving changes in Mom's work schedule or the court situation, that I had grown bored of them. There wasn't much that could surprise me anymore.

I hadn't seen or spoken to my dad since the night he intentionally crashed the car with us in it. That was at least five months ago. We don't know much about him these days, just whether or not he pays child support (he hasn't) or whether he shows up for court (he won't).

Luke's stiff demeanor is odd, but I don't take much notice. I'm in too good of a mood. I don't sit next to him at the breakfast bar, and instead go to the fridge and grab the orange juice. Mom doesn't talk until I've already got a glass down from the cupboard and have begun pouring my drink.

"Your dad is missing." She blurts out. Luke flinches and closes his eyes. *So that's why he's acting so weird.* "Your grandpa called me today at work. He disappeared sometime late last night."

I can't hear her over the pumping sound of my own blood rushing through my ears. My arms are frozen in their spot of pouring orange juice into my glass.

"They think he went on a binge, Alex."

Her voice snaps me out of my reverie. I look down at my hands and see that orange juice is overflowing the cup I'm pouring it into, spilling over the sides and onto the counter.

"Sorry." My voice comes out as a forced whisper as Mom rushes to grab a towel to clean up the mess I made. I set the juice container down. "I'm sorry, Mom."

That's the last we speak of it. Looking up at my brother, I see that Luke looks dangerously close to punching a hole in the wall. His knuckles are white, his hands clenched together. Next to him, hanging on the wall, is the calendar.

Today is June nineteenth. Father's Day.

after

The memory slowly comes back to me, that afternoon in the meadow with Carlie. My best friend. A whole new wave of sobs begins to shake through my body, but I shut them down. I absentmindedly wonder how she took my death. Standing up, I realize I'm wearing the same thing I was that day – the flowing white dress that stops just above my knees, the messy braid with flyaway strands. I reach up to the top of my head and feel the reassuring softness of the flower crown. It's still moist, as if I'd just picked it two seconds ago. My bare feet dig into the soft soil and I want to cry at the beauty of it all. The sun is setting, and I've been obsessed with sunsets ever since I can remember. I smile – this would be a good place to spend eternity. Way better than what I'd first been in.

before

Fifteen Years Old – Summer

Exhausted by my excursions with Carlie and today's tribulations, I shut my light off just as there's a whisper-soft tapping at my window. Luke had just fallen asleep beside me, curled up against my back like he did when we were kids. *He's still a kid*, I thought. I creep out of bed and over to my window. Daniel stands there, dressed in his usual outfit of all black. His hands rest on my windowsill and he grins up at me like I was Christmas and he was eight years old. I scowl down at him.

"Hey there," He whispers in an overly cheery voice.

"You look like the cat that ate the canary. What are you doing here?" I hiss.

"Whoa, kid, what's with all the negativity?"

I look down at his feet. His Converse sneakers were dirty, like they always were. I avert my eyes to hide the puffiness from the crying I'd done a few minutes before.

"Hey." He speaks in a softer voice, pulling on my wrist to free my cheek. "What's wrong, Ally?"

I smile sadly and stare at him through my lashes, then quickly look back down at his feet.

"Alex, look at me."

My eyes immediately go to his face. His beautiful, perfect face. He knows he's pretty. Hell, the whole town knows he's pretty. Daniel is my best friend, and he's been there for me through everything. He's fought every bully, made me laugh at every obstacle, but how can he help me with this? How can he fight the bully if the bully was me?

"Alex, please." He pleads.

Daniel is the only one who knows the truth about my family. He's never failed me before. Somehow, sharing this with him felt like *more*.

"My grandpa called my mom today. They can't find my dad."

He doesn't say anything, only rests his hand on mine.

I continue. "He's been missing for a really long time. They say he's on a binge or something, but it's not like him. He wouldn't just disappear like that, even after all this time."

"Where do you think he is?"

I shake my head repeatedly, trying to shake something *into* it instead of out of it. "I don't know."

"I'm coming in." He puts his hands on the windowsill and starts to lift himself up, but I place my hand flat on his chest.

"No, Luke's in here. My mom—"

When I touch him, his entire body freezes mid-climb. He looks down at my hand that rests there so innocently on his chest and I can't decipher whether he is angry, sad, or happy. Probably a lot of all three. Flushed, I start to remove my hand, but he catches it. I think he's about to make some stupid inappropriate joke about me making a pass at him or me still being Little Virgin Alex. But he doesn't. Instead, his fingers interlock with mine on his chest. I avoid his eyes. We've held hands before, of course, but only out of necessity.

But this time, it isn't a necessity. I push away the evil thoughts that pop into my head. *He's only doing this because he feels sorry for you.*

"I hope you know that I didn't come here just to put the moves on you in such a vulnerable state." Daniel whispers. I close my eyes at the sound of his soft voice.

I breathe out a laugh. "Why did you come here, then?"

He backs away just a fraction so he can look into my eyes, but keeps ahold of my hand. "I came to take you to a party."

I frown. "I don't want to go to a party."

He grins. "Yes, you do."

I pull my hand away from Daniel's and cross my arms tightly, looking back at my brother. "I can't leave Luke."

"Luke will be fine. Come on, please?" He pouts.

A few seconds go by, and I'm having an internal battle with myself. I can't leave Luke all by himself, not right now. If Luke wakes up in the middle of the night and finds me gone, I don't know what he'd do. But I *really* want to spend more time with Daniel. The moment crackles between us a like a fire, and I don't know how much more time like this I'll get.

I turn back to Daniel. "Okay. I'll come."

after

I remember that night now: the night that changed everything else. Why did Daniel want me to remember that? I feel like there's much more to it, but it's all so foggy. I think I'm going to be sick. Suddenly the sunset that seemed so dazzling just seconds ago feels dizzying, and it burns too brightly for my tired eyes. I sink to my knees and cover my face with my hands. I hear the voices of everyone at that party, all screaming and laughing and drinking. There was so much alcohol, and I had never tasted it before. I'd had sips of my mom's wine or champagne at holiday parties, but nothing like that.

The voices become too much and I want nothing but to go to the hell I deserve just to make it stop. *Maybe this is hell.* I cover my ears with my hands and scream above it all as I'm sucked back down into the labyrinth.

That night, Daniel tasted of cheap beer, sweet-smelling sweat, and mint. Kissing him was indescribable, so I won't even try. I'm not going to be cliché and say that I fell in love with him right then and there, and all I could think about was having his babies and living happily ever after. I didn't think about any of that. Kissing Daniel was heaven on earth, plain and simple. I could never get enough of it.

before

Fifteen Years Old – Summer

His soft words felt even softer against my cheek. Cheap beer was making me lose my self-consciousness, and I looked up at him through my sleepy lashes. My thumb fit right against his bottom lip like they were made to pair. We both tried to forget reality and imagine that this was what heaven felt like. I kissed him again as we slow-danced together in our own little piece of paradise.

after

Oh God. Please, no. Not this. Not Daniel. Please, God, no.

The last thing I could ever want to remember is how it felt to fall in love with Daniel.

Please, God, if you exist, please don't do this to me...

That night, after I got home, Luke was still sleeping soundly in my bed. Mom must have come in sometime during the night and shut off my desktop lamp, but I never received any consequences. Despite being divorced for years, I think she was too worried about where Dad had gone to have time to worry about where I was.

When I wake up, I have a searing headache. I open my eyes, but find it to be too bright, so I close them again. Am I still dead? Shit. My eyes adjust to the brightness and I sit up. I'm sitting on my couch. Literally, *my* couch. In *my* home. It feels like the house of a stranger now. I swing my legs over the edge. It's cold in here; involuntarily, I shiver. Luke must've been playing with the thermostat again. He likes – correction, *liked* – to do that just to bug me.

I stand up and look around. I'm alone again. I walk over to the front windows and tentatively reach my hand up to touch the vintage lace curtains that everyone in my family despised except my mother. She loved them – said they reminded her of when she was a little girl. I wish I could go back and listen to her tell stories. She was the best storyteller. I always said she should've been a writer.

"Please come back to us, honey..." I hear the whisper of her voice, but it's too far away. I strain my ears to hear more, but the words fade away.

I spin around as tears well up in my eyes. "Mom?" I call out. Silence. "Luke!" Nothing.

"We miss you so much..."

"Mom!" I'm screaming now, running through the house, trying to find something. All the bedrooms are locked. Everything I've ever known is locked away from me forever.

"I can't do this without you, Al. Who's going to take care of me if you're gone? Who's going to protect me?" My brother's voice. I close my eyes and choke up at Luke's voice reverberating through my eardrums. I would give up anything, do anything, just to have him back.

I curl up into a tiny ball in the middle of the house. I'm numb. I rock back and forth and wish for it to be over *so badly.* I fall asleep sobbing, "Please, please, just let this be over. Just let me die. I can't do this anymore. *Please let me die, God."*

before

Fifteen Years Old – Summer

"Jesus, can you two get any cuter?" Carlie hisses as Daniel and I approach her at the mall. His arm is around my shoulders and mine is around his waist. I'm wearing a stupid grin that never seems to leave my face.

"Put a lid on the jealousy, please," Daniel jokes.

She rolls her eyes and continues sifting through racks of clothes. "Cue the annoying falling-in-love summer montage."

I laugh and continue to shop with her. We make plans for the rest of the day, and the rest of the summer. Daniel is old enough to work now, so he got a job at an ice cream shop in town. I don't say anything, but my summer plans include ogling him as he scoops ice cream.

Later that night, Daniel and I lay in the meadow alone. Our thighs brush against each other as we lie in the flowers looking at the stars. I play slow music from my cell phone. We don't talk, or touch each other in any significant way.

I feel Daniel's head shift so he's looking at me, but I don't look at him. After a few seconds, he says, "Alex, can I tell you something?"

Turning my head to meet his gaze, I whisper, "Sure."

"The first time I saw you, I thought you were an angel."

I laugh quietly in disbelief. "What?"

He grins and I want to kiss him but hold myself back. "It's true. It was in the hospital, and I was feeling like absolute shit, because of my mom and whatnot. I was wandering around looking for shit to mess with. Then, out of nowhere, you appeared in your pink princess dress—" I laugh in disgust. "—and your dad sat you down and told you not to move, that he'd be right back. I couldn't stop staring at you, but it was from around the corner. There was blood on your neck and chest, and it made you look like some badass warrior, but you looked sad. And when you went to the bathroom and came back with a ripped up dress, I couldn't help but laugh and go sit down across from you. I practically shit my pants when I heard your voice."

I smile, lifting my hand up to touch his cheek. "Why are you telling me this?"

"I don't know. I guess my point is, I've thought you were the most beautiful thing I'd ever seen since that moment. I've never felt different."

"What a line," I smile.

Somewhere deep in my heart, I prayed that wasn't a line. I prayed he meant it, believed it. I kissed him, and continued kissing him until my brain turned to mush and my heart was carved out in his hands.

before

Fifteen Years Old – Fall

Geometry sucks. Big time. I'm on my bed trying to wrap my head around it when my phone starts buzzing on my bedside table. It's Daniel.

"I am *trying* to study here." I answer with a grin on my lips.

"Alex." He chokes out.

I sit straight up, my smile quickly disappearing. "Daniel? What's wrong?"

Quietly, he was crying. "My mom…" His voice catches in his throat and I can hear him sobbing. "I didn't know who to call."

"Daniel, you're scaring me. Please tell me what's going on."

"She's dead, she's lying on the ground not moving and I should call the cops but I don't know what to say. Oh, God. I should've been here, Al, but I wasn't. Oh, God."

The words spill out in a matter of seconds. He's unrecognizable through the phone. I'm taken back to a time when I sounded a lot like him, filled with fear, dread, and a lot of confusion. I jump up and run into the living room.

"Are you home?" I ask frantically.

"Yes."

Mom looks up frantically from the couch. "Is everything okay?"

"Call the police right now. Tell them to go to Daniel's house." I answer her, pulling the speaker on my phone away from my face. I quickly slip on my shoes and open the front door.

"Please come, Al."

He sounds so lost and sad that I start crying too.

"I'm coming, Danny."

Daniel is on his knees in front of his dead mother's body, screaming into the old wooden floor with tears streaming down his face. I sink to my knees like him and touch his arm. He swings around to face me and crumbles.

"She's *dead.*" He wails into my chest. "She's dead, Al, she's *dead.*"

"I know." I wrap my arms around him and kiss the top of his head. Tears squeeze out of the corners of my eyes.

"I never got to say goodbye." He weeps.

"I know, Danny. I know." I scrunch up my face in an attempt to keep the tears from coming, but they come anyway.

Loretta Easton-Walker died of liver and heart failure at the ripe age of 34. Her heart seized up after so much alcohol intake over the years that it just... stopped. It happened quicker than you could say, "Holy shit, I think she's dying." The ambulance put her lifeless body on a stretcher and ask Daniel if there was anyone around to plan the funeral. Questions, questions, questions, no answer. Danny just stares at the floor with his mouth open, the blanket the medics gave him strung around his thin shoulders. I've never seen him look so similar to a skeleton – or a ghost. Even in the worst of situations, he usually is always the one to see the glass as half full. I think his whole glass broke today.

"Is he in shock?" I ask one of the medics. His name tag reads: JEREMY. *Are medics supposed to wear name tags?*

Jeremy shakes his head, giving me a quick once-over. "No. I don't know the kid, but people usually take it pretty hard when their parents croak."

Jeremy was an ass.

After all the ambulances, police cars, and too-curious-for-their-own-good neighbors left, it was just Daniel and me. Well, Daniel, me, my mom, and Child Protective Services. We might as well have been alone. His eyes are red-rimmed and filled with tears. I put my arm around his shoulders and he lays his head on my shoulder, closing his eyes.

"Tell me this is a nightmare." He mumbles. "Tell me I'm gonna wake up tomorrow and everything is gonna be okay."

I kiss his forehead. "Everything is gonna be okay."

He squeezes his eyes together, and his next words come out so low and hushed that I'm not sure I'm supposed to hear them, "You're lying."

I hardly have time to react before a female social worker carrying a large manila folder approaches us.

"Daniel? It's time to go." She speaks in an apologetic voice.

He bolts upright. "What? Go where? I can't."

"Daniel, all of that will be taken care of. We haven't been able to contact any other available family members at the time, and until we do, you will need to stay in a foster home."

"Can't I just stay here?"

"You're under 18. You have to stay with a guardian, honey." The social worker shares a long silent look with me. "My car's out front. You should get a few things for the next couple days together. You'll be able to collect all your things another time."

She walks away, and Daniel and I are left alone again. Suddenly, I feel like crying. But not for Loretta, or even for Daniel – for me.

after

I wake up back in Loretta and Daniel's old house. His bed is unmade, his sheets covering my body haphazardly. I want to go back to sleep, but I'm plagued with restlessness. The thought of Daniel being in the house somewhere keeps me awake. After a while, I sit up, wrapping his thick quilt around my shoulders and pad, barefooted, around the small house.

I find him sitting on the steps of the back porch, his back to me. He's leaning forward, his elbows resting on his knees. I recognize he's wearing his favorite shirt, the black one that reads, *"Tres bien."* At first, seeing him startles me. It's the first time in… a while. Timelines seem to elude me here. Silently, I sit next to him on the step. His eyes glaze over as he watches the sunset.

"Why did you do it?" I ask quietly. At first, I don't know if he can hear me. Then, slow as a slug, he sighs and opens his mouth.

"Did you know that the colors we see during a sunset are actually caused by dust particles in the sky?"

"Daniel, I need to know."

"The light from the sun bounces off the dust particles and creates the light we see in sunsets."

"Answer me, God dammit!" I scream.

He turns his head sharply and looks at me, his eyes wild. "It's all an illusion, Alex. The colors we see aren't really colors at all. It's just an illusion."

"Why are you doing this to me?" I sob. I blink and I'm back sitting on the edge of the cliff, with Daniel standing right next to me dangerously close to the edge. I scream and scoot away, tears streaking down my face.

Daniel raises his arms like a bird and smiles. He steps backward into the nothingness with me screaming his name. I lunge forward and manage to catch his hand; he dangles in the air, the wind howling around us. His eyes briefly flash with terror, but then he looks at peace. I don't know much longer I can hang on.

Daniel whispers, "Wake up."

He lets go of my hand, tumbling through the air, and I watch him leave me all over again. *What if I don't want to remember?*

before

Fifteen Years Old – Winter

Somehow, the glitter and confetti permeating the room had fermented itself in my hair. As I stood in the bathroom, trying to detangle my hair that I spent so much time on, the floor shook with the beat of the music coming from downstairs. There was a knock at the door, and Carlie called my name through the thin wood.

"Yeah?" I shout back.

"Everything alright in there?"

I take a deep breath and stare at my reflection for a few seconds before unlocking the bathroom door and allowing her to come in. She has a glass of champagne in her hand, which she sets on the counter.

"I'm trying to get this gunk out of my hair." I explain, looking back towards the mirror.

"Alex, you *have* to get out there. Daniel is talking to the *cutest* guy."

I give her a look. "I don't think I have to worry about Daniel with another guy, Carlie."

This sends her into a fit of giggles. "Not for him. For me."

"Oh, yeah?" I ask blandly.

"Yeah. But I need my wing-woman out there."

"How come you didn't ask Daniel to be your wing-woman? I'm sure he would've thoroughly enjoyed that."

"He's too drunk to do anything too productive." She rolls her eyes and leans her head against the doorframe. I clench my jaw just a bit.

"I think you're *both* too drunk to do anything productive."

There's a tiny bit of malice in my voice, and she hears it. However, she really does sound too drunk to do anything productive, and her wits have lost her.

"Oh, quit being so *uptight*, Alex. Nobody likes a goody-two-shoes. You've never had any problems with booze. Just because your dad did doesn't mean you will."

I drop my hands from my hair and stare at her, daring her to say anything more. She obviously realizes her mistake, her eyes widen, and she stands straight up.

"Alex, I'm sorry, I didn't—"

I smile at her tightly. "I'm just taking precautionary measures, Carlie. Let's go."

Daniel is refilling his red solo cup just as I walk down the stairs. He has the sleeves of his dress shirt rolled up to his elbows, and he's taken off his jacket. I pull down the hem of my dress, feeling self-conscious.

Carlie grabs my arm, demanding my attention. I look over at the boy. He's cute, with sandy blonde hair and a broad smile. He's surrounded by a group of good, wholesome kids – he should be good for Carlie. I look over at her and she's practically foaming at the mouth. I smile.

"Go talk to him," I say quietly.

She looks over at me, horrified. "I can't just go up and talk to him."

"Why not?" I grab her arm and we walk down the stairs together, towards the keg. Out of the corner of my eye, I see Daniel staring at me. I ignore him.

"Because he's… cute, and…" She stares at him lovingly.

"And what? Totally unapproachable? Out of your league? I don't think so." Instead of pouring her beer, I grab two of the shot glasses the host was passing out. "Liquid courage."

She grins at me and takes the shot. Someone announces to the room the countdown will begin with a shot at New Year's, then a kiss with whoever we're standing next to.

"I think I'm gonna go situate myself next to that boy," Carlie says and takes a deep breath. I laugh, and Daniel comes up next to me just as she goes off.

"Having fun?" He asks.

"Yeah," I nod and smile. "I am."

Ever since Loretta's death, Daniel asked to be given space to clear his head and think about everything. Technically, we were on a "break," but lately it felt more like a permanent breakup. We were playing a deadly game; he who gives up their pride first loses.

"Me too." He looks down at the shot glass in my hand. "You gonna drink that at midnight?"

"Maybe. We'll see."

And the countdown begins. The entire room is filled with drunken laughter and happiness. Daniel is next to me. I see Carlie, awkwardly talking and smiling with the boy she'd pined after the whole night. I'm surrounded by joy, so much so that it's contagious.

Five…

Everyone around me joins in on the countdown; everyone except us.

Four…

He says something that makes me laugh, and grabs my hand.

Three…

My laughter halts and he smells of alcohol and anxiety and pine trees.

Two...

Everyone drinks their shot glass, including me.

One.

after

He kissed me, even after everyone else stopped kissing. Not stopping after the shot glass at midnight, my head became fuzzy and my inhibitions were not altogether in line, but I wouldn't have changed a single thing.

It was common knowledge that the house hosting the party was caked in two inches of glitter and confetti. It took a whole day and a half to clean up. I never knew the name of the person who threw the party. Shortly after midnight, the kids got too rowdy and the cops were called.

Daniel and I ran together, buzzed and laughing. We both fell down at least twice, and we got lost on the way home. His lips were blue, from the cold, and mine were too but we continued mashing them together anyway.

We were just a couple of kids who loved each other too much, or maybe not enough. To me, that was poetry.

I remember it had finally started to snow as we found our way back home. He pushed hair away from my face, and my fingers trembled with either cold or nervousness, I couldn't tell.

"How am I ever going to survive you?" He whispered, just after pulling back from my lips. In the moment, I didn't know what he meant. I was a bit too drunk off the cheap beer, too heavily intoxicated off him.

But I finally understand what he was trying to say. *How am I ever going to survive you leaving me?* I realize now that it shouldn't have been him who was afraid.

before

Sixteen Years Old – Spring

I remember Daniel wanting to get trashed every night. I remember the look in his eyes when he sobered up: dead, lifeless, cold. Blank. That's what he had become: A Blank. They were the group we were warned about as children – the group we were supposed to stay away from.

It's the day before spring break began, five months after Loretta died, an hour before the last bell rang commencing a week of sleeping in and eating too much junk food. Daniel has nowhere to go but his foster parent's house, and he was dreading it. It's the warmest day of the season so far. Everyone leaving town for vacation was buzzing around, talking about their plans and making promises to send pictures to their friends.

Daniel is sitting in the desk next to me with his cheek pressed against the desktop, looking out the windows with that open-mouthed, blank-faced expression that he'd had on his face ever since his mom died.

"Danny, you still coming to the party tonight?" A fellow student questions, leaning over to his desk.

NO! I want to scream at him. I wait for Daniel to answer, but I'm met with silence. The rest of the class is in a joyous uproar, too enthralled in their own conversations.

"Danny," he says again, louder this time. "Daniel." He puts his hand on Daniel's shoulder and shakes him. I crane my head to look at Daniel's face; his eyes were wide open. Carlie is starting to take notice and panic, which draws the teacher's—and all the other students'—attention.

"Is everything okay over there?" Mr. Ramone asks, standing from his desk.

That's when I notice how pale and lifeless Daniel *really* looks, and then drops of blood plop from his nose, and a girl screams, and my veins turn to ice.

after

I open my eyes to a bright, pulsating light beating down on me. My head throbs to its own beat, nearly doubling me over.

Then, all at once, the white light snaps away in the blink of an eye and my head is clear. I'm lying flat on my back on the blue linoleum floors of a hospital I recognize instantly.

Quincy Jones Medical Hospital – this place is a maze, but I've been here a million times. I was born here, everyone I know (or knew, whatever) was born here. Hell, even my parents were born here. Between Luke's broken bones from sports and my dislocated elbows (four times, the same elbow) this place might as well be a hang-out spot for my family.

Of course, Q.J.M. is abandoned right now. I have no idea where I'm supposed to be going, so I slowly get to my feet and wander aimlessly. All of the patient room doors are closed except for two, right next to each other in a flickering hallway.

Suddenly, the hallways are filled with an eerie silence and I'm overcome by an urge to walk a little farther. Almost as if in a trance, I walk a few extra feet into the first open room. *I've never been on this floor before... why is it familiar?* Outside, on the patient chart, is my name. Perplexed, I turn around in the corner into the room and see Luke on the edge of his seat next to the bed, but it's empty and perfectly made just like all the other rooms.

Luke looks disheveled, unwashed, worried, frantic… his eyes tell me that he's been crying. His body isn't all the way here, though. His image is hazy and discolored, as if he's floating between two different realms. His hands are clasped together as if he's been praying. He doesn't look at me as I enter the room; rather, he talks to the bed. He is older than I remember him.

"Alex, please…" He pinches his eyes together, as if in pain. "Please, just come back to us. I won't be mad, and neither will Mom or Carlie. We all just miss you so much." His face contorts to hold back a sob. "I love you so much. I'm sorry I couldn't be a better brother. I'm so sorry."

I want to take him in my arms, tell him whatever he's talking about wasn't his fault, but as soon as I move so does he.

Luke stands, leans forward, and kisses the air gently above the pillow on the bed. I'm frozen in my spot. *What is going on?* He turns toward me, but he doesn't see me. As he walks away from the bed and toward the door, he still doesn't acknowledge my presence. He walks right through me on his way to the door.

I stumble backwards, running into the door hinge. As soon as I turn around to chase after him, he disappears. I walk back into the hallway in a daze, clutching my forehead, trying to collect my thoughts.

Somehow, I find my way into the next open hospital room. The chart on the exterior of the hospital door is empty, but when I walk into the room I see Daniel lying on the bed hooked up to a million machines and tubes.

The room is disturbingly silent, putting me on edge. Daniel doesn't move a muscle when I walk into the room. His eyes are open, but lifeless. The television hooked into the corner of the room is on, but only loud static is coming through. A terrible, inexplicable feeling of dread and anxiety washes over me.

I walk over to his bedside and stand stock still. Suddenly, his eyes turn to me, soliciting an audible gasp from me. I notice his face is ghastly pale and he's shaking. His hair begins turning soaking wet, as if an invisible force were slowly pouring water over his head. His blue eyes are wide, fearful. Slowly, his lips turn blue and his cheekbones sink, revealing how gaunt he is. All at once, he begins looking like a skeleton. I back away from his deteriorating body.

Dark green ivy begins to crawl from beneath his hospital bed and curls around his fingers, then slowly encapsulates his entire arm, then wraps itself around his torso and legs. His face is the only thing the ivy doesn't touch, and I watch helplessly as he chokes on it. I watch for a while as the phantom ivy engulfs him and starts snaking to its next victim: me. Stumbling back, I trip and fall on my own feet. The ivy pushes its way toward me and tickles my index finger, but I crawl away fretfully, trying my hardest not to scream at the top of my lungs.

I sneak a peek at Daniel, whose face is now completely covered by dark green moss and branches. His body has not moved an inch. The ivy continues to pursue me as I regain my footing from the cold linoleum and sprint away from Daniel's hospital room. I'm running forward with my head turned back, watching for any sign of some ghost to pop out and snatch me up, when I lose my footing once more and fall face-first into the unforgiving, hard floor.

before

Sixteen Years Old – Spring

Quincy Jones Medical Hospital smells wretchedly of disinfectant and sick people. No matter how much Febreeze you spray, the stench of clustered, dying white blood cells is always stronger.

Daniel has no family. I'm sure he's got estranged grandparents or aunts, but he never knew any of them and wouldn't know how to contact them if his life depended on it. He has no one to visit him in the hospital, except his friends, which I guess are the Blanks now.

Daniel has been in and out of consciousness since they brought him into the hospital, but I refuse to leave his side. I don't want him to wake up and be scared. He went into cardiac arrest after mixing alcohol with Adderall – 16 years old and he's having heart attacks. Jamie, his new best friend and drug supplier, has been intelligently staying away from the hospital. I'm the only one in the room when he finally shows his face.

"You *bastard*." I leap up from my chair by Daniel's bedside and lunge for Jamie. I end up pinning him against the wall with fistfuls of his shirt in my grip. He's already a scrawny kid, but my adrenaline is pumping and I'm stronger than I thought.

"Chill!" He squeaks out, trying to free himself from my iron grip.

I let out a noise which can only be described as *growling* as I pull him back from the wall and slam him back up against it.

"*Chill?*" I scream at him, slamming him again. "Tell that to Daniel!"

"He said he needed it to study! I was just trying to help him out!"

I growl again and pull him back to slam him once more when two male nurses clasp their hands around my biceps, dragging me away from Jamie. I writhe in their grasp, quite literally foaming at the mouth, eager to bash Jamie's face in.

"I will have them forcefully remove you if you don't settle down, Ms. Sinclair." Daniel's doctor threatens. At the thought of not being able to return to Daniel, I calm down and stand on my own, still glaring daggers at Jamie. *If only looks could kill.* Seeing that I've returned to a peaceful state, the doctors and nurses disappear.

"*Believe it or not,*" Jamie says as he smooths down the wrinkles I caused in his shirt. "He was my friend too."

"Bullshit." I spit out, my words laced with venom. "He was your pay day."

"Get off your high horse, Alex. You're wrong."

That just makes me angrier, so angry that I shake. "*Adderall,* Jamie? *Really?* Are you a moron?"

"I didn't know he would take it *all,* let alone with booze! I thought he was smarter than that." Jamie sighs and runs a hand through his messy, greasy hair.

With the audience gone, it's the perfect opportunity to lunge at Jamie's neck again, but I refrain. My body is drained of all the adrenaline and anger. I'm left with only sadness and a heavy weight on my shoulders that never seems to lift.

"I know you think we're all just a bunch of deadbeat potheads, but you've got it all backwards, sweetheart." Jamie says it ironically, like I'm the one at fault. He sits in the chair across from me, on Daniel's other side. "I never thought it would get this bad with him."

"You have to promise me not to give him any more," I say quietly, then look up at him intensely. "*If* he ever wakes up."

He shakes his head, his eyes flicking to Daniel's sleeping face. "It's not that simple. The kid has a goddamn death wish."

I grind my teeth. "Whatever he does to you to get it, just know that I will do ten times worse if you *do* give it to him."

His eyes flash up to mine. "Is that a threat?"

"More like a promise."

Jamie shakes his head again, not breaking eye contact. "You don't get it," I wait for him to elaborate. "It won't matter if I don't give it to him. You think I'm the only one selling in this town? If you think *I'm* sketchy, you would shit your pants if you met the people he's been hanging around. I'm a walk in the park compared to those guys."

I clench my jaw and close my eyes. "This is your fault."

Jamie looks taken aback. "*My* fault?" He laughs sardonically, almost in disbelief. It seems like an inappropriate reaction for the situation, and I frown in response. "Alex, you really are warped. *You* were the one who is supposed to look out for him, not me. I mean, that's kind of your job, being the girlfriend and all." He gets up, stretches, and starts to walk toward the door to leave. Calling over his shoulder, "But we see how good you are at that."

His words make my blood boil. "Go to hell, Jamie."

"I'll save your boy toy a seat." Jamie grins and waves behind his head as he strides out. I want to throw one of these stupid plastic chairs at his head. I was going to, but Daniel groans next to me. His long eyelashes flutter open, revealing bloodshot—but still beautiful—eyes.

"Alex?" Daniel's voice is hoarse.

I call for the doctor. Before I even get to squeeze his hand, a swarm of people were all around me, pushing me away from him, buzzing like little flies.

A few hours later, after the hype dies down, they allow me back in to see him. Daniel is so apologetic it makes me sick. He tells me it was a one-time thing, tells me that it was a mistake. I don't reveal that Jamie came to see him, or what he said to me. He wants to hold me, kiss me, but I keep him at arm's length. He looks like shit, but I bite my tongue and refrain from telling him so. He looks weak, sick; the realization of it makes me quiet. Much like my father used to shapeshift from one person to another, I don't recognize Daniel now.

I feel so overwhelmed by this stranger in front of me that I find the first possible excuse to leave. I turn away from Daniel just as the disappointment begins to show on his face. I try to keep my composure as I leave the hospital and find where I parked the car I borrowed from Mom.

Once in the safety of my own vehicle, I softly bang my forehead against the steering wheel. The weight of what Daniel has done hasn't fully hit me yet, and I'm scared for what I'll do when it finally does. My ringtone chimes, startling me from my fetal position against the steering wheel. I compose myself as best as possible before picking up.

"Hello?" I answer quietly, then clear my throat so I sound more at ease.

"Hey, Alex." It's Carlie, sounding worried as ever. "How are you doing? How's Daniel?"

"He's..." I know I should tell her how he's he doing, but I don't even know where to begin. "He woke up for a while today, but the nurses said he should rest."

"Really?" Immediately, she sounds relieved. "That's great. Did they let you see him? Did you get to talk to him?"

"Yeah. Yeah, I was there."

There's silence on the other end of the line as Carlie waits for me to continue. "And?" She finally prompts.

I run a hand over my weary face and sigh. A million thoughts run through my head all at once, and I finally settle on one: *What did we do to deserve this? We're just kids.*

"I feel like I'm watching him disappear right before my eyes," I whisper into the phone.

"Oh, Alex," Carlie sounds distraught as she mutters my name like a prayer.

"I can't let him do this to himself, Carlie."

"I know, honey. It's okay."

"I don't know what to do. I don't know how to help him." I cover my mouth with my free hand as sob escapes.

Carlie is silent for a few seconds as silent tears flow down my cheeks. Finally, she speaks. "Alex, there isn't enough love in the world to make Daniel want to stop. He has to want that himself," She pauses. "Even if the love is coming from you."

"He wants to change; I know he does." I sniffle. *Maybe if I say it loud enough, say it enough times, I can convince myself it's true. Maybe it'll actually be true.* "If he could just remember how we all used to be, then he'd want to change."

Carlie sounds defeated. She speaks slowly. "Alex, he lost his mom. He wants to shut the pain off. This is the only way he knows how."

"No," I whisper and shake my head. "I refuse to accept that. Daniel is not the type of person who would lose himself like this. He didn't want to end up like his mother."

"*Alex, I don't want to see you go down with him!*" Carlie suddenly shouts into the phone, and I'm taken aback.

I don't understand, and immediately, I go on the defensive. "Carlie, what are you talking about? I'm fine."

"I'm sorry, Alex. I know you're hurting. But Daniel would get help if he wanted it. You have to protect yourself now—"

I can't stand to hear anymore. I pull the phone away from my ear and hang up on her. After sitting in the quiet for a few seconds, I give up on trying to be strong and start to sob into my steering wheel.

after

I thought I was past the point of crying. Turns out I was wrong.

before

Sixteen Years Old – Spring

Mom is waiting on the couch with a cup of hot tea steaming on the coffee table as I walk through the front door. I shake the rain from my coat and run my hand through my damp hair. I'm too preoccupied with myself to notice how tense she looks. It's only been a day since my fight with Carlie on the phone, and I haven't heard a peep from her since. Daniel said she hasn't been in to visit him, either.

"Hey," I approach carefully. "Shouldn't you be at work?"

She ignores my question. Her back is straight as a rod, and her face looks sour, as if whatever information she's holding in is poisoning her from the inside out. "Were you just visiting Daniel?" Even her voice is off, too quiet for everything to be alright.

"Yeah," I walk over to her. "They're gonna release him tomorrow. His foster home was threatening to kick him out if he didn't stop that stuff."

She nods slightly, looking away from me to her cup of tea.

"Mom?" She looks up at me. "Is everything okay?"

She takes a deep breath. "Sit down, Alex."

I shake my head. "I don't understand. What's going on?"

"Please sit down." I do as she says, plopping down with no grace. I'm too worried to care. "Alex, I don't quite know how to say this. You know I love Daniel, and I understand that you two are very close and have been since you were kids. But he is going down a very dark path, Alex." I know what she's going to say before she even says it. "And as much as I think he needs someone in his corner right now, I don't think you should date him anymore."

Profusely, I shake my head. "You don't understand. This was a one-time thing, Mom. He's a good person. He won't do it again."

"I know he's a good person, Alex. Good people make incredibly bad choices every day. You have so much at stake here that he doesn't. You might not notice it, but Luke looks up to you a lot. If he sees you hanging around people like Daniel, he might—"

"'People like Daniel'? What are you trying to say?" My voices raise involuntarily in pitch as I start to get defensive.

"He was hospitalized for a *drug* overdose, for God's sake!"

Quickly, I realize who is going to win this argument. Tears pool in my eyes. "Mom, you can't do this to me. Daniel has been there for me through everything. I can't just abandon him."

"You can still be his friend, honey. I just don't think it's a good idea for you two to see each other romantically anymore."

Anger flares. "This is bullshit! You know nothing about us. Or him, for that matter."

"Alexandria, I am your mother, and you will do as I say. That boy is no good for you, and you will no longer see him."

I stand up and shout something I never thought I'd say to my mother. "Fuck you!"

It all happens so quickly. Before I have time to react or even blink, she stands up and smacks me across the face. Pain slices my right cheek and I cup it with both hands. I am equally shocked and hurt that she hit me. *She hit me.* I look back at her, and she's covering her mouth with both hands, eyes wide with shock that

155

match mine. Dead silence ensues. Slowly, my senses come back to me as I try to catch my breath.

"Oh, Alex," She sobs. "I'm so sorry."

She reaches out toward me, and I flinch away. That only makes her sob harder. I'm still standing, lower lip quivering in fear and sadness. Mom plops down on the couch, sobbing into her own hands. I walk backwards until I back into the front door. Mechanically, I put my boots and coat back on. I grab her car keys, and leave.

Carlie's father answers the door. The sputtering of rain has turned into a torrential downpour, and I'm entirely soaked. I hardly feel it. All I can think about is my mother. The raindrops dripping from my hair mingle with the tears on my cheek.

"Alex! Come on in, honey. You're soaking." Her dad touches my shoulder and I, inadvertently, flinch and draw in a gasped breath.

"Ally?" Carlie asks as she walks down the long winding staircase, her socked feet padding on the slippery hardwood. "Are you okay?"

I don't know if it's her face contorted in concern, or her soothing voice that I've shared countless jokes with, but I finally start to break down again. Her father still stands next to me, awkwardly. I had kept it mostly in control the whole car ride, until now.

Carlie speed-walks toward me and wraps her arm around my shoulder. "Dad, why don't you go order some pizza for us or something?" He readily takes this excuse to leave.

Carlie ushers me up to her bedroom, which is probably bigger than my whole house. Her family has always had a nice house. They've always had money. Her parents are happily married. She's beautiful, and smart, and funny. Though they're friends, she would never get mixed up with a boy like Daniel. I'm nothing compared to her. I've always been nothing.

"What's wrong, Ally? Is it Daniel?" She asks gently, rubbing my arms up and down. I cry harder, but shake my head.

"My... mom..." I'm sobbing so hard, these words come out slowly and in between hiccups. "She... hit... me."

We're sitting on her bed, cross-legged and facing each other. The door is closed. I watch Carlie's reaction through blurry tears. Her mouth goes slack, and she blinks quickly almost like she's just been hit. She whispers, to herself, "Oh my god." Then, she leans forward and wraps both of her arms around my shoulders and lets me bury my sobbing and snotty face into her neck.

After I calm down, Carlie gets the full story out of me. I even tell her I said "fuck you" first. I deserved to get hit, and I felt terrible for saying what I said. But I knew Mom only felt worse.

She holds me for a long time after that. I assume she's trying to stick all my broken pieces back together, the way only a best friend can.

I don't drive home until much later, past midnight. When I pull into my driveway, my house is dark. I shut off the engine and let out a shaky breath. Closing my eyes, I try to calm myself down and fail miserably. I explode, pounding at my steering wheel and raging. *She hit me. She doesn't want me to see Daniel anymore. I cussed at her. She hit me. She hit me.* I keep punching at my dashboard until I've exhausted all my energy. Resting my forehead against the top of my steering wheel, I close my eyes once more. I know I should go inside, or there'll be hell to pay tomorrow morning.

But I can't bring myself to walk through that door. There are too many painful memories in there. Every footstep is like walking through hell. I miss my dad. I miss him so much. *Why did you leave me, Dad? I'm sorry. I'm sorry I've ignored you. Please, just get better. That's all I ask. I promise I'll love you. I promise.*

My heart hurts too badly. I look down at my fists, and they're shaking. My knuckles are red from the violent outburst. Suddenly, I know where to go. I don't know if I'll be able to stomach it, but I have to try something.

Driving through a city at night is the loneliest thing in the world. My small town all but rolls up the sidewalks when the sun sets, but there are ghosts scattered everywhere, paying no attention to what time of day it is. They like nighttime the most; it's when the living goes to sleep and the world isn't bothered by their humanity.

It's still spring break, but the weather is only just recovering from winter despite all the snow having already melted. The meadow isn't full of life and flowers, but instead full of dry, brown grass and scraggly stems. The trees haven't gotten their leaves back yet. I suppose I shouldn't be so upset; this is what happens in winter, after all. Things die. And then they come back. But the meadow was my home, and now it's turned on me and died like everything else.

after

I was so selfish that night. I should've just listened to Mom and got Daniel the help he needed. I was so stupid, so self-centered. Such a child. I *deserved* to die.

before

Sixteen Years Old – Spring

In the bottom of my mother's closet, there are a few shoeboxes full of scrapbooks from Luke and I's childhood. Taking photographs used to be a passion of hers, before our world spun out of control. Mom always had a camera around her neck, ready to capture even the simplest of memories.

She's at work now, so I can go through her room undisturbed. I kneel in front of her closet, sifting through clothes and old shoes looking for the boxes. After digging profusely, I find them. There, in big black Sharpie, is "OLD PHOTOS + SCRAPBOOKS."

When I was searching for them, I had been filled with determination. As if a switch was flipped, that mood evaporates and is replaced by melancholy. My heart fills with dread, and the boxes feel like a dead weight. I can't remember why I wanted to look at these in the first place.

They're just pictures, not the boogeyman.

Despite every gut instinct telling me it's only going to hurt to look at the albums, I open the first box. This one is just full of pictures Mom hasn't put in a scrapbook yet, and probably never will. I pick up one that stands out; it's of me and Dad, on my seventh birthday. Money was starting to get tight, but Mom and Dad still believed it would all be okay, that it was just a rough patch they would get through somehow. Dad and I were smiling above an alit birthday cake. My front tooth was missing, showing proudly through my broad grin. He was watching me and I was watching the candles. The worry between my parents had dissipated, for that day at least. They even held hands. I can't help but smile when I look at the picture now, even with tears forming in my eyes.

"Alex?" Luke asks, standing in Mom's doorway. "What are you doing?"

"Oh," I fluster, hurriedly putting the picture in my pocket before closing the box back up and putting it back. "Just looking at old pictures."

"Okay..." He gives me a funny look as I stand back up and wipe my sweaty palms on the back of my jeans. "Well, Daniel is here. He wants to talk to you."

All previous thoughts of the pictures become moot. I nod at Luke, trying to smile, and tell him I'll be out in a minute. When he leaves the room, my smile fades and I try to take deep, even breaths. Daniel is outside. He wants to talk to me. I haven't returned any of his calls, and hadn't visited him in the hospital, since that argument with my mom only six days earlier. I can't just leave him out there; I have to go out. With one last look in my mom's vanity mirror, I sum up as much confidence as I can.

When I walk out into the living room, Luke has disappeared into his bedroom with loud music blasting. I can see Daniel through the skinny window beside our front door. He's facing away from the door, with his hands shoved into his jacket pockets. I can only see his back, but his hair is disheveled and he's tapping his foot impatiently. My heart races.

Slowly, I open the front door and look at him. He turns around quickly, looking at me like I'm the first person he's seen in days.

"What haven't you been answering my calls?" Daniel asks suddenly, his voice harsh.

Daniel's eyes are bloodshot; his hands won't stop shaking, even inside his coat pockets, despite the warmer weather. A thought pops into my head.

"Are you high?" I ask quietly, furrowing my eyebrows.

"What?" His voice is high-pitched. "No. Why would you ask that?"

"Quit lying to me," I snap.

He opens his mouth to say something, then closes it and looks away from me. "Okay. Me and Jamie got a *little* high earlier today."

I scoff and shake my head, anger flaring.

"I'm fine, Alex. It was just pot, and it was barely a buzz. It's already worn off," He continues.

"You're unbelievable, Daniel."

"It's not a big deal, Alex. Jesus."

"No, Dan, it is a big deal. Do you not remember who our parents are? What happened to them?"

He clenches his jaw and stares at me. "Don't use that as an argument."

"I will, because it's a damned good one. We promised each other we would never get into that shit, and here you are – getting high after being released from the *hospital* for a *drug* overdose."

"That was an accident."

"It doesn't matter, Daniel! Jesus Christ!" I yell. "All it takes is one mistake, an *ounce* too much, and you're dead. Do you wanna die, Dan? Is that what this is?"

He doesn't answer me, just shakes his head. His jaw muscle twitches.

"You can shake your head and tell yourself that I'm a crazy bitch all you want, but deep down you know I'm right."

Daniel stares at something on my cheek, perplexed. "What happened to your face, Alex?"

"What?" I quip, perturbed at the subject change. He reaches forward and touches a tiny cut on my cheek, made by my mother's fingernail when she hit me. His thumb brushes against my cheekbone softly, but I flinch away from his touch. "Nothing."

"Alex," Daniel's voice cracks, and the hurt finally begins to show on his face.

I take a deep breath, and feed him the half-truths that collectively break our hearts. "I can't do this anymore, Daniel. I can't watch you destroy yourself."

"No," He whispers. "You don't know what you're saying. You're upset, and that's okay."

"I do know what I'm saying. I love you," I whisper, and his macho-man façade crumbles entirely. It's the first time either of us has said those three little words. "That's why I have to end it."

"Ally, please don't do this. I love you too. Please don't do this to me. I'll do anything you want. Please."

A tear slips down my cheek. "I think you should go."

"Ally—" His tortured voice cracks out just before I close the door in his face.

I can hear him rest his forehead against the closed door, and I turn around and slide my back down until I'm sitting on the floor, a crumpled mess of a person. Now that I don't have to face him, I let the tears flow freely. I cover my mouth and nose so he doesn't hear it through the door. After a few minutes, the weight against the door from him lifts and I hear him walk away. His car engine revs a few seconds later, and he speeds away. I only cry harder.

I tell myself that I'm worthless, and ugly, and no one could possibly care about me. The pain is never-ending. I want to kill myself. I'm going to kill myself.

These voices, these thoughts… they're all mine. There isn't an illness or some brain disorder or a drug addiction that I can blame this on. It's all me. Maybe that's the worst part.

I should've never left Daniel. I miss him so much. He calls me every day, telling me how sorry he is and how much he loves me. He tells me that he got a job, and he's been clean. He wants to work it out, but I can smell the bullshit through the phone.

Every time I close my eyes, I see my father. Sometimes smiling and happy, but usually leaving. I dream about him screaming at me, telling me it's my fault he left and never came back. Nightmares plague me every night, so I don't sleep.

I've become obsessed with death. I fantasize about all the ways I could die, both accidentally and intentionally. The days all blend together. Go to school, try to pay attention, come home, do homework, choke down food (for no one's sake other than Mom's), pretend to sleep. I'm a fraud, a fake, a phony. I can't deal with who I've become.

Luke and Mom have gone off to see a movie. Mom finally has a few seconds off of work, and I convinced her to spend it with her only son. She'll have to spend all her time with him when I'm gone, anyway.

She has chronic back pain, resulting from a car accident in her teens. I've known this all my life. Today, I steal the pain pills out of her medicine cabinet. Once they've been gone for a few minutes and I know they aren't coming back, I grab the medicine bottle from its hiding place and go into the bathroom, locking the door.

My phone sits on the counter next to me. My note is on the desk in my bedroom. The pill bottle sits on the counter in front of me, unmoving and menacing. *Should I really do this?* Yes. I should. The pain won't stop any other way. I'd do anything to just make the pain stop.

Using tap water, I pour myself a glass of water and tighten my hand around it. Hesitantly, I open the pill bottle. I stare down at them, contemplating. *I have to do this. I have to do this. There's no other way.* Without giving myself too much time to think about it, I pour a handful of pills into my palm and shove them in my mouth. One hard gulp of water and they're down.

But I don't stop. I keep going until the bottle is empty. It was only half full to begin with, but it should do the trick.

After a while, I begin to panic. I can't feel anything yet. Surely, if it were going to work, I'd feel something by now. Right? I try to reach for the bathroom door knob, but my face suddenly feels very fuzzy. I look down at my outstretched hand, and the colors swirl together in front of my face. My knees begin to feel unstable just as my phone starts buzzing on the bathroom counter. I see Carlie's picture on the screen and fall to the floor.

I'm running – running through this blue hallway. My calves and lungs burn, but I keep going. I keep running and watch the blue pass me by. But then, I just stop. I stop, and catch my breath, and I turn around. I don't know why I stop running, or why I turn around and walk the other way, but I do.

after

Luke,

Don't drive yourself insane by worrying about me, or where I am, or why I did what I did. Wherever we go when we die, whatever happens to us, I have a feeling I'll be happier there than here. Tell Daniel and Carlie and Mom that I love them, no matter what. Remember that you're smarter, braver, kinder, and stronger than even I could imagine. I'll see you soon, little brother. I love you.

With love and best wishes,
Ally

before

Sixteen Years Old – Spring

I open my eyes to the taste and feel of vomit dribbling down my chin. Carlie is sobbing beside me, and tears have already streaked down my face from the vomit. I notice bits of puke on Carlie's index and middle finger.

"Why would you do that," She sobs hysterically, but it doesn't come out as a question. Her voice sounds underwater. "Why, why, why, Alex."

Another wave of nausea rolls over me, and I bend over the toilet again to puke my guts out. I don't know how to stop crying. I don't know how to make this right.

"No, no, no," I sob. *Why am I still alive? It wasn't supposed to happen like this. You weren't supposed to find me yet.* Through the thick fog, I hear Carlie calling 911, but all I can feel is overwhelming despair that it didn't work.

I'm put on a "suicide watch list." The doctors have to pump my stomach. I don't know if I regret it.

Being here, having just attempted my own death, doesn't feel real yet. It almost feels like a dream, or maybe more of a nightmare – like I'll wake up any moment now and everything would go back to normal.

It's dark out when I wake up. Mom is asleep in the armchair in the corner, Daniel is lying on his stomach on the floor with his head resting on his crossed forearms, and Luke is curled at the foot of my bed. He's lying on my left foot, and it feels fuzzy, but I don't want to disturb him by moving it.

Carlie has pulled one of the far-too-heavy chairs next to my bed and is sitting there with her head down. Her hands are clasped tightly, her elbows pressing into her knees harshly. Apparently I've stirred quite a bit since waking, because she looks up at me and then looks back down. It looks like she hasn't slept at all since she's been here, and she hasn't changed her clothes. There's a yellow stain at the bottom of her shirt.

"I had to put my fingers down your throat, Alex." She speaks, her voice quiet but sounding so loud and out of place at a time like this. Her throat is hoarse, I can tell, and her eyes are red-rimmed and puffy from crying. I'd hate to see what I look like right now. "I knocked the door handle off and found you in the bathroom. I had to save you." Her voice cracks on the last sentence.

I'm unable to look her in the eye, unable to say anything. There are never any words for this kind of pain.

"Why would you do something like that? Why?" She looks up at me, tears already coming down her cheeks again. Her eyes are pleading for an answer. "Why would you do that?"

Thickly, I swallow. I, myself, am fighting the urge to hold back tears.

"They're gonna put you in a mental hospital, Alex."

My blood runs ice cold. "What?"

"They do it to anyone who tries to kill themselves. It's part of the whole 'suicide watch' thing."

"They can't do that," I say hurriedly, frantically. "They can't put me there. I have school, and friends, and, and…"

Carlie stands up, trying to assure me, but that only makes me panic more. I push her away and try to stand up, only to get dizzy and fall back down again. In my efforts, I have woken up the rest of the room. Daniel looks up at me and doesn't say or do anything – he just stares. Luke looks terrified. Mom rushes to my side, trying to get me to sit down. I'm shouting at them and telling them to take me out of here. Suddenly, a nurse comes in and stops when she sees us; I see her say something to another nurse that comes in, then leaves, but I hardly register it.

"Please, Mom, don't let them take me away! I promise I won't do it again!" I'm sobbing, screaming, for my mother to take me home.

I try to push my mom away, but Daniel is up and pinning my arm by my side, and then Luke has the other one. They pull me closer towards the bed, with me kicking and shouting the entire time. "I want to go home! *Let* me *go!*" I shout at Daniel and Luke.

The nurse that left previously comes back with a syringe full of clear liquid as they try to get me flat on the bed, but the syringe only makes me thrash more.

"Please, no, no…" I cry to Daniel and turn my head to look at him. His eyes are full of sorrow and his lips part slightly, wanting to let me go. The nurse pushes the syringe into my arm and I cry out in pain and clench my eyes together.

Quite quickly, my muscles begin to feel like lead. I urge my body to fight, fight more, fight harder, but that only makes me more tired. A tear rolls down Daniel's cheek as he loosens his grip on my arms, soothing me, and my world goes black.

The next time I wake up, I'm strapped to the bed.

It's an odd thing, being in the psych ward in Q.J.M. I wasn't even aware Q.J.M. *had* a psych ward until a few days ago. The people in here have glass eyes, not real ones – everyone stares, but nobody sees.

My roommate is bipolar, and tried to kill herself too. I've heard rumors that they're moving her to a long-term facility somewhere down the coast. There are bars on the windows, and the walls are sickly white. Everyone I see is no longer human; instead they've become their own illness.

To the nurses and doctors, you aren't a person. Instead, a face, a name, and a diagnosis. I'm not Alex Sinclair anymore – I'm 16-year-old female diagnosed with depression; suffers from suicidal thoughts and panic attacks; father absent since early teens; occasionally violent and temperamental; belligerent toward staff and overall stay here. Those are all the ways they describe me, because that's what's written in my chart. What happened to all the good things I used to be?

The good – or bad, however you want to take it – thing about this place is that I have a lot of time to think. Actually, that's probably a bad thing overall. Left to my own devices, I'm quite unreliable in my own train of thought.

Before being involuntarily committed here, Mom packed a bag full of my favorite books and comfy clothes, so I wouldn't get bored. She visits every evening, for an hour; sometimes she's with Carlie, sometimes Luke. Daniel hasn't visited me yet, but we talk on the phone every night that I'm here after visiting hours.

"If I had known this would've got you talking to me again, I would've tried to kill you weeks ago," He says to me one night, trying to get me to laugh. I snicker for his own benefit and lean against the wall. He's silent for a few seconds.

"This doesn't change how I feel, Danny," I pause. "We still can't be together."

He sighs. "I know. I'm sorry I screwed it up."

I contemplate what I say next. "I just want you to get better."

He lets out a breathless chuckle. "Ditto, Ally."

The nights are the worst. In the daytime, there is a normal buzz around. I meet with my social worker and appointed therapist every day (usually when I'm just getting to a good part in my book) and they seem nice. They give me medication, which I take in the morning with all the other patients. We've found a therapist I'm going to see after I get out of here. In the second day, after moping around alone in my room, I actually attend group therapy and craft time. I was expecting something along the lines of *One Flew Over the Cuckoo's Nest*, but it's really not like that at all. The people are kind. The nurses are respectful. My doctor is overwhelmed, but that's understandable. The only real thing I have to complain about is how bored I am all the time.

But in nighttime, the hustle fades away and all you hear is the sound of your own heart beating, or your own roommate's snoring. The silence is unbearable, and it plagues you, molding you into a sleep-hungry zombie.

The worst night was when the screaming started. A few days previous, a new guy with severe Asperger's was admitted. I was just starting to feel my eyes grow heavy when I heard the earth-shattering screaming. I bolted awake, slowly rising, trying to get my bearings. My roommate sits up and rubs the sleep from her eyes.

"What the hell?" She says to me, her voice dripping with contempt.

"It wasn't me," I retort. The screaming picks up again, and I hear the scuffle of nurse's orthopedic shoes running past our bedroom door. I rise from my bed and go the small cut-out window in the door; my roommate does the same and we bump heads a bit, trying to get a clear view. The new guy was thrashing around, screaming bloody murder. The nurses were trying to calm him down, but nothing they said or did helped. It was like the guy became Superman in just a few short seconds, acquiring new strength and adrenaline.

He tried running away a few feet, towards the direction of our room, but they caught and twisted his arms behind his back. A nurse speed-walks toward him, wielding an all-too-familiar syringe full of clear liquid. I look away as I hear his screams immediately satiate; I can practically hear his body sag with the drug they pump into his veins.

My roommate is still at the window, watching them take him away, as I go back to my bed and lay down. I never fall asleep that night.

after

I'm going insane I know I am I can feel it in my bones in my
bones
I feel everything and nothing everything and nothing
This isn't real
It can't be
There has to be more
I just want to go home
I want to go home
There's no ruby slippers for the hell I'm in.

before

Sixteen Years Old – Spring

After four days (Mom couldn't pick me up on the third day), I'm released from Quincy James Psychiatric Facility with a slap on the wrist and scheduled appointments with my therapist. I beg Mom not to make me go back to school, to please let me be homeschooled, but she says it isn't an option. *I'm still paying back your medical bills,* she says. *How do you think I could ever afford for you to be homeschooled now?*

When I walk back into my home for the first time after trying to kill myself, it's like a breath of fresh air. I never realized how many things I took for granted until now. Number one was sitting right there on our couch.

Luke's hands are folded together, his elbows resting on his knees. My baby brother looks as if he's grown ten years older in the short time I've been away. He avoids eye contact, but stands when we enter. I put my duffel bag down and we stand there for a few seconds, just staring awkwardly at each other. Then, almost as if we could read each other's minds, we cross the floor simultaneously and meet each other halfway. He wraps his arms around my shoulders and I put mine around his back. I can't remember the last time I hugged him, even before the hospital visit.

"Jesus, it's like you grew a foot in four days." I whisper to him, my voice muffled by his shoulder.

Despite everything, he laughs through his own tears. "The steroids are working wonders."

I smile and pull back, getting a good look at him. After a few seconds, I hug him again.

"I'm so sorry, Luke," I say quietly. "I never meant to hurt you."

He doesn't say anything as he pulls away from my hug. Again, he won't look me in the eye. Who can blame him? I almost ripped this family apart, again.

"How are you… feeling?" He asks tentatively.

"I'm alright." It's a lie. But it's all I can do to fix the mess I made.

"Are you hungry?" Mom asks, walking toward the kitchen. "What do you want to eat? I bought all your favorites."

"I'm not really hungry right now," I say sheepishly. "I think I'll just sleep for a while."

"Oh," She pauses, looking around the kitchen, as if searching for something else to say. "Okay. I'll wait until later to cook dinner, then."

I smile at her, but I think it probably comes out as a grimace. I grab my bag and head down the skinny hallway to my bedroom. The door is closed, and I'm not sure I want to open it.

But I do, because I have to face it eventually. It still looks the way I left it. It still smells like lavender, the scent of the candles I used to burn religiously when things like that mattered to me. The candle smoke must've permeated into the walls. My bed is still unmade. Slowly, I walk over to my desk. Pictures in frames of me with Carlie, me with Luke, me with Mom and Dad, me with Daniel—they all still stand proudly in their same spot. I pick up a picture of me and Dad; I was eight. We were in the meadow with

Mom and Luke. We had a picnic. Dad was chasing us around the field. It was summer, so Luke had an advantage of hiding in the tall flowers. Mom had taken the picture just as Dad lifted me up in the air and spun me around. Dad's looking at me. I'm looking at the camera. I set the frame back down on my desk and I look over all the others.

There's a lot of pictures of Carlie and me, some taken during summer, some taken at our school's football games, some taken at birthdays, or holidays, or school dances. Then there's Daniel. One is a candid photo Carlie took in school, where we're both looking at each other, sticking our tongues out. Another is of Daniel, Carlie, Luke and me. We're in a line, arms all around the other's shoulder. Our grins are contagious, and I remember Daniel made a particularly dirty joke just before Mom snapped the picture. She took it on our first day of school, when I was 14. We each have a copy.

There's a picture taped up on the wall above my desk, without a frame. It's the most recent picture I have, taken right before Daniel's stunt in the hospital… and right before our breakup. We're at a party. Daniel is kissing my cheek, and I'm smiling into the camera. I remember he smelled like booze that night, but his kiss felt the same.

I turn back around and look at the posters on my walls. Most of it are band posters, some artwork. What would they have done with all my stuff if I had succeeded in killing myself? Then I remember something: the note. I left a note. It was on my bedside table, but it's gone now. *Who found it?* The thought makes me sick. It was addressed to Luke, but I hope it wasn't him who found it. I don't know who would've been less distraught in finding my note.

I look out my bedroom window, at Daniel's now-empty house. His treehouse is still there, and they can't seem to find anyone willing to buy the place. There are memories of us up in that treehouse for hours on end, when we were kids. As we got older, we outgrew things like that. I wish we hadn't.

Every day of life outside of the hospital is a blessing. I can step outside whenever I want to, and stay there for as long as I want. I begin to realize how lucky I was to just have a roof over my head, and food in my belly. Sure, Mom might be gone a little more than I would like. But I have Luke, Daniel, and Carlie, when they aren't working. Luke had to take on a job when I was admitted to the hospital to help Mom pay my medical bills. At first I feel really guilty for it, but my therapist is helping me get past that.

My therapist's name is Dr. Moore. He is short and stocky, with a thick dark beard and glasses always perched on the edge of his nose – reminds me of Robin Williams in *Good Will Hunting*. He is a no-nonsense sort of guy, and he tells it to me straight. I like that. I like him. I think he can really help me. He starts off every session, including this one, with, "Tell me all of the good things that happened today."

I've never cried in front of him. I made myself a promise that I wouldn't, not ever, not unless someone died or something. We've kept it light, mostly, just focusing on me. And it helped, for a while. But no matter how hard I try, the darkness always creeps back in. I can't breathe without feeling the never-ending weight on my chest.

I'm trying to explain that to him when he asks me, "Do you love your depression, Alex?"

"What?" I ask, taken aback by his question. "What do you mean?"

"Do you love your depression?" He says it slower. I asked what he meant, but I already know.

"No," I answer quickly. "Of course not. I hate it. I hate it so much. I just want to be happy, and normal, and fun, like I was."

"There is no such thing as 'normal.' We're all a little strange."

I stay quiet.

Dr. Moore regards me for a few seconds, considering his next answer. I watch him stroke his beard intensely. "That's a good sign, that you don't love your depression. Do you know why?" I shake my head. "It means you want to get better, Alex. It means that you can." He smiles at me. I look away.

"How's your brother?"

"He's okay, considering the circumstances." Circumstances that I caused. "I'm worried about him."

"Why?"

"Because I think he might've been the one to find my… suicide note. And it's got to be hard for him, knowing that his sister tried to kill herself after everything that happened with Dad."

"Of course. It sounds like you care a lot about him, Alex."

"I do."

"Most sisters and brothers butt heads a lot, but you two seem to get along very well, and even have an unusually close relationship. What makes him so special to you, aside from the obvious?"

My throat tightens, as does my chest. "Well… when my parents were getting divorced, and even before then, they'd fight all the time. Mom was starting to work a lot, and Dad was always off doing whatever it was that he did. So the only people Luke and I had been each other." Dr. Moore motions for me to continue. "I have a lot of respect for him."

"Why?"

"I think I underestimate him a lot, which I probably shouldn't do. He's one of the toughest people I know. I mean, I wish I was as strong as him sometimes. And he can make me laugh no matter how upset I am."

My voice cracks, and I feel the tears coming on. "He was all I had, for a really long time. Protecting him kept me alive. I just love him a lot."

"I can tell. What makes him so strong, to you?"

"He just rolls with the punches, I guess."

"So if you think he's so strong, why don't you think he can deal with your suicide attempt?"

I frown. "It's different."

"How so?"

"Because this is *me*. He's supposed to know that I'm the one that'll always protect him. How can I do that if I can't even protect myself?"

"You said yourself that you underestimate him too much. In healthy family relationships, it's important for everyone to know that their family member will be there for them if they're down in the dumps. You've protected Luke his whole life. Maybe he believes it's his time to protect you."

Dr. Moore gave me coping mechanisms, to help raise my self-esteem. He told me to go look in the mirror tonight and pick one thing, just one, that I thought was physically "beautiful" about myself and focus on it.

So, here I am, staring into my bathroom mirror like a total idiot. I take a deep breath. Okay, this is totally normal. Right? I just have to focus on something that I like. How hard could it be?

I like my eyes. I've always liked my eyes. And I like my teeth. *Who likes their teeth?* God, this is so weird. Okay. I like my… hair. It's a nice brown color, and it's shiny and thick. I have freckles; I like those. I look like my dad – I like that. I have good bone structure. I like that too.

Every day, the darkness finds a way to creep in. And every day, when it does, I close my eyes and tell myself, "No. I am better than that. I am happy, and I will be okay."

Soon, the darkness doesn't creep in so often anymore. After a while, it stops altogether.

before

Sixteen Years Old – Summer

The end of our sophomore year ends with a bang: Oliver Fitzpatrick's annual beach bonfire. I had never spoken to Oliver Fitzpatrick, personally, but Carlie's new beau from New Year's Eve had scored us an invite.

Carlie always had good grades, and so did I, but mine had been understandably slipping these past school years. But at the end of the year, I come home with a report card full of A's. Carlie and I have already been planning what colleges we were going to visit together this summer. We can't visit the ones we really wanted to, which were all the way across the country, but it was fun planning short little road trips.

The party is already in full swing when we get there. Loud bass music thumping out of huge speakers standing on truck beds make the ground shake, and the kids are already acting crazy. In the middle of all the partying and drinking is the biggest bonfire I'd ever seen; they must've had to cut down a whole forest to find enough wood to keep the thing burning.

"Look, there he is!" Carlie grabs my arm and points across the crowd, over to a cluster of boulders closer to the water. I recognize the boy from the New Year's party laughing with his friends, standing on one of the boulders messing around. Daniel is one of the boys in the group, and my heart starts pounding a little harder than before.

"I want you to meet him. Come on, let's go," She starts tugging me toward them, but I dig my heels into the sand.

"I think I'm gonna get a drink first. Why don't you go get him, and I'll meet you over by the fire in a few minutes?" She gives me a perplexed look, then says okay and walks off. I look back at the group once more before turning toward the keg. Daniel hasn't noticed me yet.

We haven't spoken much since I was released from the hospital. He wasn't allowed to come over, and I got too busy with schoolwork and making myself better to call him. For the first few weeks, he would always try to talk to me in school; I would be polite, but distant. He'd be warm; I'd be cold. Pretty soon, he stopped trying to reach out altogether. It made me sad to think how I had just ignored him the whole time, but what was I supposed to do? Every time I tried to talk to him, it was a reminder of what we used to be and how we could never be *that* again. And when I saw him around Jamie, it only fueled my anger. I couldn't risk my entire future on him – not even if I loved him.

Maneuvering through the thick crowd turns out to be harder than it looks, especially while carrying two full cups of beer. I make it to the fire before Carlie does, so I'm left standing there like an idiot all alone. To calm my nerves, I gulp down half of my beer.

"Better slow down," Daniel says behind me. I whirl around, knocking into a few people. I mutter a half-assed apology to them, buying as much time as I can before I have to look Daniel in the eye.

Eventually, though, I do have to. My heart pounds against my rib cage at the sight of him, aching to jump out of my chest and into his hands. His eyes are cold and protective, but he's not malignant.

183

I can tell he has his wits about him, so far. He looks cool, calm, and collected – the opposite of everything I feel.

"With the beer," He continues, nodding at my hand. "You've never drank much."

When I don't say anything, he looks me up and down from head to toe. Suddenly I feel very self-conscious, as if he's scrutinizing me. He meets my eyes again. "You look good, Ally."

I gulp, smiling half-heartedly at him, and find my voice. "Thank you."

"Carlie sent me here to tell you they're *congregating* under the pier." He voices "congregating" ironically.

Looking at him in the firelight hurts my heart. "Will you be coming, too?"

He stifles a smile, but says, "Unfortunately for you."

That stings a little bit. I sum up whatever dignity I have left and wedge the solo cups into the sand, leaving them behind. "Thanks for telling me."

I walk away, towards the pier, and he follows me. We walk in silence, me ahead of him with my arms crossed. Eventually, though, he catches up and walks in step with me. I walk as far away from him as possible, until I'm on the edge of the water line.

"Sorry. I guess I was kind of a dick back there." Daniel looks over at me, searching my face for something.

I thaw a bit, then look over at him. "Can't really blame you."

"No, I guess you can't."

Awkward silence ensues, but I start to hear the laughter and music coming from underneath the pier. There's another, smaller, fire there as well.

"Ally," He grabs my arm, his fingers brushing against my bare skin. I spin around to face him, and we're closer than before. "I just wanted to say that I'm sorry. For everything."

I don't know what to say. I know I should say something, but what? I don't know whether it's the darkness or the beer has made me confident. "You shouldn't be sorry for it all."

He smiles at me, a genuine smile. He still hasn't let go of my arm yet. "I'm not sorry for everything." My skin sizzles and his eyes go dark. "But I am sorry for hurting you."

I open my mouth to say something, but I hear Carlie calling my name. We both look over and she stands, silhouetted by the fire, waving us over.

"Guess that's our call," Daniel releases my arm and leaves me, walking toward the pier, shoving his hands into his front pockets.

"Alex, this is my boyfriend, Mike. Mike, this is my best friend, Alex."

I shake his hand, smiling politely. "It's nice to finally meet you, Mike."

"You too. Carlie's told me a lot about you."

I laugh. "All good, I hope."

"Of course," Carlie grins, wrapping her hand around Mike's forearm and leaning her head against his shoulder. It's nice to see Carlie so happy, no matter how much it makes my heart ache for Daniel.

We all sit around the fire, Daniel sitting directly across from me. We share awkward eye contact more than once, but after a few beers, I no longer care. It feels so good to be among friends again, and to laugh freely.

I am sufficiently buzzed by the time our group returns to the bigger party. The music has been turned up louder, and the heavier liquor has been brought out. Carlie and I run to the designated dancing area and jump along with the bass, singing the few lyrics we do know. The air has gotten chillier, but I'm still sweating.

Daniel and Mike join us, but I don't mind. Mike grabs onto Carlie's hips and sways with her.

I don't know how it happens, or who grabs the other first, but all I know now is that Daniel and I are dancing together. Against my better judgement, I reach up and wrap my arms around his neck. His eyes are hooded as our foreheads touch. For a second, I think we're going to kiss, but then Carlie pulls me away to dance with her again.

Mechanically, we all gravitate towards the fire again. My exhaustion gets the best of me, and Daniel and I settle for just sitting around the big fire and talking. I think Carlie and Mike go back to the makeshift dance floor, but I lose track of them.

Daniel is happy, laughing at all of my jokes and making jokes himself. We talk about what we've been doing in the time since we've been together.

"How's your home life?" I ask him tentatively.

"It's okay. It's stable, you know? It's better than what I had growing up, but… I just don't feel a connection with them. They're kind of just… there." He looks up at me and I nod at him. "It feels like I'm just renting the place out sometimes." I stay quiet because I don't know what else to say. "I forgot how good it feels to talk to you, Alex. For the longest time, I forgot what it's like to enjoy myself and be sober at the same time."

The tension between us suddenly reaches its peak. "And I forgot how you beautiful you are."

To dissipate the awkwardness, I laugh and roll my eyes. "What a line."

He laughs along with me. "I'm serious."

Pausing before, I say, "Daniel—" But he stops me.

"You said you love me, before you…" he trails off, and I want to finish the sentence for him. *Before I tried to kill myself. You can say it, Daniel.* "Is that past tense now?"

I should shut this down right now. Daniel is clean, he's doing good in school, he's doing what he's supposed to do – but does this change anything? Inside, I know it shouldn't. He hurt me. He *hurt* me.

But I love him, present tense. How can I possibly lie?

"I—" I start to speak, unaware of where it's going to go, but we're interrupted by someone who claps Daniel on the shoulders. I jump, involuntarily, and look up to see Jamie standing above Daniel with a smug grin on his face.

"Alex, you're looking stunning, as always." Jamie says sardonically, with a tight smile. When he leans down and gives Daniel a wet kiss on the cheek, I know he's drunk. "Daniel, have you won her back yet?"

"What are you doing here, Jamie?" Daniel's voice is clipped, and it's evident he does not feel as warmly to his "old friend" as Jamie does.

Jamie stands up tall, suddenly, and opens his arms wide regarding the scenery. "It's a party, Daniel! Where else would I be?"

"I don't know, maybe rotting in a hole somewhere," I mutter under my breath. I peek up from under my lashes to see Jamie staring at me coolly.

"Daniel, your girlfriend's *attitude* certainly hasn't improved in the months since I've seen her last. Perhaps a little *pick-me-up*—" He plops down next to Daniel and reveals a plastic baggy filled with white pills. "—is in order."

My blood runs cold, and I hold my breath for Daniel's reaction. I don't know what kind of drug he has, and I don't want to. Daniel refuses to look at Jamie's hand, the one holding the bag, and clenches his jaw.

"Get out of here, Jamie."

Jamie is silent for a few seconds; I risk a look up and our eyes meet. I can see that dilated look in his eyes; the faraway look of someone on a trip. He had always been a Blank, devoid of emotion, but now all I see is rage on his face.

"What, you don't want to party anymore now that your booty call is here?"

"Don't talk about her like that," I can see the anger forming behind Daniel's tensed muscles, and I start to grow scared. But what Jamie is saying grabs my attention.

Jamie holds his hands up in defense. "I'm just saying; it's a little coincidental you don't want to party now that Alex is paying attention to you again. That wasn't your attitude last week."

Oh. Does this mean Daniel lied to me about being sober? After hearing this, all I want to do is get away from *both* of them. Jamie doesn't even stop talking.

"Last week, you were pretty intent on partying." Jamie smiles and winks at me.

I've had enough. I set my plastic cup down into the sand and begin walking in the other direction, toward where I parked my car. Betrayal and hatred for Jamie runs through my veins.

"Alex!" Daniel shouts, trying to weave his way through the crowd to follow me. "Alex, wait!"

I shouldn't be surprised Daniel was lying. So why am I?

The commotion is all too much. The sting of Jamie's words, the adrenaline of trying to get away from Daniel, the thumping music, the sweaty bodies – they're all closing in on me, and suddenly the little alcohol I had comes rushing up to me. My head begins pounding and nausea rolls through me.

Thankfully, I break from the crowd and my foot hits the sandy pavement of the public parking lot. Daniel is still following, closely behind me.

"Alex, wait! Please!"

"Just let me go home, Daniel."

As quickly as I can, I unlock the driver's side door on my mom's truck. Daniel catches up to me before I can climb in.

"Alex, you can't just leave. You can't seriously believe Jamie after everything I've said tonight." He's out of breath only slightly from chasing me down, and puts his hand against the door to keep me from getting in.

"Why wouldn't I? All you've done is lie to me."

"Jamie is jealous, Alex. He's jealous and he wants you. He was one of the people who told me how much I was screwing you over when we were on-and-off." He steps closer and touches my cheek. "I have a job; I have a stable home. I'm trying to win you back," He smiles at me, just like he used to, and my heart melts. "If I was partying last week, I wouldn't be standing in front of you like this right now. Once I start, I can't stop. I know that. *You* know that."

He's going to kiss me; I can feel it. Or, at least, he wants to. Anxiety sets in and I begin to panic; all I can remember is him lying to me, him hurting me, him breaking my heart.

"Stop," I say as he starts to lean in. "I can't go through this again, Daniel. I'm sorry."

Before I can stop myself, I push him away and get into my car, speeding out of the parking lot. He could've easily stopped me, grabbed me, or tried to convince me to stay… to give him just one more chance. But he didn't. He let me go.

When I get home, Mom is already in bed and Luke is staying the night at a friend's house. I tip-toe through the house and drop her car keys in the bowl on the kitchen counter. By the time I reach my bedroom and put on my pajamas, exhaustion is rolling through me. I don't have time to think about my night; I fall asleep as soon as my head hits the pillow.

Mom gently shakes me awake. I startle, and she starts smoothing my hair down from my forehead.

"Honey, you're sweating," she says quietly. "Did you have a nightmare?"

"No," I murmur back, still trying to catch my breath. "Sorry. I'm fine."

"I thought maybe we'd hang out today; it's my first day off in a while," she smiles. "And Luke's on a date. It's been a few years since we've had a day just for ourselves."

"Yeah," I grin at her. "That sounds nice. I just need to get ready."

When I get out of the shower, I wrap my hair up in a towel and wipe away the mist collected on the mirror. I stare at my reflection. With all the makeup wiped off from last night, I look a lot younger. My skin is fresh and clear, my freckles more evident now that I've gotten a little sun. I think I look pretty, and young, but I look away from my reflection anyway.

I stare down at my cell phone, expecting some sort of text message or voicemail from Daniel, but there's nothing. Only a few texts from kids I go to school with, telling me it was great to see me last night.

Feeling like a normal teenage girl is still so fresh to me. It used to be hard to just get myself out of bed, let alone get dressed and have a day out with my mom. But now, everything is different. I wake up early – now that it's summer, I usually drive over to Carlie's house to wake her up, or wait a few hours reading or hanging out with Luke. Feeling so incredibly happy every day is such a unique feeling. Life isn't a burden anymore.

It was harder in the beginning. My emotions were up and down, and happiness felt so raw that I didn't know how to trust it and just let myself enjoy the moment.

Mom knocks on my bedroom door just as I finish dressing. "Almost ready?" She calls through the door.

"Yeah!" I shout back. "Be out in a minute."

I look over at my bed, and see my phone lying face down. Still no word from Daniel. I decide to leave it here for the day. When I walk out of my bedroom, Mom is waiting for me, rather anxiously, on the couch. As I appear from the hallway, she stands up and wipes her palms against her jeans. *Jeez... how nervous do I make her?*

"I thought we'd go shopping, and get some lunch. Sound good?" She asks, grabbing her keys from the bowl by the door and walking out the front door with me.

"Yeah, sounds good."

In the car, Mom blasts oldies and we sing along together, laughing at each other whenever we messed up the lyrics. It was the hardest I've laughed in a long time, with the exception of last night.

Growing up, my dad and I were always closer, but my mom was my backbone. She was my confidant, there whenever I needed her. I don't think Dad would've been comfortable giving me the talk about "growing up," and the open dialogue about sex, boys, and relationships. After I got depressed, I retreated into myself, and that relationship dissipated. I had nobody. There aren't enough words to describe how good it felt to have my first best friend back.

We sit over a plate of hot pretzels and fries, filling each other in on the latest gossip in our very different lives. My cheeks hurt from laughing so much. After a while, the laughing dies down and we sit there in silence for a few seconds.

Mom still has a smile on her face when she says, "It makes me happy to see you laughing again, honey." I don't say anything. "You were always the most beautiful when you were laughing."

I think I mumble a stunned "thank you" after that, but I can't remember. For some reason, her words stick with me long after we've finished our food and I've flopped down on my bed in exhaustion. Before now, I'd never thought about someone getting joy from seeing me laugh.

There's a buzzing against my stomach. My face twitches, and I groan in frustration. I roll over and search for my cell phone, the culprit of the buzzing.

Groggily, I answer, "Hello?" And drop my head back on the pillow.

"Alex?" It's Daniel.

I perk up. "Um, hey, Daniel."

"You wanna come to a party tonight?"

"Uh…"

There was lots of music and noise in the background, making it hard to tell what he was saying. "Come on, Al. It'll be fun. I heard Carlie and Mike were coming too."

I think of last night and respond as calmly as I can. "I think I'll just stay home, Danny."

There's a bit of silence on the other end. "Okay. Well, if you change your mind…"

"Yeah," I cut him off. "Thanks. Have fun."

"I will. Goodnight, Alex."

I hang up and lay there in bed, staring at the wall. My heart aches to be with him, to let myself settle with him – but still I know, deep down, that he'll never be good enough for me.

There is knocking. *Who the hell is knocking on my door?* I stuff my face deeper into the pillow, but the noise doesn't stop. I punch the bed beside my face and open one eye, looking around. Mom must've come in some time during the night and shut off my lights and tucked me in.

"Doesn't anyone sleep around here?" I half-shout into my pillow. When I realize the knocking sound isn't coming from my closed bedroom door, I look over at the window.

"Alex, it's me." A muffled voice says beyond my window. I reach over to my bedside table and turn on the light. He knocks on the window again, and I throw my covers aside and go to him.

"What the hell are you doing here?" I whisper as I slide up my window. It's mid-June, but a cool breeze hits me when I stick my head out the window, sending shivers down my spine.

"I came here to see you."

From the soft light coming from my bedside lamp, I can see that his eyes are bloodshot and his hair is messy, like he's been running his fingers through it.

"Why?"

"Because you didn't come to the party."

"I told you I wasn't going."

"Will you take a walk with me?"

I should be sleeping right now, peacefully in my bed. And in the morning, I should wake up happy and refreshed, without a care in the world. But instead, Daniel is at my window, reeking of pot and beer.

"Please, Alex? Just come outside." He snaps me out of my reverie. "We need to talk."

I take a deep breath, and as I do, catch a whiff of potent booze coming off of his breath. My face hardens. "Daniel, you're drunk. I think you should go home."

Daniel's face contorts in a sob. "Please, Ally. Why are you doing this to me? I did everything you wanted. When will I be good enough for you?"

My cool façade snaps, and I have to maintain lots of self-control in order to not wake my mother. "You *were* good enough, Daniel. God, how dumb are you? You were everything I needed before you started partying all the time—before you chose *drugs* over me, just like our parents." I add the last part icily, just to hurt him.

"I lost my mom. What would you have done?" Anger is evident on his face.

I'm silent for a few seconds. "I lost my dad. And then I lost you."

Without another word, I slam the window back down and close my curtains rapidly. For a few seconds, I try to calm my quickened pulse. When I do, I get back into bed and sleep like a baby.

Mom is working the next day, and Luke and I unanimously decide it will be an old-movies-and-ice-cream day. We don't even bother to change out of our pajamas.

"So," I say in the middle of *The Breakfast Club* over a plate of pizza we're sharing. "Mom told me you went out on a date yesterday."

His faces changes from white to red in a matter of seconds, and he tries to hide his ear-splitting grin with a mouthful of pizza. "Yeah."

"Yeah?" I adjust myself on the couch, looking sideways at him. "Who was she?"

"A new girl. She'll be going here next fall."

"Did you have a nice time?"

"I think so, yeah. It wasn't, like, a real date. We just went out with a group of people."

"Ah, a double date," I tease, and he laughs. "Where'd you go?"

"Bowling,"

"You suck at bowling."

"I know that *now*," I laugh, and so does he. "It was pretty embarrassing."

Things are quiet for a while, until I say, "So, when do I get to meet this girl?"

He rolls his eyes. "I just had my first date with her *last night*. She doesn't even know how crazy I am yet, the last thing we need is for her to be introduced to your crazy."

We laugh some more because it's true, and that's all he says about the girl.

before

Sixteen Years Old – Summer

Weeks of the summer blur by. Carlie and I take the road trips we'd planned—sleeping in our car and eating the cheapest food possible—along the coast, and manage to visit a few colleges along the way. She thinks she wants to attend USC, despite that being on the other side of the country.

"Where do you think you'll go?" Carlie asks just before taking a bite of the ice cream from her spoon.

"I don't know," I admit. "I don't really know even know what I want to do."

"Well, you were always in astronomy and stuff. You could do that."

I don't say anything for a few seconds and look down at my ice cream. "I don't know. That was kinda something I just did with my dad."

"He wouldn't want you to give it up, Ally."

I roll my eyes at her, faking any other emotion but the overwhelming one I was feeling. "It has nothing to do with him. It's just not my scene anymore."

"So, Alex. Tell me. How has your day gone? Anything exciting?" Dr. Moore asks me. I sit across from him, on the uncomfortably starch leather couch. I wonder if they make them uncomfortable on purpose. Trying to situate myself as best as possible, I fidget and cross my legs.

"Uh, nothing, so far."

He hesitates for a while. "Would you be willing to talk about your father today?"

I ice over. "Well, for starters, how have you been dealing with his absence?"

"I'd rather talk about something more interesting."

"Alright. What did you have in mind?"

I look down at my fingernails and pick them. *Nervous habit.* "I've been avoiding Daniel."

"Why?"

Why wouldn't I? I'm transported back to a time when I wasn't just in love with Daniel – back to a time when he made me laugh; we could spend hours just laughing together. I have so many questions Dr. Moore would never be able to answer for me – questions that I would never have the courage to ask Daniel.

I finally answer. "I left him when he needed me most." Looking down at my fidgeting hands once more, I continue. "I don't know if he'll ever forgive me for that."

"Well, try to put yourself in his shoes. I'm sure he's feeling some resentment towards you, if you really did leave him when he needed you most. From what you told me, it sounds like you two had a pretty tight relationship. Why torture yourself about it, when you could just call him and talk it out?"

"I don't know."

"Alex," I look up at him. "Let's look at the big picture together. He was getting in with the wrong crowd, he wasn't going to school, and he was lying to you about if he was partying or not. Arguably, he was bringing your relationships with your family and other friends down and dragging you into his world. You distance yourself from him and, with the exception of a few bumps in the road," I scoff. "You flourish and are able to be happy again. Looking at all of that information in one piece, do you really think it's healthy if you pursue a romantic relationship with him again?"

I shake my head.

"Of course not. With that said, I do believe it will be healthy for you to air your grievances with him and talk it through, and if you're comfortable being friends, then feel free to do so as long as there's no toxicity."

I take a shaky breath and blink away the tears in my eyes. "I don't even know where to start."

Dr. Moore smiles. "I think an appropriate place would be 'hello.'"

This is so crazy. Why am I even doing this? I can't believe I'm doing this. Mike, Carlie's boyfriend, gave me Daniel's address a few days ago. His foster parents live in an affluent neighborhood, and everything looks so cookie-cutter. Growing up where we did, I could see why Daniel wouldn't fit in here. Still, we lived in an even nicer neighborhood before Dad lost his job. Nevertheless, Mom always made sure we had what nice things we *could* afford. Daniel never had that luxury.

Anxiously, I walk up to the door and knock on the thick wood. I stand there for a few seconds and listen to a dog bark inside at the sound of a visitor. The door is opened by a petite woman, a few years older than my mother, with graying hair. There are laugh lines around her eyes, and I warm to her immediately.

Confusion flits across her pretty features at my unfamiliar face. "Can I help you?"

I smile charismatically. "I'm sorry to disturb you, ma'am. I was told by a friend that Daniel Walker lives here. Is he around?"

"What's your name?"

"Alex Sinclair," I supply. "I'm an old friend of Daniel's."

"I'll go get him," She closes the door half-way, but I'm able to see a sliver of the living room. It looks cozy, and spacious... very much like a home. *How could Daniel not love this place?*

She walks up the carpeted staircase a few feet away from the front door, much like the one I used to have in my childhood home. I turn away, towards their cul-de-sac road, in hopes to prevent the onslaught of flashbacks. I hear the tell-tale padding of fast feet down the stairs. The door swings open and I twist back around. Daniel is there, looking as disheveled as ever. His t-shirt is thin and wrinkled, and he's wearing basketball shorts. He looks like he just woke up. His face has brightened with curiosity and bewilderment.

Despite myself, I can't help but feel a little breathless at seeing him. I'll never get used to that face.

"Alex," He says, surprised. "What are you doing here?"

I stutter for a few seconds, feeling like a total idiot. I should've never came here. I was so stupid. Suddenly, I remember who I am. *I'm Alex Sinclair. I can do this.* I square my shoulders and the stuttering goes away. "I came to invite you to lunch."

Disbelief pours throughout his face. "You came to invite me to lunch?"

"Yes."

"Why?"

"Because it's been a long time since we hung out like normal people. And I was rude to you the other night, when you came to my window."

His face hardens. "Normal teenagers don't 'go to lunch.' They go to parties."

199

I grow tense. "I don't want to go to a party, Daniel. I want to hang out, just like old times."

"What, you want me to take you on treks through the woods and write signs for you from my treehouse?" He says it with such a hurtful tone that those beautiful memories will be forever tainted by his cruelty now. He doesn't stop there, either. "We're not kids anymore, Alex."

Daniel's words slice through me, but I don't show it on my face. In that moment, I realize that the Daniel I fell in love with is gone forever, just like my dad was gone before he ever left. I feel nothing for Daniel Walker but hate.

"You're right, Daniel. We aren't kids anymore. Sorry for wasting your time," I look over his shoulder at his foster mother, frozen in her spot in the hallway watching us talk. "Thank you for getting him, ma'am."

I turn on around on my heel, walk down the short concrete walkway, and unlock my car. I get in, start the engine, and pull out calmly – as if nothing had happened. As I drive away, Daniel still stands in the doorway of his big, plastic house; a house that is not, nor will ever be, his home; a house homing a boy who is not someone I ever want to see again.

I drive for a long time. I drive until the sun sets. I try to drive until it doesn't hurt anymore, but that only works for so long. The stars are shining bright in the sky and all the neighbors' houses are dark before I finally pull into my driveway. I shut off the engine, get out, and lean my back against the outside of my driver's side door. Then, I explode.

I turn around sharply and begin slamming my palms against the side of the car and finally turning my palms into fists. I keep punching and kicking and crying until I finally stumble backwards and land on my back in the grass. I'm *so damn angry*. I'm angry at Daniel, for not being who I remember. I'm angry at him for being just like his mom. I'm mad at him for not loving me back. I'm mad at him for being so stupid, and not being who he should've been. *He could be so much more. We could be together.*

The stars captivate me, and stop my angry tears. I'm still sniffling, but barely. The stars remind me of my dad, and I find the only constellation I know.

"I miss you," I whisper, talking to my dad. But he's not here. It's just the night sky and I. "Please come back. I just need you to tell me what to do, Dad. Please, just tell me what to do." I close my eyes and cry harder. "That's all I want."

My front door opens. "Alex?" I hear my mother call. I sit up, still sobbing; she rushes toward me, quickly fastening her robe tighter. "Alex, honey, what's wrong?"

It all comes out in a rush, in between hiccups. "I went... to... Daniel's, and..." I cry harder, and she kneels beside me and wraps her arms around my shoulders. "I... miss... Dad, Mom. I miss him so much."

Mom freezes, only for a second, then she helps me stand up and guides me toward the house with her arm protectively around me. "I miss him too, baby. I miss him too."

I don't stop crying, not even when she puts me to bed and rubs my head to soothe me. It takes a long time for the crying to die down, but she doesn't leave. She stays with me, because that's what a mother does.

That night, I dream of the stars.

before

Sixteen Years Old – Fall

"Oh my god, can you believe this is our *junior year?*" Carlie exclaims to me as soon as I open the door. "We're *juniors!* This year we'll be picking out *colleges.* Can you believe it?"

She put emphasis on all her words, and her hand gestures were just as grand. The sun's shining so bright on the first day of school, and it perks me up despite all my nerves.

"I know," I respond to her. "I'm actually really excited."

Carlie fakes a heart attack. "Did Alex Sinclair just say she's *excited* about something?! Someone pinch me, I must be dreaming."

I laugh and shove her playfully. Mom walks into the living room, scatter-brained as usual. In her hand is our old digital camera.

"Alright, kids, out on the porch." She ushers Luke toward us. I stand in the middle of them both, and we wrap our arms around one another's shoulders. Mom holds the digital camera up to her face, and says, "Smile!"

The flash goes off, blinding us all for a second, but we're all still smiling happily. When Mom is done taking pictures, we all turn to each other and laugh.

"I'll see you after school, Mom," I kiss her on the cheek and jiggle my car keys at Carlie and Luke, signaling we're late.

"Have fun on your first day, guys! Drive safe! Don't talk to strangers!" She shouts at us when we're all in the car, buckling our seatbelts with the windows rolled down. I roll my eyes at her, but smile nevertheless.

The campus is bustling with all the faces I know, and a whole new class of freshman that I don't. The familiar faces smile at me, and I smile back. When we get to the gates and start walking forward, Luke immediately spots his friends and starts running toward them, but I grab his backpack and yank him back.

"What?" He demands, looking at me as if I've grown two heads.

"I'll meet you in the parking lot, right after school, alright?"

"Yeah, I got it," He turns toward his friends again, but I pull him back once more.

"I don't want to have to come track you down."

"Alright."

"Have a good day, Luke,"

He smiles at me sarcastically, and I let him go. Carlie has already gone off, no doubt to find Mike and our other friends. I look down at my schedule, folded up nicely in my hand. Taking a deep breath, I prepare myself for the first day of my junior year.

Between second and third period, Carlie sidles up to me at my locker as I'm exchanging my books.

"So, I've decided how to present myself to these new freshmen." She's talking fast, and I can tell she's had an exciting day.

"Pray tell," I say, and shoot her a playful look.

"Since I'm being elected class president this year," She holds her head high as she voices her goal for the year. "I've decided to come across as friendly and approachable, rather than the scary upperclassmen, but still intimidating. You know? Like, not quite Beyoncé, but maybe Solange. Or Beyoncé's mom. Coolness by association."

I laugh and shake my head at her choice of words, then slam my locker shut. "You've got my vote."

"Hey," She brings her voice lower and steps closer. "Have you seen Daniel today?"

"No," I answer, and start walking towards my next class. "I haven't even talked to him since that time I went to his house."

"He looks… bugged out."

Nonchalantly, I say, "Hmm."

Trying to gauge my mood, Carlie treads lightly. "Mike came up to me and asked if Daniel was on drugs again. I think it's really bad this time."

I take a deep breath. "He's not my responsibility anymore, Carlie. You, of all people, should know that."

"Sorry. I'll drop it."

Just then, I see Jamie turn the corner we're walking towards; he walks on the left lane of the hallway, in the throng of people. His hands are around the straps of his backpack. He walks with his head held high, cockiness oozing from his every pore. I stop in my tracks, right in the middle of the hallway. Carlie stops mid-sentence, looking at me with perplexity.

As he gets closer, he sees me staring at him. His mouth transforms into a smirk, and he winks. *He winks.* My blood boils, and I tighten my palms into a fist. Absentmindedly, I register that Carlie is saying my name, but Jamie and I have locked eyes and it takes every ounce of will-power I have left not to cross the small space and punch that stupid smirk off his stupid face.

"Alex," Carlie nearly shouts in my face. I'm snapped out of my reverie, and look over at her. I blink a few times. She looks from me to Jamie's retreating back, with a horrified expression on her face. "What the hell was that?"

The warning bell rings, saving me from an explanation. "I have to get to class. I'll see you at lunch."

But by the time lunch rolled around, my anxiety was already clawing at my brain. Seeing Jamie had sent my thoughts spiraling, all I could think about was how much I wanted him to pay for what he gave Daniel, what he created of Daniel.

The bell rings, signaling lunch, but the thought of eating makes me sick to my stomach. I dump my books in my locker and scurry off to the bathroom to hide away.

I lock myself in the bathroom stall, already feeling the heavy weight of gravity pounding on my chest. I take in big, quick gulps of air, trying to fill my lungs with healthiness instead of this horrible feeling. I can't feel anything, I can't feel, my brain is on fire and that's all I feel. My limbs shake like an earthquake and I try to breathe, I try to remember how to breathe, but the air won't come. Who sucked up all the oxygen and left me with none?

My thoughts jumble together. *Breathe, in, out, out, in, Daniel, Carlie, Daniel is here, no he's not, Daniel is not here, home I wanna go home, home, let's go home, the meadow, I want to go to the meadow, Jamie, Jamie, stars, stars collapsing and exploding and breathing, music everywhere.*

When I was a little girl, even before my brother came along, my family used to drive all the way to the coast and stay in a family friend's house on the beach. I was young, young enough to not be able to recognize the significance of these family trips. I remember we would be able to walk along the wooden paths through the beach grass, leading down to the water.

The ocean was so loud, so powerful, yet so peaceful. Each day, I would run through the shallow part of the waves and squeal with joy. Mom would have to reprimand me for wandering out too far, and Dad would come and splash around, sweeping me up and throwing me over his shoulder.

And then Luke came along, and Mom's attention was always divided between watching me in the ocean and making sure Luke didn't swallow a handful of sand. One day, Mom kept her back turned just long enough for me to wander out farther. Dad went back to the house, because we'd forgotten beach towels. I saw something out on the water; being an ever-curious four-year-old, I was determined to find out what it was.

The current caught me, and the saltwater filled my lungs before I had a chance to scream. I didn't know how to swim yet. The waves, which had been my friend before, suddenly turned into the thing that was killing me.

I don't remember Dad pulling me out of the water, or pushing the water out of my legs and blowing breath into my mouth. I don't remember Mom's heavy sobbing and her cries of, "My baby, my sweet baby," when I finally opened my eyes. I don't remember any of that. But I remember what it felt like to drown. I remember what it felt like to feel the water push its way into my lungs, filling them with the salt of the sea. I remember what it felt like to not be able to breathe—to die.

That's what this felt like. That's what a panic attack feels like.

I went to the nurse after that, saying I'd thrown up. She called my mom, who obviously couldn't drop everything at work and come pick me up. After I realized how selfish it was of me to expect her to drop everything just because I had a panic attack, I claimed I felt better and asked to go back to class.

The nurse looked at me with disbelief. "Are you sure, sweetie? You don't look so good."

"Yeah, I'm okay," I try to smile, which I'm pretty sure comes out as a grimace.

"Alright." She still looks skeptical, but lets me go.

The rest of the day, I'm withdrawn and quiet. Carlie asks me what's wrong, and I say I'm fine, but I couldn't be farther from it. I can hardly pay attention to my teachers' explanation of the syllabus. *I don't know what's gotten into me.*

When the bell rings, I don't wait at my locker for Carlie like I usually do. Instead, I quickly back up my backpack and scurry out to the student parking lot. I wait patiently for Luke to show up, but I can't sit still. In the car, I turn the radio up loudly for a few minutes then get a headache and turn it back down. I tap my fingers against the steering wheel impatiently, then look at the clock on the dashboard. It's been fifteen minutes since the last bell rang. Where the hell is Luke?

I take the keys out of the ignition and start walking towards the school again. Going into the sophomore building, the halls are silent. I furrow my eyebrows and walk around a little more before hearing voices echoing down the hallway.

"...swear he didn't know, Will. Please don't do this." A girl's voice.

I peek around the corner and see a group of guys cornering Luke and some girl, who's placed herself protectively between Luke and the guys. Luke's lip is bleeding and he's holding his stomach.

"I don't give a shit, Samantha," The one she calls Will, clearly the pack leader, says and steps forward. "Get out of the way."

Samantha says, "No. This is stupid, Will. Let's just go."

Will pushes toward Luke again, but Samantha pushes him back. He pushes her out of his way, and she falls on the floor. Even behind the lockers all the way down the hallway, I can see the rage flare in Luke's eyes. He gets one good punch in before Will and his friends start beating on him. He does his best to fight back, but it's no use.

My adrenaline spikes and I reveal myself to them. I'm not stupid enough to believe I'll be able to fight them off, but I could probably use my authority against them. Right?

"Hey!" I yell out, speed-walking towards them, and their heads turn. Samantha is crying, but she looks up when I speak. Will's fist is raised mid-air, but he drops it and releases Luke's shirt. "What the hell do you think you guys are doing?"

"Who are you?"

I help Samantha off the ground, and she wipes the tears from her cheeks. "Does it matter? I could've been a teacher, you dumbass."

Will looks from his friends to me. "Who are you?"

"Luke's sister. What's going on?"

"He had sex with my girlfriend."

"Jesus H. Christ. This is *high school*, and she's not your God damn wife. Break up with her and get over it." I grab Luke's arm and yank him off the ground, but Will knocks him down again.

"Who the hell do you think you are?" He shoves me against the locker, and I'm momentarily stunned. Luke stands and shoves him back while shouting, "Keep your hands off her!"

I hear footsteps approaching rapidly, most likely drawn by all the noise, and Will's friends abandon him. Luke keeps beating on Will, finally able to get out his pent up anger. My mind flashes back, briefly, to a memory of our father and his rage.

"Luke," I say, but he doesn't stop. His expression is one I don't recognize – one I can only remember, but on a different person. Someone comes into my line of vision and pulls Luke off of Will and holds him back.

My entire line of vision is blurry. All I can hear is the sound of my own breathing. Someone grabs me by the elbow and pulls me up, and I'm forced out of my reverie to look this person in the eye.

His brown eyes are bloodshot, but from lack of sleep rather than intoxicants. His mouth is moving; he must be saying my name, but I can't hear him. All I can hear is Luke's fist hitting Will's face. All I can hear is my dad's fist hitting some poor man's face.

"Alex, let's go!" Daniel pulls on my arm, yanking me down the hallway. I can hear teachers coming. We run away, run so fast that I feel like a new person. Pretty soon, we're back in the student parking lot and I can see my car in the distance. I unlock it while we're still running, and we all get in together.

"Gimme the keys!" Daniel shouts, as we near the car. I throw the keys at him, and we hop in and speed off.

It takes us a while for us all to catch our breath. When we do, I explode on Luke, who sits sullenly in the backseat.

"What, the *hell*, was *that?*" I yell, then turn to Daniel. "And what the hell were you doing?"

"Seriously? Luke would've just been suspended, if not expelled, had I not showed up and saved the day. A 'thank you' would suffice just fine, princess."

Daniel hasn't called me "princess" since we were kids. Instead of gagging on the nostalgia, it only fuels my anger towards him *and* Luke.

"What the hell, Luke?!" I shout once more. "Did you really have sex with that guy's girlfriend?"

"No, I didn't," He says, snarky. "I'm fine, by the way."

"What were you *thinking*, Luke?"

"Her name is Samantha; in case you were wondering."

I narrow my eyes. "I wasn't, but thanks."

We continue arguing the whole car ride, with Daniel sitting silent in the driver's seat. As we pull into our driveway, Luke and I get out and slam our doors before Daniel even takes the keys out of the ignition. Mom isn't home yet, so we storm into the house still screaming at each other. Solemnly, Daniel follows.

"What are you trying to accomplish with her, Luke? She has a *boyfriend*. Are you *trying* to be like Dad?"

"Oh, fuck you, Alex."

"*Luke*," Daniel shouts, slamming his palm against our kitchen counter. "Don't talk to your sister like that. She's just trying to help you."

"What the fuck are you even *talking* about?" He shouts back at Daniel with malice in his voice. "Where have you been for the past year, man? You show up and get us out of some shit and think you own the world again. Do you have any idea of the shit you put my sister through?"

"Luke," I plead, begging him to stop before he spills my entire guts out to Daniel.

"She tried to fucking kill herself, man. All because you had to be a selfish, dumbass prick who turned out to be everything she'd been scared of becoming her whole life."

"You have no idea what—" He tries.

Luke cuts him off. "Rot in hell, Daniel." With that, he turns on his heel and walks down the hallway, slamming his bedroom door so hard it shakes the house.

Daniel and I stand in awkward silence – me, twiddling my thumbs, and him, staring into the space where Luke would've been. I take a breath to start talking, but he interrupts me.

"Carlie called me, after she found you. You were already in the hospital and stable, but she was still crying. I was such a dick to you, Alex."

I stare at his back, gritting my teeth, trying to blink away the tears.

"I loved you, and I fucking ruined it." His voice cracks.

"It wasn't just you, Daniel. I completely ignored you."

"Yeah, and for good reason. I don't deserve your forgiveness, Alex," He turns around to face me. "I really don't. But I'm so sorry."

I don't know what to say. I open my mouth, but I'm interrupted by the sound of my own cell phone ringing. It rings for a few seconds, and Daniel and I stand there staring at each other. Eventually, I reach across the counter and pick it up.

"Hey, Mom," I answer quietly, almost breathlessly.

"Hey, sweetie. Everything okay?"

Daniel gives me one last emotional look, then walks silently out of my house. I don't speak again until the door shuts behind him. "Yeah," I sniffle. "Yeah, I'm okay. What's up?"

"I just wanted to remind you about my business dinner tonight. I'll be home pretty late."

"Right. Sorry. I forgot."

She chuckles. "I figured. There's money for you and Luke to order pizza in the bowl by the door, or you could cook something."

"Okay. Thanks for calling." I'm still sniffling.

"Are you sure you're okay, Alex?"

"Yeah, I'm fine. It's just allergies or something."

"I hope you're not getting a cold. Anyway, I'll see you later. Love you!" She hangs up, and I put my phone back on the counter and sit down heavily.

I said so many mean things to Luke. I feel terrible. I need to go in and apologize to him, but I don't move from my seat. Music blares from Luke's bedroom, and I know he's too angry to go near him right now. I lay my head down against the cool wood of the table and close my eyes.

The meadow is aglow with the bright sun; the orange, yellow, and purple wildflowers have caught fire with it. I look around, the flames nipping at my exposed skin. Char and smoke are staining my white dress.

I see someone standing a few yards away from me. They're completely charred from head to toe. I walk forward, into the stinging flames. I feel nothing. I get closer and closer to this strange person made black with ash until I can see that it's a man.

"Ally," It's Dad's voice, and I can see the remnants of his cheekbones and hairline, but he's made of ash instead of flesh. His black arm reaches out to me, and I should be scared, but I'm not.

I want to burn with him.

I grab his hand, and we go up in flames.

I wake with a start, sitting straight up in the uncomfortable wooden dining room chair. It's dark outside, and only the lamp beside our couch is on. There's no more music blaring from Luke's bedroom. I rub the sleep from my eyes and try to forget the disturbing nightmare I just had. I haven't had a dream about Dad in a long time; I'll have to bring it up to Dr. Moore at my next appointment.

Looking at the clock on our wall, I see that it's only eight o'clock. I walk down the hall and see light spilling out from under the crack of Luke's bedroom door. I knock tentatively.

"Luke? Are you in there?" I ask through the thin wood.

"What do you want?" He shoots back.

"I just wanted to ask if you're hungry."

"No."

I wait a few seconds, shuffling my feet. "Okay. Can I come in?"

"No."

"Are you naked?"

"No," He scoffs.

I open the door and step into his bedroom.

"What the hell, Alex? I told you not to come in." He sits up in his bed and yanks his headphones off his ears.

"I don't care."

"What do you want?"

I sit down on his bed and make myself comfortable, all while ignoring the furious scowl on his face. If only looks could kill. "I'm sorry for yelling at you like I did."

Luke rolls his eyes and plops back down. "Fine. Apology accepted. Now get out."

"Nope," I'm not done yet. "Is that the girl you went on a date with over summer?"

He waits a few seconds to respond. "Yeah, it is."

"Did you know she had a boyfriend when you went on a date with her?"

He hesitates again.

"Don't lie to me, Luke."

"Yeah. I knew."

"Does he abuse her or something?"

"Something like that."

I take a deep breath and shake my head. "You do realize this is only going to get worse for you, right?"

Luke nods. "I know."

"Why are you doing this for her?"

His face twists into confusion. "Why wouldn't I?"

I can't help but smile, even though I try to hide it. *My brother.* "I can't let them hurt you, Luke."

"I can't let *him* hurt *her.*"

"Why won't she leave him?"

"She has, but he hasn't accepted it. He still goes around being possessive of her and calling her his girlfriend. She doesn't know what to do."

"Why doesn't she talk to someone? An adult."

"She's scared."

I want to ask, *Of what?* But I realize, then, that I don't need to. Maybe I can help her. "Do her parents know?"

"God no," He scoffs. "Her parents are crazy protective. They'd lose their minds and press charges and have him expelled and shit if they found out."

"Maybe that's what needs to happen," I offer delicately.

He plays with a piece of loose thread from his blanket and won't meet my gaze. "She'd never forgive me."

"It doesn't have to be you."

"I'm the only one that knows," He meets me with a pleading gaze. "You can't tell anyone, Alex. You have to promise me you won't."

I wait a few seconds, weighing my options. I could try to convince Luke to tell someone, but would that benefit in the long run? "Alright. I promise."

That seems to satisfy him, because he doesn't say anything more. I speak again, in a lighter tone. "Alright, now what do you want for dinner?"

before

Sixteen Years Old – Fall

The weather gently grew colder without anyone really noticing, as it always does. Carlie won student body President. Luke's bullies were an omnipresent and intimidating force, but they hadn't touched him again yet.

He was meeting with that girl, Samantha, in secret every few days. She had broken up with Will, and he was *not* happy. I told Luke it was best if he stayed away from her at school, just for the time being.

"What do you mean, 'stay away from her at school'? We can finally be together and now you're trying to ruin it?" He asked incredulously, one night after I tried convincing him of it.

"I'm not trying to ruin anything, Luke. I totally understand. But just think about this for a minute. He has the whole football team on his side, and you're about to walk around the school with his ex-girlfriend on your arm. He'll rip you to shreds."

"He's gonna do that no matter when the timing is."

"Possibly. But right now the wound is still fresh. You need to give him time to cool down."

Luke looks at me like he wants to say something more, but he keeps his mouth shut. That's the last we speak of it.

The first snowfall of the season comes a week before Thanksgiving break. Everyone skips their lunch period and spends it outside, throwing snowballs (and getting in trouble for them), rolling around in the snow (and regretting it 30 minutes later when their pants were all wet), and catching falling snowflakes on their tongue.

I am one of the many outside, just playing around. Carlie and her boyfriend, Mike, are canoodling somewhere nearby. One of our friends throws a snowball and it hits me right in the back, and I laugh and reciprocate, initiating a full-fledged war.

That's why I don't notice Jamie, or that he's running towards me. Carlie looks at me quizzically when Jamie screeches to a stop in front of me, halting my laughter and gasping for breath.

"Alex..." He puffs. "Daniel's flipping out. We tried to calm him down, but he keeps saying your name over and over again. He told me to come get you."

"What did you give him?" I ask in horror.

"It wasn't me. He got it from someone else." Jamie is still huffing and puffing. "And he's having a bad trip."

I take off running towards the direction Jamie came from, towards the band room. It's abandoned every period except one, so that's where the Blanks usually hang out if they're skipping – which is always. Carlie and Mike run after me, also following Jamie.

We're a few yards off from the band-room entrance, and I can already hear him yelling.

"*Get them off me, Alex! Get them off! They're crawling through my skin, I can feel them, Alex! Get them off!*" Daniel hasn't seen me yet, but he screams my name anyway.

I skid to a stop in front of him, and see claw marks up and down his face, with him still scratching. I kneel down next to him and pull his hands gently away from his face, but that just increases his twitching and screaming.

"Danny, I'm here. It's Alex. I'm right here." I try to speak soothingly.

Daniel looks into my eyes, but it's like he's staring at a blank wall. He stares right through me. He's already been sobbing for quite some time, and now he's rocking back and forth under my hands.

"Get them off me, Alex, I can feel them. Get them off." He speaks frantically, his eyeballs moving every which way.

"Get what off, Danny? What's wrong?"

"There's bugs on me, Alex!" He shrieks, and begins clawing at his face again. "There's bugs on me! Get them off! Get them off!"

I sit back in horror. I should be grabbing his arms and keep him from scratching his own eyeballs out, but I can't. He's too far gone. *What has happened to him?*

"Jamie," I say, and get off my knees and step away from Daniel. "You need to take him home before a teacher finds him like this and gets us all in trouble."

"I can't do that. His foster mom is home."

"Then take him to your house, or somebody's else's house, or something! Just get him out of here."

He nods at me and looks back at Daniel. Mike says something to Carlie, then walks toward Jamie. "I'll help you guys get him out of here. I have a free period next, anyways."

There's more said, but all I can see is Daniel. His eyes are bloodshot and fleeting, as if he's seeing things that aren't really there. Carlie has to drag me out of the room.

"Alex, what's wrong? You've hardly eaten any of your dinner." Mom asks quizzically.

"Oh," I say, trying to come up with an answer. "I just don't feel good."

"I got a call from the nurse today saying you'd went there and asked to go home. I'm sorry I couldn't pick you up." *That was after Daniel's freak-out. I stayed in the nurse's office for at least an hour, trying to calm down. The school nurse is ancient, and has probably been deaf for 100 years, so I could cry quietly if I faced the wall.*

She says it sincerely, and I know she really is sorry, but I can't meet her gaze.

"It's okay."

Luke gives me a look across the dinner table. He heard about what happened with Daniel; all of the students did. I silently plead with him to keep quiet; he looks back down at his plate of food.

Mom looks between Luke and me. "Am I missing something here?"

We look at each other again, and I rack my brain for something to say. Thankfully, Luke speaks first.

"No," Luke shakes his head, perfectly calm. "I was just looking at her to see if she's okay."

"Do you want to go rest?"

"Yeah, I think that's probably best."

I go through the motions like a champ. I clear my plate and put it in the dishwasher, then walk calmly into my bedroom and close the door. I lay down on my stomach and stare ahead of me like a zombie. I don't remember ever closing my eyes, but I must have at some point. Absentmindedly, I wonder if the bugs Daniel was screaming about have crawled into my brain too.

before

Sixteen Years Old – Winter

The bell rings, signaling the end of another headache-inducing day. It's Friday, the week before finals begin. My pre-calculus teacher, Mrs. Boone, looks up as I walk past her desk toward the door.

"Alex, stay behind a minute," She finishes grading a packet and folds her arms together, leaning on her desk. I give my friends a look and sit back down at the desk across from hers.

"So, we've got finals coming up," Mrs. Boone says and raises her eyebrows at me.

I raise my eyebrows back. "Yeah…" *And?*

"I'm going to be blunt here, Alex. Your grades are not satisfactory, and not only in here. Every teacher in this school knows how intelligent and capable you are. In all of your transcripts, you have not gotten below a C. And yet, you're lucky to get above it these days." I swallow thickly and break eye contact. "So what's going on?"

Can I trust her? She's never given me a reason *not* to. Speaking to her like this, like she genuinely cares about me, is comforting.

But she's a *teacher*. The only thing she cares about is getting her paycheck and going home.

"Yeah," I muster a fake smile. "I'm okay. I guess I just don't understand the new material."

Mrs. Boone doesn't look like she believes me at all. She puts her hands up in surrender. "You don't have to tell me anything, Alex. But don't bullshit me here." Tears prickle the backs of my eyes. I swallow again and open my mouth to say something, but nothing comes out. I just look at her – *what do you want me to say?*

She seems to take the hint. "So, since absolutely nothing's wrong, what can we do to help you get your grades up enough in time for finals?"

"Um," I try to gather my thoughts. "A tutor, I guess."

"We'll start with pre-calculus. I'll meet you here every day after school, with the exclusion of Thursdays. I'll talk to your other teachers about getting a tutor for those, but until then I'll try to help you with those too." Mrs. Boone shuffles her papers on her desk while she talks, and I sit there stunned. She looks at me over the tops of her glasses. "Sound good?"

"Why are you doing this?" I question in a hushed voice.

Mrs. Boone looks me directly in the eye for a few seconds without speaking. "I think you're a good kid who's a little stuck in the mud right now. I want to help, in any way I can."

I don't know what to say except, "Thank you."

She nods at me. "You're welcome. Now, run along. We'll start Monday."

By the time I make it to my locker to pack up my stuff, the hallways are deserted. When I walk out to the parking lot, it's even more empty. Luke must've gone home with a friend. I settle myself into my car and crank the heat.

I don't know what to think about Mrs. Boone's comments. What could she possibly gain from saying nice things about me?

I don't get it. Maybe she really does just want to help me pass the class.

Either way, I grab my backpack and begin digging through it for my cell phone. I take it out and see that I have on voicemail from an unknown number. Perplexed, I open it.

"Hey, Alex. It's Daniel. I just wanted to, uh, talk about some stuff and maybe grab a cup of coffee. Or something. Um.... Alex, I'm sor—"

Message erased.

"So I heard Jamie's, like, freaking out because Daniel has totally cut him and all his buddies off. He won't buy or sell *anything.*" Carlie says as she paws through the racks of our town's only dress shop.

I pause, only halfway paying attention to my own clothing rack. I don't say anything.

"I just thought you might want to know," She continues innocently.

"Well, I don't," I take a deep breath and hold up a dark blue chiffon dress. "Do you like this one?"

"For me or for you?"

"Me,"

Her eyes sparkle and her face lights up with a mischievous grin. "I love it. Go try it on."

It was our first week back from winter break. Mrs. Boone had tutored me enough to get my Calculus grade up to a C, and I got an A on the final exam, knocking my grade back up to a B-minus. It wasn't what I was used to, but at least it didn't screw up my transcripts too terribly. My other classes went just as well, and my lowest grade for the semester was that B-minus. She still tutors me sometimes, to make sure I'm still on the right track. I'm slowly getting back to where I was before Daniel messed me up again.

221

Winter formals are in just a few weeks, right before my birthday. We're shopping for formal dresses. Mike was taking Carlie, of course, but I was going alone. Even Luke is going with someone – that girl, Samantha. It's supposed to be their "debut" as a couple.

The navy blue dress is strapless, and chiffon, with no sparkles or anything; just how I like it. It's tight around my waist but hung down to the floor from there. I loved how I looked in it; for the first time in a while, I felt pretty.

"Oh my god," Carlie whispers, wide-eyed, when she sees me in it. I expect her to make some sort of a joke, but she doesn't. She looks at me with serious eyes. "You look beautiful, Alex."

I blush and look down, smoothing the dress with my hands. "Thanks."

I end up splurging on the dress, silently cursing myself. I'll have to take up some more babysitting jobs to pay this one off. Carlie buys a more expensive lavender dress, and winks conspiratorially at me.

We go back to her house for some girl time, watching scary movies and eating junk food. We stay up all night together, laughing about things that aren't particularly funny. It's the most fun I've had in a while.

It's snowing outside – the perfect, big-flake kind of snow. There's no wind; only huge flakes drifting down. Luke is as nervous as ever, a wilting corsage in his hand. I watch him slide it on Samantha's frail wrist; I watch her smile at him like he's the sun and she's all the trees and flowers in the world. It reminds me of Daniel, and I can't help but turn melancholy.

Her dress matches his tie. They look like the perfect version of high school sweethearts. Mom takes pictures and sheds a few tears, and I smile big for the camera. Carlie and our other friends arrive shortly before Samantha and Luke leave. Mom takes more pictures. We all laugh together, and someone sneaks vodka into the limousine. I respectfully decline, and they don't force me. Carlie doesn't take any either.

Everything is in full swing at the dance, and some of the Blanks even showed up. Soon, my melancholia subsides and I'm dancing along with everyone else. Some of our other friends went stag, and we all hang out together. One of our friends introduces me to a boy named Jack, and we begin talking. I try to find Carlie and tell her, when I see her in a heated conversation with Mike over in a secluded corner of the dance. I decide to go back and let them work it out.

I see Luke and Samantha dancing together happily. Jack is nice; he goes to a different school, but was invited by the girl who introduced us. Apparently they're cousins, and she didn't have a date. I laugh when he tells me the story, and he shyly laughs along with me. I think he's a nice person.

Carlie approaches me with a scowl on her face and taps on my shoulder. "Alex," She says somberly. "Can I talk to you for a second?"

"Uh," I look at Jack. "Sure. I'll be right back."

She doesn't wait for his response, just grabs me by the elbow and steers me a safe distance away. "Daniel and Jamie just showed up."

I wait for her to continue. When she doesn't, I say, "And?"

"What do you mean 'and'? It's *Daniel*."

"And I'm Alex, and you're Carlie, and that's Jack. And he's really nice, and I'm having a really good time. So I'd appreciate it if you didn't ruin it by supplying commentary on *everything Daniel does*. I'm *over* it, Carlie, and I've been trying to get over it for a long time."

Carlie stares at me with steel in her eyes, her mouth set in a hard line. "Well, maybe I'm not. He was my friend too, Alex." She turns on her heel and walks away, getting lost in the throng of people in our school's gymnasium.

Her words settle heavily in my mind. *He was my friend too.* I walk back to Jack, who is now leaning against one of the decorated pillars alone. Our friends must be on the dance floor.

"Sorry about that," I say apologetically and smile.

Jack smiles back. "Don't worry about it." He gives me a quick look, then fixes his eyes back on the dance floor. "Everything okay with Carlie?"

"Yeah," I sigh. "She just saw an old friend of ours, that's all."

"Old boyfriend?" He asks innocently and nonchalantly, but I can tell by his body language there's a more serious note to it.

I laugh awkwardly. "You could say that."

Jack opens his mouth to say something, but the DJ interrupts him. "Alright, guys, we're winding down for the night. Here's one for all you old-school Stones fans."

A slow song begins playing, one that I recognize. My ears strain to hear it better, but when I do, my breath catches in my throat. This was my parents' song, the one they'd dance to every time it came on.

For a few moments, I'm frozen in my spot. Jack says something to me, but I don't hear him. I turn my head, dazed, and ask what he said.

"Um," He shuffles his feet awkwardly and smiles. "I was just asking if you wanted to dance."

"Oh," I stutter, and butterflies ruffle my stomach. "Yeah. Yeah, sure."

Jack grins and I take his outstretched hand. He dances properly, with my right hand in his, and my left hand resting on his shoulder. Just like my parents danced. As the song progresses, we drift closer together and closer until our chests are pressed together and my arm is wrapped under his armpit, resting on his shoulder from behind.

It feels like a movie, dancing with this person I barely know. But, crazily, I feel safe with him, and I feel happy. Then, in the last few bars of the song, my eyes flicker up and meet the gaze of a boy who looks like he's just had his heartbroken, permanently.

Daniel is surrounded by people, but he doesn't see any of them. He's wearing a skinny, navy blue tie – one that matches my dress. His dark curly hair is slicked back and to the side, revealing his eyes; the eyes I fell in love with – the eyes that look like the inside of an old tree. His face transforms from heartbreak, to impenetrable sadness, to bubbling anger. I could see the storm brewing beneath those eyes; I needed to protect this poor boy from the ultimate wrath of Daniel. The only way to do that was to leave Jack.

"Jack," I say and pull back, looking away from Daniel's brown eyes and into Jack's blue ones. He meets my gaze, perplexed. "This has been really fun, but I have to go. I'm sorry."

"Oh," I can see the hurt in his eyes. I look back to where Daniel was standing, but he's no longer there. Anxiety prickles underneath my skin. "Okay. Can I get your number, though?"

"What?" I ask, totally distracted. Then I realize what he just asked me. "Oh, um…"

Chaos erupts in the back corner of the gymnasium, near the punch bowl. The music stops suddenly and I whip my head around to the sounds of shouting and fists hitting flesh. The crowd breaks for a split second, and I see Will pounding on a boy who looks an awful lot like my brother. Students were already crowding around the fight, but I take off running.

It's harder than it looks to run in heels, but I try my best. Jack takes off after me, calling my name, but I'm too fast and we lose each other. Teachers are pushing their way through the crowd to break up the fight, but somehow they keep getting held back.

225

I scream Luke's name, my eyes wide with horror as I watch blood splatter from my brother's nose, and then his eyebrow, and then his lip, onto the hard gym floor with every *whack* of Will's fist. I get to the front of the circle crowding around them; some people are cheering, some booing, but everyone in the room is buzzing with the adrenaline of a fight at a school dance.

"Luke!" I try to pull Will away from him, but someone grabs me and holds onto me. I kick and scream, but I'm left useless by the strong athletes who hold me back, no doubt friends of Will's. "Luke!" I scream and scream his name.

Daniel gets to Will before the teachers ever do. I watch him pound away at Will's face, just like Will pounded away at my brother's. He takes all his rage towards me out on this boy, who struggles at first, but quickly goes limp underneath Daniel. My voice is hoarse from screaming and tears are streaking down my face. The boys release me and I go to my brother. He's not unconscious, but his face is cut up and already bruising and swelling. Samantha stands there, her face pale as a ghost. Carlie is right by my side, and Mike is dragging Daniel off Will. Teachers are screaming at him, their faces red, but it all moves in slow motion for me. I register, briefly, that Mrs. Boone kneels by Will's head and tells someone to call 911. Daniel has gone slack, his energy drained, as Mike drags him away. For a split second, we make eye contact but he doesn't move. His hair is no longer combed neatly, as it falls over his eyes again, and he's sweaty. His expression is emotionless as he stares at me. The paramedics come, but Will never gets up.

Mom screams at the dance chaperones until she's red in the face, making threats to sue and have all of them fired for negligence. Apparently, the punch (which neither Luke nor I drank) was spiked, fueling Will's anger with loss of common sense. They separate Luke, Will, and Daniel; I stay with Luke and wait for Mom as they stitch him up and give him some ice.

Mom speeds home, with me in the front seat and Luke in the back. She's still too angry to drive safely. This time, though, her anger is turned on us. "How could you be so stupid, Luke? I mean, really. Getting involved with a girl you *knew* was trouble?" Her voice is incredulous, and she shakes her head with rage.

"I'm sorry," It comes out as a whisper, and he drops the ice pack from his face. I look at him through the rearview mirror.

"He could've killed you, Luke! How many times did Alex warn you about her? How many times could you have gotten her real help instead of just messing around?" She's yelling now.

"I thought she loved me," His voice cracked, and he sounds so broken. He leans forward with his elbows on his knees and begins crying into his hands. "I thought she loved me. I thought she loved me."

Mom and I are both silent. I can feel her rage sizzle out, and she visibly slouches with it. When we get home, Mom makes sure we're emotionally alright and sets out an ice pack for Luke, then retreats to her bedroom. His eyes are red and puffy from crying, but also from the black eye that has sufficiently formed.

"Sit down," I point to the couch and he does as I say, sniffling. I grab the ice pack Mom set out, and wet a wash cloth in warm water. I adjust my dress before sitting on the coffee table across from him. He's staring down at his hands, caked with dried blood in a few spots from holding his face. "Look up."

Luke, once again, complies. I hate to see my brother so broken. I want to kill both Will *and* Samantha for what they've done. Samantha, for being such a stupid, petulant child; Will, for being such an incomprehensible douche.

"I'm sorry, Ally," Luke says quietly as I wipe away the dried blood with the wash cloth with one hand and hold the ice pack to his face with the other. Briefly, I meet his gaze and then look back to his injuries.

"I know." I let the wash cloth rest in my lap and finally look into Luke's eyes. "Don't waste your time feeling sorry, Luke. At least not to me."

It takes a few seconds, but his face scrunches up in a silent sob. "She said she loved me. Why'd she lie, Ally? Who does that to a person?"

I grab his hand. "She was scared of him, and she let her fear control her," I pause for effect. "Some people don't care who they hurt." He nods and lets his head hang, plopping fat alligator tears on the lap of my dress.

"She meant everything to me. All I wanted to do was help her. I let my ass get fucking *beat* for her."

"Yeah, but what are we gonna do about that now? Nothing, because it's over with. All you can do now is focus on yourself."

He stares at me like I'm crazy.

"It's harder than it looks, believe me."

Luke is quiet for a while. "Daniel pulled him off me."

I dab at his injuries again. "I saw."

"He got expelled. So did Will."

"Good."

"Are you gonna talk to him?"

My hand stills. "Why would I?"

"I just thought he did it to get back with you."

Remembering Daniel's face when he saw me dancing with Jack, I can't quite believe Daniel would ever talk to me again. Not that I care, or want him to. "I doubt that very much. Do you think you'll be alright for the night? I'm gonna go to bed." I stand up and start walking toward the hallway.

"Yeah, I'll be fine. Sorry for this whole mess."

"Oh, quit it. Don't stay up too late, alright?"

Somewhere is a grunt in response, but I don't listen for it. I stop in the bathroom first, to try and clean the spots of dried blood on my hands from holding Luke before the paramedics arrived. My beautiful blue dress is ruined. My makeup that took a way longer time than necessary is smudged underneath my eyes. There's even a small rip at the bottom.

Quickly, and without much thought, I take it off and dispose of it on the floor. My bathrobe hangs on a hook next to the shower, but I feel dirty. I turn the showerhead on full blast; the hot water scalds me, but I don't move. The night hits me in flashes. I let the water wash away the mascara and the hairspray and the blood, but I don't let myself cry. I can't; I won't.

before

Seventeen Years Old – Spring

It's my 17th birthday, only a few weeks after Luke's fight at the winter formal. I had dinner planned tonight with Carlie, Mike, and all of our friends; including Jack, whom Mike swore was not freaked out by the showdown at the dance. Mom's working today, but we planned to have dinner tomorrow. I hadn't seen Daniel since the night of the formal.

Luke's lying on his bed with his legs propped against the wall throwing a basketball against it and catching the ball when I walk into his room. He turns his head to look at me.

"Hey, have you seen my phone? I've looked all over for it," I ask and lean my head against his door frame.

"Yeah, it's in the bowl by the door." He continues throwing the ball back and forth against the wall.

I've got one voicemail. I walk into the living room and sit on the couch, then click it. Daniel's voice pours through my phone, slurring his words. He sounds like he's been crying.

"Hey, Ally," He starts, sniffling. "How you been? I'm sorry I didn't call sooner. I should've called to ask about Luke." There's music playing and people laughing in the background, but Daniel's voice is the most somber I've ever heard. "Listen, Ally. I don't know when I'll see you next, but, uh... take care of yourself, okay? And take care of Luke, and Carlie, and your mom... thank her for everything she's done for me. I'm sorry I screwed it all up. I'm sorry I couldn't be what you needed." He doesn't speak for a while, and I can hear his sobs, muffled by him holding the phone away from his face. "I'll see you on the other side, Ally."

My whole body freezes like ice. I sit, still as a rock, unable to comprehend what this could be. *A goodbye – Daniel's version of a suicide note.* All too quickly, I spring into action. I dial his number again and again, clutching my face and begging him to pick up. *Come on, Danny. Just pick up. Please. Just once. Pick up, pick up, pick up.*

Voice message system full.

Hitting the end button, I dial Carlie's number.

"Carlie speaking," She answers.

"Carlie? It's Alex."

"Hi, Al," She answers cheerily. "What's up?"

My stomach twists in knots, my face flushed. Everything felt *wrong, wrong, wrong.* "Have you heard from Daniel?"

"No, why?"

"I'm worried about him. I think something's wrong."

"I saw him going up to the Cliff with some of Jamie's friends. I didn't think it was a big deal."

I shake my head and race to my car keys. "He left me this weird voicemail. I think he's gonna hurt himself."

"I'll meet you there in ten with backup."

She hangs up, but I barely noticed. I'm already in my car racing toward the Cliff. *Please, don't let me get pulled over today.* The Cliff is a notorious hangout for Blanks. It is, technically, private property; countless kids have been busted by the cops for "reckless behavior" and trespassing. It's surrounded by dense forest, and is as tall as a skyscraper from the ocean. The trek from the road for the Cliff was through uphill forestation, and it takes a good twenty minutes to get there. I run the entire way, ignoring the burn in my calves and lungs, adrenaline pumping through my veins.

My feet hit the tell-tale gravel of being near the edge and I increase my pace, despite my body's protests. I hear shouting and hyena laughs, and I increase my pace evermore. Then, I hear joyous screaming and Daniel's voice. I lift my eyes from the ground up to the Cliff and see him standing on the edge with a lazy grin on his face, holding an empty liquor bottle. The sight of him makes me stop in my tracks; his hair is disheveled like always. He looks so young and carefree. Then I see the sloppiness to his movements and how dangerously close he was to slipping. The adrenaline starts pumping once more.

"Aaaaaaleeeex!" He greets happily when he sees me. He opens his arms wide and starts walking to me, then loses his footing and falls forward.

The liquor bottle slips from his hands and tumbles over the edge. I never hear it break at the bottom. Daniel falling sends him and his crew into hysterics, while I'm still standing there looking like a deer in headlights. Daniel's rolling around on the concrete, slamming his open palm down to how loud he's laughing.

"Daniel," I say cautiously and step forward, open palm towards him. "Come here. Get away from the edge."

"No!" He suddenly shouts, stopping his wild laughter. "You don't love me!"

It was clear he's talking more to himself than anyone else. He tries to stand up once, then falls back down again. It takes him three tries just to get on his feet. My heart beats against my rib cage.

"Daniel," I say again, inching forward. "That's crazy talk. Of course I love you. Please come here."

"I don't deserve you! I never deserved you!" He starts smacking himself in the head just as Carlie and Mike skid to a stop beside me.

I barely see them. I barely see anything. All I can focus on, all I can think about, is how close Daniel is to that edge.

"It's all my fault, Al! My mom's dead! Your dad's gone! Luke hates me, and you do too." He's screaming, and his friends are still laughing their heads off. I want to shoot them in the face. I want to scream *WHY ISN'T ANYONE HELPING HIM?* But don't. *Daniel.*

"I let you go, Ally," His voice cracks and he looks so *broken*. "I tried to help, but I couldn't. I let you down. I let everyone down. You left me."

"Danny, I'm right here. I'm not going anywhere. Look, Carlie and Mike are here," I wave frantically to them, my voice cracking like Daniel's. *How do I fix this? How do I confess I've lost my mind loving him?* "We still love you. I still love you. Don't do this. Please come here." Tears fall from my eyes, blurring my vision of him. My pale hand is still outstretched toward him, dangling in mid-air. "Danny, please come here, baby, please."

The edges are blurry but he's still right there and he's still sharp and he's still all I can see and I see him backing away away away and I want him to come closer but he won't. He's leaving. I can see it in his eyes and I'm so helpless I don't know what to do.

"Daniel, you don't know what you're doing, man. We can get you help. Just come to us." Mike says.

"I was supposed to save her. I was supposed to save everyone. That was my job, and I messed it up." Snot is dripping from his nose and his face is contorted in a sob but he's still beautiful and he's still mine. Please still be mine, Daniel.

The back of his heel is off the edge. "I love you, Alex. I'm sorry."

And then he's gone,

And their laughter has stopped,

And I'm screaming,

And suddenly I want to be gone too.

233

after

I can still feel the pain in my heart like it happened two seconds ago. I'm back on that Cliff, back in his arms, back there screaming and sobbing for him to come back to me.

It was cold that day. The clouds were gray, and it was even windier up on that cliff. It would have been easier to believe that he was pushed back by the wind, but he wasn't. He walked off that cliff by his own choice. He left me on purpose.

I'm back on the Cliff. I'm staring up at the gray clouds and I can see the trees surrounding me in all directions but one. I can't feel any body parts, and I don't want to. My mouth is slack. My body is numb. I close my eyes; *finally, a death I can actually enjoy.*

When a star collapses on itself, as all stars do eventually, its physical properties no longer exist in that galaxy. In its place is a black hole, something both there and not there in the same space. Black holes are made of magic; they swallow everything in their gravitational pull and turn it into nothing, but its energy still exists. I think grief makes people the same way.

The truth of the matter is that Daniel's death had turned me into something I'd never thought I'd become. His death was kryptonite and I was Superman. Despite having ignored him, pushed him away, I knew that I could always reach out whenever I needed to. A part of me had always hoped, one day, things would return to normal. At seventeen, I thought I had done all the growing up I would ever need. I thought I had suffered enough heartache for a million lifetimes. I was wrong.

This is what he left behind: two grieving friends and one shell of a girl, left with a husk of a boy to remember. The love of a mother who didn't birth him. Two foster parents who had never cared enough to wonder where he spent his nights. Blank-faced people who weren't really people at all.

The list of people impacted by his death could go on and on, because he simply was alive long enough to leave behind a footprint in the shape of a human soul. He wasn't a celebrity, or the president, or a Nobel Prize winner, but he was almost a man. He was my best friend. And that counted for something.

That is the crater he chose to leave. That is what he chose to give up.

before

Seventeen Years Old – Spring

There's lots of things your parents never prepare you for; things the cruel, cold world has to teach you all on your own. My parents never taught me how to deal with the death of my first love. They never taught me just how much it truly hurts to lose someone.

The pain radiates through my whole soul. It started in my chest, then slowly moved onto my brain. The cold, numbing ice swept through my face and filled my fingers and toes. I can't breathe through the pain. All I can feel is the empty hole in my heart where Daniel's life should be.

Paramedics have to lift me from the ground; I'm too weak to stand on my own. I haven't stopped shaking, no matter how many blankets they layer around my shoulders. They tell me he's dead, but I don't believe it. Teenagers don't *die*. We've barely even lived. How could God possibly let him die?

Daniel's foster parents arrange the funeral. It's closed-casket. His body was barely recovered, but what was left of it was unrecognizable. I throw up when I hear the officers say that.

I'm standing in a dark room, with my love's casket ten feet away from me. There are no windows. Everyone in town showed up. The air is stuffy, and smells of old people. Daniel was not old. He should not have died. It should have been me.

His name is escaping through strangers' lips. I hear people tell me that I'm so *brave* for showing up today, so *strong*. Who are they? I do not know. Their words mean nothing. I feel people squeezing my hand, or my arm, or wrapping their clammy limbs around my thin shoulders.

They should not be here. Neither should I. Neither should Daniel. If I had just grabbed him and pulled him to me, none of us would've been there, and nobody would've had to force compassion into their eyes and apologies into their voice.

What are they apologizing for? I decide they must've killed him. He could not have left willingly. Daniel would never do that to me. These people, with all their *I'm sorry for your loss's* and *He was too young's* sicken me. They didn't know him. They couldn't possibly care like I did – like I do.

"Alex," My mother says tentatively, touching my shoulder.

Daniel's casket is ten feet away from me. I think I am going to throw up. I turn quickly on my heel and bolt out the door. Everywhere I look, people are watching me. Everywhere I turn, I hear his name, see his face. I dropped to my knees on the cold concrete of the parking lot, scraping them up. I stand up and kick off these blistering flats my mother made me wear and run straight for the woods across from the funeral home. When I'm a good distance away and I can't hear Mom calling my name anymore, I collapse on the forest floor. I take a fistful of the frozen soil and pine needles and throw it forward, smashing my fists over and over into the dirt. I try to sob until it no longer hurts, but that moment never comes.

Firefighters find me long after the sun sets. When I ran from the funeral home, it was just under 50 degrees. It dropped to below 35 as it got dark, and I was purple and shivering in my black dress by the time they found me. They told me I was saying Daniel's name over and over again, but I don't remember that.

Mom was in a frenzy when I got back. After warming up a bit, I felt fine. Minor headache. While I was in bed pretending to sleep, she casually walked past my bedroom door pretending not to spy on me. I briefly fall asleep, only to be woken by night terrors.

Every night, I see him falling from that cliff over and over and over again. Every. Single. Night. Dark purple bags grow under my eyes. I run on an average of three hours of sleep each day. I do everything I could to avoid sleeping, because I see him the most in my dreams.

I'm a zombie in the school hallways. A ghost, drifting through the crowds, seeing nothing and staring at everything. I hear their whispers, see their faces turn cold and bitter when I meet their gaze. I talk to no one, not even Carlie; *especially* her. "Why can't she just get over it already?" They question. "It's been two months," They state.

The only people who never treat me any differently were the Blanks. They're just as empty as me. They know that Daniel died, and they know I loved him. No, not loved; I love him, present tense. Yet they still stare at me with that blank-faced expression. Even the ones who were there offer me no pity.

As I was rummaging through my locker for books for my next class, Jamie bashes into the closed locker next to mine. He's been wearing the same wrinkly Hawaiian shirt for a week. I heard him say it was vintage. The bags under his eyes are almost as profound as mine, but he hides them with sunglasses.

"You look like shit, Sinclair," He says as he surveys me up and down with a grimace on his face.

I raise my eyebrows, then drop them back down without saying anything.

"So this whole mute widow thing is really true?" Jamie folds his arms against his chest and huffs. I say nothing.

"I brought you a present." He digs through his pocket and returns with a small baggy filled with white little pills. He waves it front of my face. "Answer to all your troubles."

I slam my locker door and start walking the other direction. Jamie quickly catches up with me and is still waving that bag around. No one is in the hall but us, which gives him more confidence than he needed.

"It'll help you stay awake. Give you the best high of your life."

"I'm not a Blank, Jamie."

My voice is scratchy and sounds foreign coming from my lips. I'm startled that I had actually talked, but Jamie isn't. His voice grows hard.

"Really? Cause from where I'm standing, you look worse than most of the regulars."

I stop walking and look up at him. He towers over me, but he hangs his head. Anger bubbles up and I yank the sunglasses off his face and throw them on the ground, breaking them. "Get those stupid fucking glasses off your face."

His eyes show compassion. I didn't know he was capable of that emotion. "I know you want to forget, Alex," He says quietly. "I do, too." Jamie grabs my closed fist, opens it up, and then drops the baggy in. "This will help."

I look from him to the bag. The pills look so innocent and dainty. "What's the catch?"

Jamie shakes his head. "No catch. First bag's free."

"What if I try to kill myself? Then you'll have two deaths on your conscience."

"You won't kill yourself. You're not that stupid."

I scoff. "Do you really think I'm that naïve? I don't want to end up like Daniel, and I *certainly* don't want to end up like *you*."

He grabs at his heart and leans back, feigning hurt. "Oh, ouch, careful folks, her bite is just as big as her bark."

"Go to hell." I turn on my heel and walk away briskly.

He calls after me, "Those were good sunglasses, by the way." I give him the finger behind my back.

Mrs. Boone takes a quick phone call during our tutoring lesson after school. While she's on the phone, I lay my head down on the desk and close my eyes. I'm not gonna fall asleep, I'm just resting my eyes...

The waves crash around us. Daniel gives me one last smile before raising his arms like a bird and tumbling down, down, down, towards the cresting sea. All you can hear are my own screams.

"Alex," Someone's shaking me. "Alex, wake up."

My eyes shoot open and I sit upright, taking a good look at my surroundings. Mrs. Boone stands up straight and eyes me carefully.

"Oh, sorry," I say and rub the sleep from my eyes. "I must've fallen asleep while you were on the phone."

"It's okay," She continues to eye me, but doesn't go back to her desk like she normally does. "How are you sleeping at night, Alex?"

I shrug.

"Do you wanna talk about it?"

I look up at her, blank-faced. "That's very considerate of you to offer, but I'm alright. Thank you."

She stares at me a beat longer, then shakes her head and sighs. The only other thing we talk about from then on is calculus.

It is four in the morning and I'm still awake. My heart still pumps, despite the grief. My bones still ache with loneliness.

Most days, I think I won't be able to live beyond this. Wouldn't that be the most ironic thing you've ever heard? That Daniel's death was the thing that finally killed me. The final bolt in my coffin was the lowering of his.

His funeral was almost a week ago, and I still can't get the smell of death and wet dirt out of my nostrils.

I am too tired to continue being strong for my brother. I am too weary to be accommodating to my mother. I hurt too much to even look at Carlie. It doesn't feel right to have any emotion when, in reality, my heart has been surgically removed from my ribcage. It's floating around somewhere in outer space, right up there with my sanity.

What did Daniel think he'd accomplish by doing this? That I'd feel better, feel like a weight was lifted off my shoulders? I feel the opposite. Instead, I feel like planet earth is sitting on my chest and refuses to move.

Jamie doesn't approach me again the next day, but he doesn't have to. I find him in the band room, already clad in another pair of sunglasses, lying down on several chairs pressed together. He's surrounded by his "friends," but not talking to any of them. He stares up at the ceiling.

"You said these'll make me sleep, right?" I whisper after he takes me behind a row of instrument lockers. He drops the Ziploc baggy into my hands.

"Yeah. Should make you sleep all night." He eyes me as I hide them deep in my backpack. "You sure you wanna do this?"

"Please," I scoff. "Don't pretend to care about me. Consider yourself lucky you've got another customer."

Jamie doesn't say anything, just gives me a weird look. Then, as suddenly as it had come, it passes. He retreats back into the distant, smartass Jamie I know and assumes the role of seller to buyer.

"Don't take them with booze. Don't take them in the morning, and definitely don't take them at school or you'll get both of us in trouble. Last thing I need is a rookie like you selling me out."

I give him a fake, condescending laugh and glare daggers. "Personally, I think I'm the last one you need to worry about. It's those dipshits you call 'friends.'"

Jamie actually laughs. "Really? How's that meathead you were dancing with at the winter formals?"

My demeanor turns icy. "Don't be a dick."

"'Dick' is my middle name, sweetheart. Have fun with your Wonder Pills."

before

Seventeen Years Old – Spring

Jamie takes me to a Blank party the same night he gives me the pills. When we get there, he hands me more pills that are a different color than the ones he gave me earlier. He doesn't force them down my throat. He doesn't even pressure me into taking them. I take two, snaking them back with some mystery drink in a red Solo Cup.

And then the world spins to gold.

Jamie and I run in just our underwear through the forest, and every color blends together. Glowing butterflies flutter around me, tickling my feet and arms and thighs. It's like the stars in the sky are thumping and spinning around me, dancing along to the music in my head. I go back inside and see a beautiful. The most beautiful I've ever seen. Her name reminds me of a sad color, the color I've been feeling for weeks, and it was *beautiful*. I tell her I love her. We get married. I never see Daniel. It was wonderful, wonderful, wonderful! The floors and walls ripple with every step that I take.

I feel my heart pump blood and I feel the glitter running through my veins. My senses are on fire. I was utterly *invincible*.

When I wake up, my head pounds like an iron fist. I'm in a stranger's house; crinkled sandwich bags and crushed pills are littered around the room. I'm on my stomach on a couch that smells disgustingly like piss and booze. Slowly, images from last night come back to me. Kissing a girl, running naked with Jamie… it all blurs together. After I remember last night, Daniel comes crashing back into my thoughts. It hits me with the force of a freight train. All I want is to get the hell out of here and sleep this hangover off.

I stand up and see that other people were sleeping around me, too. I search my pockets for my phone and pull it out, but who could I call? Certainly not Mom. Not Carlie. Daniel's dead, so I couldn't call him. I dial the only person left. He answers with a grunt, like he just woke up and he didn't want to be bothered. The sun had just come up.

"Luke, it's me,"

He says nothing. I keep talking.

"I need you to pick me up. Don't tell Mom, please," I beg.

I hear rustling on the other end. "Where are you?" His voice speaks quietly and cracks lazily with sleep.

"I'm at Jamie's house."

"Okay," He says after a few beats.

And that's it. No questioning, no disapproving lecture. Just "okay." He's coming to pick me up, because that's what we do for each other. When he finally pulls into Jamie's gravel driveway, I'm so relieved to see his face that I run up to him and wrap my arms around his neck.

Luke is my little brother, but he's grown taller than me over the past couple months. He had always been a skinny kid, but as he grew older, he packed muscle and dominance. My little brother is growing up. He wraps his arms around my little waist and hugs me tight. As he straightens up, my feet lift off the ground. He smells like home, and suddenly, I want nothing more than to just go.

"Take me home, Luke," I cry into his neck. "Take me home."

He pulls away only to lead me back to the truck. "Let's go."

When I get home, Mom is sitting at the kitchen table with her hands folded and a half-empty bottle of wine sitting next to her. There are dark purple bags under her eyes that I'm sure match mine. I guess she's sitting there for me, so I sit down across from her. The wooden chair creaks and wobbles beneath me. Luke stands beside me with his arms crossed.

Mom doesn't look at him, just stares at me dead in the eyes with her mouth set in a grim line. "Luke, go to your room."

Luke doesn't move, but his demeanor crumbles a bit. We share a look, and he shuffles his feet awkwardly.

"*Luke,*" She demands. "Room. Now."

Hesitantly, he scurries off into his bedroom. The room crackles with tension. She stares at me with an intensity that I've only seen a few times before.

"Where were you last night, Alexandria?"

"A friend's house."

"What friend?"

I don't say anything. *What can I tell her without her assuming I'm lying to her?* I never intended to stay overnight, but I never intended to get high either. It was stupid, and reckless, but I can't take it back now. It was the first night without nightmares; the first night without thinking of him at all.

"I'll ask you one more time, Alexandria. *Where* were you last night?"

"I went to a party at this girl's house, and everybody else was drinking. Nobody could drive me home, and it was way too late to call anybody else. I just stayed the night. I'm sorry."

Mom clenches her jaw. "You really expect me to believe that everyone else was drinking, except you? Do I have 'stupid' written across my forehead?"

I shrug. "It's the truth."

Mom is silent. She looks down and wipes away some invisible dust, then crosses her arms again and looks at me. "Carlie called me last night – said she saw you go home with Jamie Wallace." I don't say anything. "What the hell are you thinking? You saw what happened to your dad, and then Daniel. And now you think you can get into that shit?"

She looks at my backpack, which I'm clutching harder than I intended to. "Give me your backpack."

Anger flares. "What? No."

"Alex, I said give me your backpack."

"No! Are you fucking insane?"

The pills are practically burning a hole through the thin material of my bag. She stands up and starts grabbing towards my backpack, and I get up and push her hands away.

She yells, "You're grounded, Alex. Go to your fucking room right now."

"What?" I ask incredulously. "You have no right to ground me just because I don't want you to go through my shit."

"I have no right? I am your mother, and you will do as I say."

"No. You can't just pick and choose when you want to be a mom."

"Excuse me?" She stills.

"You heard me. You're gone all the time, and you don't even care. I've had to practically raise Luke since Dad left. You don't do anything for us!"

"I don't do anything for you? Are you kidding me?" We're screaming at each other now. "How about this roof over your head?

How about that food in the fridge? I've worked two jobs ever since your dad left. Luke even got a job! What have you done?"

I stare at her with contempt, stricken silent.

She doesn't stop. "I pay for everything you own, and you repay me with acting like a spoiled brat and partying your troubles away. You don't have any consideration for the people around you, Alex!"

"I hate you!" I scream. "I hate you! I never want to see you again!"

I storm out of the house, dragging my bag with me. She doesn't run after me, but I'll never forget the look on her face. She looks as if she's been slapped. Luke runs after me, slamming the front door behind him.

"Alex!" He calls, but I don't stop. The concrete in front of me blurs, and I sniffle and try to wipe the tears. "Alex, what happened? Where are you going?"

"Leave me alone, Luke."

"She doesn't mean it. You just need to calm down."

I wheel around. "Don't you fucking tell me to calm down," I screamed. "Are you siding with her? After everything she's put us through, you're really going to do this to me?"

"Al, I'm not siding with her. I'm on your side, always."

"Then leave me alone!" I yell.

"Have you gone insane? What the hell were you doing hanging out with Jamie?"

"That is none of your business," I say in a low voice.

"It is my fucking business, because you're my goddamn sister. Are you *trying* to end up like Daniel? Is that your goal?"

I go silent. I grit my teeth together and gave Luke an icy stare. His eyes went raw.

"Alex... I'm sorry..."

I run as fast as I could. Luke calls my name but I'm already sprinting down the road.

It's harder to run with my bag, but I can't ditch it. I'd always been a fast runner, but I'm out of shape. Luke could easily keep up with me on foot, but I knew he wouldn't. He'd want to take the truck, which would delay him a few minutes. That gives me enough time to get to Jamie's house if I maintain a steady pace.

My brain buzzes with electricity. Pain and soreness pump through my veins. The road in front of me blurs and I can feel the sweat dripping into my eyes, glazing them over. I can't take it anymore. I collapse onto my knees on the side of the road and wheeze. I press my cheek against the cool, wet grass and close my eyes. I feel so tired. I pull out my phone, dial Jamie's number, and fall asleep to hearing him say, "Hello? Hello? Alex, is that you?"

after

The drugs. The booze. It was all too much. I should've listened to Luke. I *should've stopped.*

before

Seventeen Years Old – Spring

I wake up face down in an unfamiliar bed. The lights are dim around me, and some kind of soft music hums through the cheap speakers beside the bed. I open my eyes and adjust them to my surroundings; Jamie is standing by a rickety bookshelf stuffed full with vinyl records and CDs. I sit up and see that I'm tangled in thin sheets. I look around the room; white Christmas lights are strung up around the perimeter of the ceiling, and the walls are painted a dark color. Band posters are tacked to the walls in a disarray – the room screams "pessimistic teenager."

"Hey," I say in a low voice to Jamie.

He turns his head around lazily and keeps thumbing through records. "Hey."

Pause. "Is this your room?"

"Yeah,"

Pause. "How did you find me?"

Jamie glances at me then away. "You called me. Don't you remember?"

I look down briefly and shake my head, then stare at his back.

"You were slurring your words pretty bad, saying something about Daniel and punching and sleep. I thought you took some more pills, and I didn't want you to be stranded and high off your ass all alone. I managed to get where you were out of you, so I came and got you." He turns around and walks toward the bed until he sits on the very edge.

"You don't have to sit so far away from me, you know."

"Yes I do."

I narrow my eyes and shake my head, then look around the room again until I see the bottle of pills on the night stand.

"What do those do?"

"It's Zyprexa. Makes you sleep."

"Can I have some?"

"Do you want to go home first?"

I shake my head once more and say, "No. Just give me some."

He grabs the bottle and shakes two out. "It dissolves in your mouth. Don't swallow it whole."

I use his advice and it takes a while to get it down my throat. "What's it for?" I ask him, lying back down and getting comfortable.

"Bipolar disorder."

"I didn't know you were bipolar," I say, my speech slurring.

Simply, he says, "There's a lot of things you don't know about me."

When I wake up for the second time, there's a loud bass thumping wildly. Jamie is nowhere to be seen. The light in his room is still the same, but I can hear people laughing and plastic cups clinking together. Signs and sounds of party life are all around me, but all I want to do was sleep. My phone vibrates in my back pocket; I pull it out and look at the screen.

Incoming Call from... *Luke*

I hit the ignore button – six other missed calls from him and three from Carlie. A swarm of "where are you???" text messages. I turn my phone off and throw it across the room, where it lands with a dull *thud* on Jamie's bean bag.

I close my eyes and bury my face in my hands. I miss Daniel. I curl up into a ball and shake because all my tears have been gone for a long time.

I drift in and out of sleep for a couple hours. Jamie is successful at keeping the party out of his room and away from me. I think he stays sober all night, because he keeps coming in to make sure I'm still breathing. He watches me for a few minutes. Then, he sighs, closes the bedroom door, and walks away.

During one of those intervals, I decide to sit up and wait for him. The bags under my eyes are dark with smudged eyeliner and puffy from crying. I have a horrible case of bed head. When Jamie walks in, his dilated eyes soften. He smells like weed.

"Hey," He says softly, his voice cracking. The bed creaks as he sits down beside me, his back resting against the headboard. The sound is unwelcome and out-of-place after all the silence.

"Hi."

"What's up?" He asks, his words slurring.

"Nothing," I giggle quietly.

He sighs and rests his head on my shoulder.

"Are you high?" I ask, trying to hold in my laughter.

"Maybe a little," He laughs. "Why aren't you?"

I frown with a shrug. "Too tired."

"Of the drugs?"

"I don't know."

"Do you miss Daniel?"

"Of course I do."

"Do you still love him?"

I grimace and get defensive. "Why are you asking so many questions?"

He smirks to himself and looks away. "You still love him. Of course you do. After all, he was Daniel. What's not to love?" There's no malice in his voice, only sadness, and I have nothing to argue against his statements. He was Daniel, and there was nothing unlovable about him. My exterior hardens and I look down at my fingers.

"He could've murdered a puppy and you'd still look at him the way you always did," He continues. "You never looked at me that way. You always hated me."

"That's because you're a jackass."

"Then why are you in my bed?"

It takes me a while to respond; my answer is not something I want to admit. "Because I have no one else."

"You're beautiful, Alex."

The change of tone in his voice alone is sobering, and it is one all females are programmed to recognize at a young age. Alarms and red flags go off in my head, and I think, *I need to get out of here.*

"Don't be stupid, Jamie."

"I love you," He makes a move toward my thigh and I jolt away from him.

I sit up straighter and try to push him off. "Get off me,"

"Alex," He grabs my hand. I get off the bed, which only ends up in Jamie being on his knees on the bed facing me. "Please. It's been *so long* since Daniel died. He would want you to be happy."

Jamie tries kissing my hand, but I pull away with a disgusted face.

"Pull yourself together. You're drunk and you're horny and you're hitting on your best friend's girlfriend."

"He's *dead*, Alex! You're not his girlfriend anymore. When are you gonna realize that? Everybody else moved on, it's time for you to, too." He reaches for me again, but I step back.

"Stay away from me."

"Why are you being such a bitch? You're the most uptight person I know. Quit being such a tease," His voice takes on an insulting tone and he looks at me like a piece of meat.

"Duly noted," I walk over to my shoes and force them on. I storm out of Jamie's bedroom with him angrily calling my name behind me.

Panic begins to take over. *Panic will get you killed, Alex. Channel your fear. Channel your anger. Don't run from it.* Flashbacks of my childhood dance through my head as I run through the throng of people as they're all laughing and dancing wildly around me. Time seems to go in slow motion, and the front door keeps getting farther and farther away from me. I see familiar and unfamiliar faces all around me, and suddenly Jamie is at my side, pawing at me. I ball up my hand in a fist and make a quick and forceful jab to the middle of his face. I hear that tell-tale *crack* and immediately see blood gush from Jamie's nose. He sputters and shouts expletives at me, holding his broken nose. My knuckles throb and I cradle them in my uninjured hand, trying to numb the pain. I turn quickly on my heel and begin running toward the door again.

When the door finally flows open, I nearly collapse in the fresh air. I'm so thankful to have made it out unscathed that I nearly praise Jesus right then and there. I take a deep breath and try not to hyperventilate. I hear shouting behind me, and then I hear grumbled voices calling out my name. I dig mercilessly through my pockets for my phone, then realize I left it behind in Jamie's room. I silently cuss at myself and frantically look around for someone, *anyone*, who could help me. There is no one.

"WHERE IS SHE?" I hear Jamie shout from inside, even over the loud music. "WHERE IS THAT FUCKING BITCH?"

I take off running into the surrounding forest. I have no idea where I'm going, and Jamie lives in the middle of fucking nowhere, but I know there's got to be a neighbor around here somewhere. Most of the Zyprexa has worn off by now, bringing my clear head back. That's unfortunate for Jamie and the other Blanks, who I could easily hear clambering behind me, trying to catch me. I hear them scream profanities at me.

As I sprint through the forest, thorns and sharp branches zip past my face and cut me. My face stings and the muscles in my legs burn. My lungs are threatening to explode, but I *have* to keep going. I don't know what will happen if I don't.

Suddenly, I get an idea. I see the road a few hundred yards away from me, to the left. I see oncoming headlights and adrenaline spikes through me again, which helps me quicken my pace. I tumble down on the road and see the oncoming headlights, still far away enough to be blurry. I run towards the light and wave my arms, screaming, "Help!"

"Hey, there she is!" A friend of Jamie's yells. I want to collapse from despair, but I kept waving my arms and screaming for help.

A large meaty hand wraps around my neck and another slaps down on my mouth, nearly suffocating me. Clearly this is not Jamie, because this person is strong, his arms thick and bulging with muscle. I struggle against his grasp but he just tightens it. I scream against his palm but he drags me back over into the woods and wraps his arms around me, still keeping one hand firmly over my mouth. As the car passes by at high speed, I bite down on his palm until I taste blood and sprint towards the road, screaming as loud as I can with another boy's blood still on my lips. He cusses loudly and clasps his hand around my ankle, causing me to lose my balance and fall face-first on the forest floor. I hit my temple on a thick branch on the way down and white dots cloud my vision for a few moments.

Jamie, his friends, and a meaty-looking guy holding his hand with his face contorted in pain stand over me. I blink a few times, trying to shake the grogginess. I see dried – and fresh – blood dripping from Jamie's nose and around his mouth. He hacks and spits down a mixture of blood and snot. It barely misses me and lands beside my waist. Jamie reaches down and I squirm and start kicking my legs in an attempt to start running, but he grabs me by the throat and squeezes. A gurgled, high-pitched sound escapes my throat and my eyes popped out of their sockets. The boys around him chuckle but the meaty one – Meat Boy – looks angry and is still holding where I bit him.

"I thought we were going to have some fun with her," He complains, then looks at me with disgust.

Um, I'm being strangled here. This isn't fun for you? You look like the type of guy to be into this.

Jamie's eyes blaze with rage and contempt, and the blood makes a little bubble from his nose like snot, then pops. It looks broken. I feel the bruises forming around my neck from Jamie's fingers. My esophagus is being contorted into a pretzel from Jamie's hands. The blood from Jamie's nose drips onto my chest.

"Do it," I manage to get out in a whisper that only he could hear. "Kill me. It's what..." My eyes bug from my head and it's a wonder I'm even able to keep talking. "...we both want."

Suddenly, like a flip being switched, his hands release their grip on my neck and he seems to breathe again, despite me being the one who's been strangled. Air flows back into my lungs and I turn over on my stomach to start a coughing fit. The color gently returns to my face. I feel so weak – physically; emotionally; mentally.

The boys around me laugh, but Jamie is still on his knees a foot away from me, staring at me like a deer in headlights. *Yeah, you almost just tried to kill me, you bastard.* I start scooting away from them again and Jamie doesn't stop me, but Meat Boy does.

"And just where do you think you're goin? Ain't nowhere to go for you but *here*, darlin'," He grabs onto his crotch, symbolizing the *here* comment. I scream and scoot faster, unsure of my ability to walk, let alone run. He grabs a fistful of my hair and yanks me back, causing me to cry out in pain.

"Come on," Jamie finally says quietly. "I know a place we can take her. It's away from the house." He looks down at me. "If we hit her hard enough, we can knock her out."

Meat Boy stares down at me and I try to move; I swear I do. But nothing happens. "I'll do it. Lights out, hun,"

I try to scream; I swear I do. But nothing comes out because I'd just been knocked unconscious.

after

I'm in the middle of the clearing where it happened. My clothes are on. I'm conscious. I'm standing. I have my bearings. And I feel free. Closing my eyes, I breathe deeply through my nose. I can smell the forest and hear the pine needles rustling around in the wind. Every memory of that night is coming back to me in disheveled clumps, but I'm okay. For now, anyway. Maybe that's all that matters.

I am eight years old. My father has taken me hunting with him in the woods behind my childhood home. The smooth, heavy wood in the barrel of the rifle feels like satin beneath my fingertips. He holds it down to my level—safety on—to let me feel it. I've seen what guns do on TV, and I'm scared to touch an object with so much power.

"Don't be scared, Alex. I'll keep you safe," Dad smiles at me. "This is a dangerous weapon, when used improperly. That's why it's important to know what you're doing with it." My father speaks in a calm, low tone. He looks at me, his daughter, with serious eyes. "It's also important to know what to do if someone is threatening you with one. What do you think you'd do?"

I stare up at him with small yet wide eyes, eager for information. He smiles down at me warmly, then rests his rifle against a tree and faces me.

"Panic will get you killed, Alex. It's alright to be scared, but don't let it consume you. Channel your fear. Channel your anger. Don't run from it. That's important in all forms of self-defense."

I nod along, as if I could understand what he really means.

"If someone is coming after you, Alex, you need to be able to think clearly. Assess your options, your strengths their strengths, your exit opportunities." He hoists the gun away from me, over his shoulder, and begins walking. I follow beside him. His eyes flicker down to mine. "And when do you stop fighting back?"

I smile. I know the answer to this one. "Never."

before

Seventeen Years Old – Spring

The first thing I realize when I come to is that a boy is on top of me. I'm still groggy, and can barely keep my eyes open. My underwear is in tatters around my ankles; my bra is nowhere to be found. My hair, body, and face are caked thick with dirt. I'm assaulted by a bombardment of senses.

First, there is a bright light being waved around my face and body that I'm almost positive is the flash on a cell phone camera.

Second, Meat Boy is grunting and groaning whilst moving in and out of me like a God damned troglodyte.

Third, all the boys are watching me.

The "place" that Jamie mentioned taking me to is a small clearing in the middle of the forest. I recognize nothing. I've never been to this part before. *I am scared. I am scared.*

Meat Boy is still on top of me. My body is fuzzy; I can't say anything comprehensible. As my head starts to clear, the place between my legs begins throbbing in pain. I groan, rolling my head around. Starting to hyperventilate, I scream at the top of my lungs and try to push him off me with what little strength I have left. He grunts loudly in response and, with one palm, shoves my face to the side and into the dirt.

Don't let the fear consume you. Think clearly.

He pulls out of me and stands up to pull his pants on rapidly.

"Jesus, man. What the fuck do we do now?" One of the scrawnier kids wielding the camera asks. My neck still feels stiff, but I roll my head side-to-side as best as I can. Their voices sound underwater. My tongue feels like lead in my mouth; an invisible elephant is pressing down on all my limbs, rendering me unable to run, to move, to *fight back.*

"My turn," Jamie says menacingly. I open my eyes just in time to see his eyes glaze over into something carnal, something animal. Something more than just hate or anger – something sinister.

My voice gets its strength back and I scream "help me" at the top of my lungs as Jamie nears me. He back-hands me across the face and I taste blood. His nose has stopped bleeding, but the dried blood was smeared to the side of his face. *How long have they been doing this to me?*

"You could've chosen the easy way, Alex," He says slowly. "If you would've just let me fuck you back at the house, none of this would've happened. You brought this on yourself." The guys laugh around him, like it's true. "You probably *liked* it." They laugh louder and harder.

"Please…" I beg, my voice lighter than a mouse's. I know he can hear me. "Jamie… please stop…"

Pain. All I feel is pain. I scream at the top of my lungs, trying to force the pain away from my abdomen and out my mouth. The pain gives me strength. The pain makes my arms, my legs, and my mouth work. Time speeds up in the next few seconds.

Channel your anger.

One: I knee Jamie right between the legs and dig my fingernails into his Adam's apple, squeezing as hard as I can manage.

Channel your fear.

Two: I get on my feet and take off running.

When do you stop fighting back?

Three: my legs fail me, but Meat Boy and the others catch me first. My head throbs with the heaviness of getting up so quickly, or the heaviness of trying to escape and failing – I don't know which.

Never.

Four: they throw me down on the ground.

Five: shouting, shouting, more shouting. There is a flashlight, I think, or maybe someone's cell phone.

Six: I surrender myself to the pain and close my eyes as I hear their running footsteps leave me behind.

Don't be scared, Alex. I'll keep you safe.

It is not nighttime anymore. That much I know.

I wake up naked and bruised, curled in a fetal position on the forest floor. At first, I am calm and motionless. I hear the birds chirping above me and see them fluttering among the branches. Then I feel the swelling between my legs and the ache in my bones and I remember *everything*. I see no sign of Jamie, or Meat Boy, or any of them. They've probably been long gone. There's a particular spot on the back of my head that's throbbing – I then remember Meat Boy yanking me back and my head getting smashed on a rock. I take in my surroundings, but am unable to stand on my own. Hearing cheery voices approach, I nearly implode with joy. An old couple wearing hiking boots and chatting happily emerge from the trails.

"Help," I croak. My voice comes out cracked, dry, and small. They don't notice. "Help me," I say again.

The old woman sees me first, gasping and clutching her hand to her heart. The old man looks – not quite, but almost – as bewildered as I.

265

"Dear, are you alright?"

Maybe it was the voice that's full of concern, or the compassionate eyes, or the fact they're someone who isn't Jamie, but for the first time in a long time, I smile.

before

Seventeen Years Old – Spring

The kind elderly couple surrounds me. The woman's face is concerned and determined, as if she knows what she's doing. My breathing slows, and I feel lightheaded. I'm increasingly unable to move my limbs, and it terrifies me, but I can't show it on the outside. The man covers my nakedness with his jacket. It must be cold, but I don't feel a thing.

The woman is holding fingers in front of my face, moving her lips; I try to make out what she's saying, but it gives me a headache to focus on anything for too long, so I close my eyes.

"She's going into shock," I hear in my head. "We need to take her to the hospital, Arthur. We'll have to carry her."

No! I want to scream, but I still don't move. Gentle fingers wrap around my arms, so I open my eyes again. My head lolls to the side, against the woman's chest.

Lights. I see lights above me, bright ones – the kind they put in hospitals and schools. I feel a gurney moving beneath me, and hear people talking. Slowly, my eyes adjust to the brightness and I'm able to look at my surroundings. There are nurses standing over me, the background blurring past them. I know I'm being whisked away somewhere. Behind the nurses is the old woman I first saw this morning – that *was* this morning, right? *I don't know where I am anymore.*

"Where am I?" I don't know if these words escape my lips, or even if they can hear me over all the commotion of the hospital. The nurses share a dark look. My skin chafes against a hospital gown I don't remember putting on.

"You're at Quincy Jones Medical Hospital," She says as they slow the gurney down into a private hospital room. A deputy approaches, looking grim. All I remember is Jamie's hands on me; Meat Boy's hands on me; all of their sweaty paws groping at me, touching parts of me that do not *belong* to them. Parts that are not theirs to touch.

The deputy sits me down and explains that I've been assaulted, that I've been drugged, that I've been raped. He asks for my guardian's phone number. In a trance, I give it to him. They wrap a scratchy blanket around my shoulders as I shiver with his words, but it does nothing to warm this cold. The cold comes from within.

I should've known this was coming. I should've been prepared for it, but I wasn't. My entire body goes numb. *This can't be right. They must be talking about someone else. They're confused; I haven't been raped. That wouldn't happen to me.* But in my heart, I know the truth.

The older couple – I learn their names are Penny and Arthur – drove me to the hospital. They're sitting in the waiting room for me, most likely being questioned by the deputies; I don't know why they're waiting for me. They give me ice packs to put on my eyes, which are swollen from crying. I reach up to touch the base of my neck and feel a bandage, then get a flashback of the night before when Meat Boy threw me down and I hit my head against the rock.

My clothes are confiscated. They test me for diseases. They test my BAC and give me a drug test to figure out what Jamie and his friends pumped into me. Rulers are held to my skin against bruises and cuts as photographs are taken. They inspect my body from head-to-toe; they take a picture of the swollen flesh between my legs and swab it for DNA. There is dried blood on my knuckles from trying to fight them off, I think   I don't remember.

Numbly, I hear the deputy say my mom has arrived through the door, since he's not allowed in. They brush pine needles from my hair and put them in a small, clear baggie. I try to stay calm, stay strong, but it's all too much... Feeling a panic attack set in, I try to push the ladies away hurriedly and begin growing frantic. The nurses set their tools—the tools to collect the evidence for my rape—aside and grab my hands.

"It's alright, honey," one of them says. "There's no reason to be afraid anymore."

But there is a reason. There's a reason to be afraid and the remains of it are crawling around inside of me, eating away the girl I was... and the girl I would've become.

When they're done, they finally let me take a shower in the private room's bathroom. A deputy still stands outside the room, and the nurses go give my mother forms to fill out. I turn the shower temperature to the hottest it'll go and stand beneath the scalding water, letting it run down my hair and back. The healing scab at the back of my head screams in protest, but I don't move.

I stare down at my bare flesh – the flesh that no longer belongs to me. There is dirt and dried blood underneath my fingernails. Whose blood it is, I have no idea. Fervently, I begin scrubbing away at my skin. I scrub away the dirt, the grime, the blood, the germs, the past, the present, the future, my entire *soul...*

The dirt, soap, and blood mix together in an invisible trail down to the drain as I wash it from my skin. It feels like an episode of

The Twilight Zone – realistically, I know I am still the same person, physically; I know I am still Alex Sinclair, but I feel trapped. I feel like a stranger stuck in my own body.

I don't want this life, this body, anymore. I want to unzip myself from it and give it up.

My mother's eyes. They're all I see when I finally walk out of the hospital room in clothes that don't belong to me. My mother's eyes—brown, unlike mine—are full of a million feelings, a million words unsaid, a million fears come true. I can tell she's trying not to cry in front of me, in order to not upset me even more, but I wish she wouldn't. I wish she would just cry. Consoling her would give me something other than the sound of my own soul coming apart to focus on.

She hugs me for a long time – the longest hug I've ever gotten from her, probably. What breaks my heart most is that she doesn't wrap her arms around me tightly, squeezing me until it's hard to breathe; she hugs me gently, carefully... fearfully. Fearful of what, exactly? Hurting the bruises, the cuts, my psychosis? I don't know. Despite trying my best, I still stiffen at the human contact. *Please don't touch me.*

She kisses my forehead and I can finally feel her tears plopping down on my neck. I've cried so much in the past 24 hours that I have no more tears left, even more a moment like this.

"I'm so sorry, baby," She whisper-sobs into my ear. "I'm so sorry, honey. I'm so sorry for yelling at you. I'm so sorry for the things I said. Please forgive me."

"It's okay, Mom," I whisper back. "I'm sorry too."

"Ma'am? I'm sorry, but we have to get a statement from your daughter, if you're still pressing charges," one of the police officers say, interrupting our moment.

"Mom..." I try to say, but they talk over me.

"She'll have to be brought down to the station, ma'am."

"Officer, she has been through a hell of a night. Let me take my daughter home."

"If we wait, she may forget pieces of the assault. It's best for everyone if we do it now."

"Mom, I can't," All heads whip toward me and my cracking voice. "The last thing I want is for the whole school to know, and that's what'll happen. I don't want to do this."

"Alex, we're pressing charges. This is not a discussion."

"No," I say definitively. "It's not your decision to make."

"Yes, it is. Whoever did this to you is going to jail. Period."

Fear grips me once again and my throat closes. I see the old couple that helped me in the corner, hugging each other's side. Penny, the woman, smiles weakly at me. I only vaguely remember them finding me, but I remember my lack of clothing when they did. Blushing with embarrassment, I look away from her gaze.

The next few hours blur by. My mother convinces – or, rather, forces – me to give my statement to the police. I tell them everything I can remember, from the moment I left my house to the moment Penny and Arthur found me. Sadly, it isn't much. They advise us to get a good lawyer, the kind that specializes in cases like these. *Rape cases.*

Mom tries to put on a good show, but I know she's just as scared as I am. I know this is ripping her to shreds inside.

My body buzzes with exhaustion. The officers here move by at a significantly lower rate than the rest of the world. Nobody seems to care that I've been raped, or that Jamie is still walking free – probably with a raging hangover, if I had to take a guess. Mom throws a hissy fit when they let us go home without telling us what they plan to do with this information, or if Jamie will be arrested. *Nothing is going to happen to him*, I think. This makes me incredibly angry, but I'm too tired to fight back right now.

By the time we get in the car, the sun is beginning to set. She doesn't start the engine, just sits there next to me for a while.

"Are you hungry?" She asks quietly. I shake my head. The last thing I could do right now is eat, even if it would make her feel better.

She starts the car and pulls out of the parking lot. When we're almost home, she speaks again. "I talked to the couple that brought you into the hospital," Mom says. "Do you know them?"

I shake my head once more, leaning it against the cold window. The coolness feels good against my hot cheek.

"Do you… remember… them?" She asks tentatively, recalling my police statement about how I didn't remember much since Jamie drugged me.

Painfully, I nod. Mom says nothing more, thankfully. I close my eyes and fall asleep, nightmares plaguing me.

When I finally walk into the house, it is nighttime. Luke is asleep on the couch with the TV on. His mouth is hanging open and he's sprawled out like he's a little kid again, despite the length of his legs hanging over the other side of the couch. I take a blanket lying on the chair beside him and cover him up with it. I then turn off the TV and kiss him on the head with tears forming in my eyes.

My bedroom is just how I left it: bed unmade; a few articles of clothing lying on my bedroom floor; notebooks, books, and pens scattered on my desk. Slowly, I walk over to the full length mirror and stare at my reflection. The borrowed sweatshirt from the hospital hangs loosely on my shoulders. I fiddle with the material that hangs over my wrist.

Gingerly, so as not to disturb my injuries, I take the sweatshirt off, revealing my nakedness. There is a large bruise near my right ribs where one of the boys kicked me. I crane my neck and move my hair to the side to look at the stitches at the crown of my head from when Meat Boy slammed me down, hitting my head on a rock.

Looking at my own body makes me sick. I turn away from the mirror and dash over to my dresser, changing into one of my t-shirts. I push the sweatpants down my hips, just as fast, and put on my own pajama pants. Overcome by my own emotions, I quickly bundle up the hospital clothes and shove them under my bed, burying them with more of my own clothes.

I walk down the dark hallway to Mom's bedroom. She's all alone in that big bed of hers, and she was still, but somehow I know she's awake. I crawl into bed beside her and she turns around so that she's lying on her side, facing me. In the light of the streetlamps coming in from the window, I see that her cheeks are wet.

"I'm sorry, Mom," I whisper. Tears fall down my face and her eyes soften. "I'm so sorry."

Quietly, I begin to sob. She slides closer to me and wipes the tears from my face.

"Shh, baby. I'm sorry too," She whispers back. Her throat sounds clogged up, like maybe she'd been trying to hold back tears of her own.

"I'm so sorry. I've been such a horrible daughter. I'm so sorry, Mom. I love you. Please forgive me." I'm babbling and quietly sobbing and she wraps her arms around me, pulling me to her chest like she did when I was a baby.

"Baby," Her hands stroke my hair. "You are the best daughter anyone could ever ask for. You have *nothing* to be sorry for."

I keep repeating my apology, but I forget who I'm apologizing to: her, Daniel, Luke, Carlie, Dad, me. She coos me to sleep, smoothing my hair down and away from my face. I fall asleep in her arms, just like that.

You are never too old to need your mom.

after

Everything is white again. It's like that cliché *"there's a bright light at the end of the tunnel…"* Only there is no tunnel. There's just me.

before

Seventeen Years Old – Spring

I wish I could've told my mom how it was to not feel safe in my own skin anymore. I wish I could've told her something to make her believe I was okay again. But I couldn't come up with anything, so I didn't. I just laid in that bed and stared at my blank wall because I took all my pictures down. They all reminded me of Daniel. They all reminded me that I was never going to be that girl again.

Carlie came every day, and Mom never told her what happened. At first, she tried talking to me. Asking me what's wrong. Saying stuff like, "Daniel would want you to be happy, Alex." *Yeah, no shit.* When I never talked back, or even acknowledged her presence, she started to grow angrier. One day she stormed into my room and started screaming at me. Apparently Mom had seen it coming and had tried – unsuccessfully – to keep her in the living room. I heard the shouts before Carlie even got to my door.

"You can't spend your entire life in here, Alex!" She yelled. "Eventually you've got to stop feeling so damn sorry for yourself and get out of bed and wash your hair and learn how to deal with this like every other person! Jesus Christ, Alex," She took a deep breath and choked back a sob. "You're not the only one who feels pain." I closed my eyes, because it was too bright in my room and my throat was closing. "You aren't the only one who loved him!" Her voice was so small and vulnerable, and suddenly I ached for my best friend. I felt so sorry and bad and horrible and I wanted nothing more than to make things right. But by the time I'd gotten my strength to move, she was gone.

Carlie didn't come back after that.

I can hear my mother talking on the phone. I had been sleeping all day, unsurprisingly, but the sound of her voice through my bedroom awoke me. I can't hear what the other end of the line is saying, but I can hear her reaction. I lie stock still in my bed, with my unwashed hair and face, wondering when their conversation will be over so I can ask her what they said.

Twenty minutes later, it happens. She knocks on my bedroom door, but enters without me having to say a word. She sits on the edge of my bed and runs her fingers through my hair like she did when I was a little kid.

"That was the deputy we talked to before," She says quietly, softly. "They found traces of Jamie, the boy you told them about, along with the others you said…" They found traces of them inside me, is what she means. "They're going to arrest them."

I don't say anything. I wonder what will happen when this news breaks at school. Carlie hasn't been around to tell me the kind of rumors fluctuating since I've stopped showing up.

"Alex…" Her voice falters and I look up at her. The pain is palpable on her face. She strokes my cheek. "Honey."

I want to cry, but I have no tears left. All I feel is the emptiness. My tear ducts have all dried up; they're useless. You cry when you feel pain. People are supposed to feel more than the pain, but I don't.

"Sweetie, you don't have to be scared anymore. You can go back to school," Again, with the "you don't have to be scared anymore." Why don't people understand it's not Jamie I'm scared of?

It's not Jamie. Jamie means nothing to me. I'm scared of everyone, because how can I trust a stranger if my own friend violated me? I'm scared of myself, because this isn't how you're supposed to react to being raped. Rape victims are supposed to feel angry, or sad; they're supposed to feel *something*, at least, anything. I feel nothing. I'm scared for Luke. I'm scared of the looks I'll get at school. I'm scared of getting out of bed. I'm scared to look in the mirror. I'm scared to remember. *I'm scared to remember.*

"Alex, you need to go back to school."

My voice is hoarse from saying close to zero words in the past few weeks. I'm surprised to hear that it, still, actually works. I guess I can still surprise myself. "I want to be homeschooled."

"What?" She asks, shocked.

"I want to be homeschooled," I say once more.

"Alex, you love school. What about your teachers? Your friends?"

I almost laugh, but nothing comes out. "What friends?"

She's silent for a second, looking dumbfounded. "Honey, I don't have time to homeschool you, and we can't afford a tutor—"

"They have online classes. I can use the library's laptop. Please, Mom. I can't go back to that school. I can't face everyone there."

For a while, she just stares at me, and I wonder if she really will force me to go back to school. Then, I see the hope in her eyes: *Maybe this is what she needs. Maybe this is what will fix my daughter, bring her back to me.* For effect, I attempt a smile.

"Give me some time to think about it," She finally says, quietly, but I know it's a secret "yes."

before

Seventeen Years Old – Spring

"Alex," Mom yells from the living room, disturbing me from my slumber. *"Alexandria Lauren Sinclair, get in here right now!"*

Rubbing sleep from my eyes, I roll over and squint my eyes. *What now?* She storms down the hallway and appears in my doorframe. My curtains are closed – I even put an extra bed sheet up to block out the daylight – so she's forced to flick on the light.

"Why didn't you tell me you'd been skipping your appointments with Dr. Moore?" She is seething with anger, and holds up her phone like it accuses me of something. I don't know what to say. I haven't gotten out of bed in so long – only to take the occasional shower and go to the bathroom. Isn't it obvious to her I'd been missing my appointments?

"I mean before this," She waves her hand at me, as if that was an explanation. "You were skipping your appointments. Why?"

I don't say anything. It's not that I don't want to; I want to defend myself. I want to tell her everything, but the words simply won't come. I sit there like an idiot, staring at her with my mouth open and my eyes wide.

"Alex," She comes to sit on my bed, most of her anger dissipating. "I am trying to be patient with you. I have no idea what you're going through. This is *killing me*," She's losing her voice from emotion. "And you don't have to talk to me, but you do have to talk to someone. You can't hide forever. You've been through so much. I just want you to get better, baby." She cups my cheek. A tear slips down her face. "I can't lose you. I want you to get up, take a shower, put clothes on, and come out of your bedroom. Please."

I wish I knew what to say. Instead of responding to her tears and anger, I do exactly what she says. I get up, I take a shower, I put on normal people clothes, and I went into the living room. I borrow Luke's cell phone to call Dr. Moore.

I stare at myself in the bathroom mirror, long after everyone else has gone to sleep. There are a pair of sharp silver scissors on the sink next to the faucet, eyeing me. My vision goes back and forth from my reflection to the scissors, and I contemplate it.

Something about me needs to change. The outside no longer matches the inside. My hair has been growing for years; it goes past my breasts, almost to my butt. Every time I close my eyes, I can still feel the dirt caked in my hair and Meat Boy's thick fingers twisting into it and yanking me back.

No one will ever do that to me again.

The loud *snip* of the steel scissors almost startles me in the surrounding silence. Long locks of hair fall one-by-one, tickling my feet on the floor. I keep cutting until my hair rests just above my shoulders. It feels like a weight has been lifted, but it still isn't enough.

I clean up the pieces of hair from my bathroom tile, put the scissors away, and go to bed.

"Alex, forgive my bluntness, but you look terrible." Dr. Moore's face transforms to shock when he sees me for the first time since

Daniel's death. I should take offense to his comment, but he says it with such kindness that I can't help but love him for it. I give him a half-hearted smile.

"Please, sit," He gestures toward the leather chair located directly in front of his identical one. His voice turns serious. "I heard about Daniel's passing. I'm so very sorry."

I clear my throat, briefly. Then, as if he meant nothing to me, I cross my legs and put on an impassive mask. With a clear voice, I say, "Thank you."

He squints his eyes at me, as if trying to see into my soul. "Your mother told me you were assaulted."

I clear my throat again, simply out of awkwardness more than anything else. "Yes."

"What are you feeling, Alex?"

It takes me a while to answer. "I don't know."

"That's understandable."

My lower lip quivers, and I swallow vomit. "I was a virgin."

For the first time in our professional relationship, I see Dr. Moore's façade crack and he shows emotion. It is slight, almost unrecognizable, but it's enough. Biting my thumbnail to distract myself, I start to quietly cry. I mourn the death of the girl I used to be, forever changed by a few angry, drugged up teenage boys. I mourn the death of my own innocence, something I'll never get back. Dr. Moore sits on the edge of his leather chair and pats my back, soothing me. I avoid eye contact.

"Alex," He almost whispers, in a calm voice. I keep my head down. "I need you to look at me."

And so I do. I look up at him, with my puppy dog eyes and nail biting. His eyes are so clear, so intent; I wish I believed in things as much as Dr. Moore does. Maybe one day.

"You," Pausing for effect, "are going to heal. I know it doesn't feel like that right now, but you will, because I'm going to help you.

What happened has not ever been and will never be your fault. Okay?"

I nod and smile, genuinely. For once, I believe his words: I will heal.

The worst part of it all is not that they took my virginity, though that is a runner-up. The worst part isn't that they chased me, brutalized me, drugged me, and left me for dead – though it probably should be.

The worst part is that I will never be able to forget them. I'll never be able to be a normal teenager, who has a healthy curiosity of sex and love. I'll never not be able to feel the metallic taste of violence on my tongue when some passerby bumps into me in the hallways at school. Even as I "heal," I'll never have the luxury of choosing who I share an untouched piece of myself with. I'll never be untouched again.

That night, when I get home, I don't retreat to my bedroom immediately. I go to sit at the breakfast bar, watching Mom make dinner. She looks at me warily for a few seconds, regarding my new hair, then goes back to what she's doing. She can't suppress her small smile, though. I want to tell her that I'm not better yet, that I don't want her to have too much hope, but that I hope I will be. I want to tell her that I'm going to try.

In that instant, I remember what really needs to happen. I remember that Jamie and Meat Boy and all of them are still in jail. I realize that what they did to me... it was deplorable. And I want them to never do it to another human being again. I want them to rot in there.

"Mom?"

"Yeah, sweetie?"

"I want to talk to a lawyer." I say and her hands stop stirring the pot of soup they were before. "A good one. I want them to go to jail for a very long time."

She hasn't said anything, but now I'm frantic to get all my words out before she has a chance to.

"All of them; I want to put all of them away. And I know we really don't have the money for a good one, but I'll get a job to help. I'll get two, if I have to. I just can't stand the thought of them being released on bail, and eventually walking free. I want them to pay for what they did."

There. It's out there. Slowly, her eyes raise up to meet mine. I see strength in them. I see pride.

"I have a friend. He's a lawyer. A good one." Mom smiles bashfully. "He'll help us out. I'll call him tomorrow."

I smile. "Thank you."

"I'm so proud of you, Alex."

Later that night, Luke comes in with a bowl of macaroni and cheese with pepper and tuna. It had aptly been named "The Alex" because it was my favorite dish as a kid. Luke sits on the edge of my bed and just eats it in comfortable silence.

"Want some?" He finally asks, holding the bowl out in my direction.

Mutely, I stare at him. I was in my bed, waiting for sleep, watching the wall when he came in. I don't say anything, so he shrugs and continues eating.

"Dad used to make that," I say quietly.

Luke nods slowly. "I know," He pauses. "I haven't had it in forever." He takes another bite. "I'd forgotten how good it is."

I sit up and rest my back against the wall, still looking at him. We're talking about Dad like normal people do. We're talking about him like he was a pleasant memory, and we're okay with him being gone.

"I miss him," I say simply. I don't know whether I'm talking about Dad or Daniel.

"Me too," Luke says back, and I don't know which one he's talking about either.

Luke holds a forkful out to me and I take a tentative bite. It tastes just like how I remember it. Luke offers me another bite and another and another until I've eaten the whole bowl and he's making more. When he comes back, he makes me smile. It isn't quite laughing, but it's progress. As we talk, I see Mom hovering in my doorway out of the corner of my eye. I ignore her, and eventually she leaves, because she understands. The only person who can bring me back to myself is my brother.

after

Of course, my mom had told me she's proud of me before. Whether it was for kicking in the winning goal when I was just a kid, or sticking up for one of my peers on the playground, or getting a good grade on a test – she's always said it. Somehow, though, that time it meant more. That time, I knew she was proud of me for surviving, for persevering. Survival is a lot harder than we'd like to admit – harder than *I'd* like to admit.

Usually, surviving sucks. It seems like it's a lot more trouble than it's worth. But, once in a while, there are these little moments of relief. These moments can be brought on by a good song, one that makes you dance; or the feeling you get in the pit of your stomach when you hear a baby laugh; or realizing that the boy or girl you've had a crush on for ages *actually* feels the same way. You have to pay attention to these moments, because they're fleeting. They're rare. When it does happen, these mere seconds of unfiltered, pure joy – notice them. Try not to take them for granted. Remember the feeling in your cheeks after laughing so hard it hurts. You're going to need the little things like that when survival becomes too hard, because it will.

When my mother told me she was proud of me that night, it cracked open a little bit of sunlight on my dark world.

285

before

Seventeen Years Old – Spring

"Hey, Carlie," I start, my voice shaking after getting her voicemail... again. "It's Alex. Um..." *Just answer your damn phone, Carlie.* "Sorry for leaving so many voicemails. Just, um... Call me soon, okay? I really think we should talk. Bye."

I hang up and tap my cell phone against my knee, wondering what to do with myself now. Maybe I should just go to her house, that way she's forced to talk to me. *Okay, psycho, cool your jets. She just needs time...*

My plan was to tell her everything before it all gets out that I'm pressing charges against Jamie and the other boys, but she won't answer my calls.

I meet with my lawyer constantly to develop a strong case. Talking about it so much helps me come to terms with what happens. I grow stronger, slowly.

Mom eventually relents about school, and lets me start homeschool. I have no friends left, so all I during the day is go to the library to get on the online school, go to work, and go to my lawyer's firm.

I try calling Carlie several more times, but she always let it go to voicemail, even after the news broke that I was being pulled from school… even after everyone knew Jamie had raped me. I understand, though. I wouldn't want to talk to me either.

before

Seventeen Years Old – Summer

No bonfire celebration after the end of my junior year, though I'm sure Carlie and Mike are out at Oliver Fitzpatrick's, having the time of their lives and drinking enough to forget it all, but I have no interest in that sort of thing. I wonder if any of them wandered over to the Cliff, and I wonder if they thought about Daniel when they did.

Instead, I stand at the brink of madness. That's quite an exaggeration, but one that suits well. Dr. Moore is always ranting and raving about "confronting my demons," so that's what I'm out here doing. Confronting my demons.

The meadow hasn't changed much. It's still the same, picture-perfect place. I can't quite put my finger on what's different, but then I realize: it's me. I was the one who changed. The last time I came here was with Daniel. It was two weeks before he died. Things were already shot to hell at that point, but that day is now known to me as The Last Good Day.

"Where are we going?" I asked him as he opened the passenger door of his car for me. He had that beautiful gleam in his eye, reminding me why I fell in love with him.

"On an adventure, Ally." Daniel grinned foolishly at me and the sun caught his eyes.

Then there was Dad – the first person who ever took me on an adventure, the first person who ever introduced me to the meadow. Without him, this wouldn't be the place Daniel had his Last Good Day. Maybe that day wouldn't have even been with me.

And now it's just me here, without either of them. Quite pitiful, really. I came when the sun was about to set, when the place is at its most beautiful. It turns all the wildflowers gold and shimmering. I sit down in the grassy hill, facing the setting sun. I close my eyes and try to remember my father – his face, his voice, the little quirks about him. He's fading from my memory because he isn't here. Why isn't he here?

Abruptly, I stand up, and the wind whips around me briefly. Goosebumps rise on my arms, no longer shielded by thick hair. I scream at the top of my lungs, for no reason at all other than to scrape the poison away from my insides. I don't stop screaming until my throat is raw and my mind is clear.

Before I can start crying again, I leave. The sun hadn't set yet.

before

Seventeen Years Old – Summer

"Alex, I'm proud of you for going to the meadow. It's a huge step in the right direction." Dr. Moore says with such intensity and without breaking eye contact.

I fidget and look away. "Thanks. I had to leave early though. Couldn't take it anymore."

Long silence. "How are you feeling, Alex?"

I scoff. "Be specific, doc."

"Jamie," I still. "Daniel. Your father. All the boys involved with your—"

"I hate them. Obviously. Not much more to say about that."

"Okay. We don't have to talk about it, if you don't want to."

"I don't," I say simply.

"That's perfectly fine. But you know you will have to talk about it eventually."

I furrow my eyebrows. "Have you ever had a friend get so mad at you, that they totally stop talking to you? They won't answer your calls; won't even acknowledge you exist. And this person... this was person was your best friend," I pause. "And you want nothing more in the world than to just hear them tell you everything is gonna be okay. You want nothing more than to just be able to hug them, but they hate you, and you know it's because you were a terrible friend. What do you do?"

Dr. Moore chuckles. "Well, those are a lot of specifics. Forgiveness is hard, and it varies from person to person. It takes longer for some than others. I'm sure you can attest that everyone processes things differently."

I sigh. "What can I do?"

"Give her time. Forgive yourself first, and the rest will follow."

Luke is sitting on the couch when I get home. I plop down next to him, and we watch movies together until the sun goes down. Mom is fluttering about somewhere, but she only catches our attention when she walks into our view, reaching up to her ear to fasten an earring.

She's dressed in a dark grey shift dress, and has her hair styled and out of its normal ponytail. She's wearing low heels, but heels nonetheless. She looks gorgeous. Luke and I share bewildered looks when we see her.

"Mom," I say, awe evident in my voice. "What are you doing all dressed up?"

She lets out a deep breath, smoothing her dress with both hands and standing up straight. "I'm going on a date."

Luke was sipping on a water bottle when she says this, and immediately chokes and begins a coughing fit. I'm in such shock that I don't even register him, just stare at Mom.

"Luke, are you okay?" She is clearly nervous, most likely about telling us.

"I'm fine," He answers, in between coughs.

"A date? With who?" I question, still in shock that she's going on a date.

"His name is Rick. I met him at work."

"Is he nice?"

"Yes," She smiles, just a tad, but it disappears quickly.

"Does he dress well?"

She rolls her eyes, and smiles. This time, she doesn't let her smile fade. "Yes, Alex. He does."

I nod slowly. "Good. Have fun."

Shock briefly crosses her face. "Are you guys are okay with this?"

Luke doesn't answer. I look over at him and kick him under the coffee table. He briefly groans in pain, then says, "Yeah, Mom. Have fun."

I turn around and smile at her, repeating what Luke said. "Yeah, Mom. Have fun."

She smiles at us. "Alright; thank you. I shouldn't be gone too long; leftovers are in the fridge. Don't get too crazy while I'm gone."

Luke laughs satirically, saying, "Oh, you too, Mom."

After watching her truck's headlights disappear down the road, Luke turns to me. He stays at the window, staring at me like I've grown two heads, as I walk back over to the couch and plop down. Briefly, I search for the remote, and un-pause the television. Luke still stands there, and I roll my eyes.

"What?" I snap at him.

"Mom's on a date,"

"Yeah," I shrug. "And?"

"Well... she's on a date."

I roll my eyes again as he walks over and sits next to me again on the couch. "Luke, she's a grown woman. It's been quite a few years since Dad left, and even longer since they've been separated. Don't you think it's time for her to get on with her life?"

Luke pauses. "I guess it's just weird to think of her with anybody but Dad," He looks over at me. "You know?"

"Yeah," I mutter. "I know. Maybe this is what she needs. To, you know, move on and stuff."

"I don't want to move on, Alex." His tone suddenly turns serious. I turn my head to look at him. "If I move on, then I forget about him. I forget all the good things about him. And I don't wanna do that."

"I don't forget. Sometimes I wish I would. And you aren't forgetting, either. It's just becoming distant; like it seems like it happened to another person." I shrug. "That's what it's like for me, anyway."

He meets my gaze. His eyes are serious. "Why do you want to forget?"

"Because it'd mean forgetting all the bad stuff, too."

"But there was a lot more 'good' stuff, Alex. You just have to look for it."

I scoff. "I don't think it qualifies as 'good' if you have to look for it."

"I don't mean it like that. I just mean..." He pauses. "Okay, do you remember when Dad was living with Grandpa and we were carving those pumpkins?" I nod. "Well, Grandpa came in all drunk and angry, and you stood up to him when Dad couldn't. You were 14, tinier than a bean pole, and you stood up to a grown man who could've easily beaten the shit out of you. And you won. That was the first time I ever started realizing how badass you actually are." I'm frozen speechless. "Anyway, that was one of my last memories with him."

"That's not a memory of him, though. That's a memory of me." I manage to croak out.

He smiles to himself. "I know. But that night," He goes on. "After you fell asleep, Dad and I were up talking. He told me," He mimics a deep, rumbling voice. "'Son, I want you to grow up and be tough, like your sister. She's tougher than I ever could be, tougher than I could ever teach you. That strength is gonna get her places, and she'll get you out of a heck-of-a-whole lotta trouble. I guarantee you that.'" Luke looks up at me, just as a tear slips down my cheek. "Turns out, what he said that night is about the only thing he ever got right."

"No," I whisper, and shake my head. "He got us right. You were too young to remember much, but he was a really good to us for a while." The tears are flowing freely, but I power through them.

Luke isn't crying yet. "I remember going to the beach. And I remember the meadow." We chuckle together, reminiscing in our own heads. "It's crazy, sometimes, the things I remember. It's little, stupid stuff. Stuff we always took for granted, you know?"

"Like his cooking," I supply, offering a smile.

He smiles back, and repeats me in agreement. "I miss him. But I don't think he's gotten better, wherever he is. If he was, he'd be here. He'd come back. Wouldn't he?"

I smile and grab his hand. "Yeah. He would."

There was no set of rules for how to be a good big sister in situations like these. No guidebook to follow, no right thing to say. I never seemed to know the right thing to say when it came to comforting Luke, because what is there left to be said? We were half orphans. But we had each other.

before

Eighteen Years Old – Winter

It is my 18th birthday. The first anniversary of Daniel's death. After a day of being out with Mom celebrating my birthday, Luke convinces her to let us have a party at the house. She's reluctant, but inevitably, he talks her into it. I think she went with that guy she had a date with a few months ago, Rick – but I'm not sure.

Luke's friends are all high-fiving him and slapping him on the back and at least a dozen girls have come over, all flipping their hair and batting their eyelashes. A few of them express their condolences to me about Daniel and wish me a happy birthday in the same breath, but I ignore them all. They're here for Luke, not me.

As I watch my brother, I realize how much of a life he has outside of home. Outside of me. I watch him interact with his friends and girls, and I realize how *happy* he looks. It's the most relaxed I've seen him all year.

It's as if everything around moves in slow motion. Or maybe I'm the one moving in slow motion, and everything around me was being fast forwarded. I try to blink, but my eyelids won't move. I think I'm going to pass out. Over in the corner, there's a drunk couple grinding on each other. If I was my old self and I was among friends, we would've yelled at them to use protection and then run away laughing our asses off. But I'm not my old self, and I don't have any friends anymore.

I walk down the hallway toward my bedroom slowly. We have a small house, but there's an incredulous amount of people here. I put my hand against the wall as I walk past for support. I collapse when I reach the threshold of my bedroom and slam the door behind me. I barely make it to the waste basket by my desk to throw up. After I'm done retching, I wipe my mouth and sit back against the wall with tears streaking down my face. *I knew today was going to be a hard day.* I feel like I'm going insane.

Suddenly, I stand up and sniff the snot back into my nose. I start with the papers on my desk, which have been sitting here for a few months. Everything is so neat. I hate it. It needs to be messy. Messy and cluttered and *horrible*, just like me. I sweep the papers off my desk in one fluid motion, sending them flying. I take the happy pictures I'd since put back up since my assault and throw them across the room, where they smash into a dozen pieces against the wall. I grab the desk lamp off my bedside table and heave it against that same wall. It breaks the light, and suddenly I'm drowning in darkness. I shut my eyes, and the next thing I know, Luke is pounding on my bedroom door.

"Alex? Are you okay?" I can hear the party going on behind him, but his voice is etched in concern. He wiggles the door handle, but it's locked.

"Yeah," My voice cracks. I clear my throat. "Yeah, I'm fine. Just dropped some stuff."

"Unlock the door."

"I'll be out in a second," I call and stand up.

Luke pauses. "Alex..." His sentence trails off. "If you don't want these people here, I can make them go. We can hang out, just me and you. Just say the word, Al."

"No, no," I say too quickly. "It's okay. Go have fun. I'll be out in a second."

Eventually, I hear him leave. I wipe the moisture from underneath my eyes and try to make it look like I wasn't just crying, but no one would notice me anyway. A few minutes after Luke walks away, I open the door and go back into the party. I must've spent at least an hour in my room, because the party is even crazier than when I left it. Somehow, I make it to the kitchen. There's a keg there and I eye it. I haven't had a drink in months; at least since my assault. I play with the empty red Solo Cup in my hands. Do I really want to risk it? I sit down on the bar stool and press my cheek against the cool countertop. *I'm so tired...*

Luke is shaking me. His voice sounds underwater.

"Alex? Can you hear me? Alex, answer me," He's shouting over the music. I love this song. Somebody turns up the volume and turns down his voice. *The waves...*

"Luke," I try to say, then blink. Luke's face is gone, and Daniel is leaning over me and smirking.

"Alex," He speaks and that beautiful smile is back. He's the only who sounds real, and clear. I want to melt in his arms. I want to be with *him*. I don't want to be in the real world anymore.

"Alex!" I blink once more; Daniel's face has been replaced by Luke's. He's shouting and shaking me, then looks up past my head. I'm lying on the ground. When did I get on the ground? *"Carlie, go get help! She's not breathing."*

But I am breathing, I want to say. *Can't you see?*

I wake with a jolt. I'm still sitting at the kitchen counter. I must've fallen asleep.

"Hey, I remember you!" A girl shouts and points at me, a big grin breaking out on her face. Her voice is sobering and I suddenly feel wide awake. I stand up straight. I don't recognize her at all. "You're Jamie's friend, right?"

I was. I nod, a puzzling look crossing my face. I still don't remember her.

"Alex?" I nod again, and she walks closer to me. "Wow, this is so crazy! I'm Blue. Don't you remember me?"

No, I really don't.

"Yeah, I remember you," I say and nod again.

Blue grins. It's very clear she's drunk – I can smell the warm booze in her breath and the musky pot on her clothes. "I saw that video he made of you, the one you got in such a big fuss over. It's why Jamie's in jail, right?"

My blood runs cold. "What video?"

Blue frowns. "You don't remember? Hold on," She pulls her phone out of her bra and clicks around on it a few times. She hands me her phone and I look at the video and I *see* it.

It's them. It's all of them. And there's me. My eyes were rolled around in my head and I was sluggish and unresponsive, nearly unconscious. I don't remember any of that. What drug did they feed me? They paw at my breasts and clothes are ripped off, and I was incoherent the entire time. I don't remember any of this. Ice seeps through my veins and my brain buzzes and i. want. to. die.

"Jamie said it was your idea, that it was some big misunderstanding. I thought this was why those guys were in trouble," Blue is speaking, but I can't see her. I can't see anything. All that matters is that video and what they did to me. I feel disgusting. How have I been allowed to walk around and actually believe I'm doing better when they'd done *that* to me?

No.

No, no, no.

nonononononono

I run the other way. I shove through people. My brain is on fire but my body is ice. I don't see Luke. Someone shoves a cup of beer into my hands, and I guzzle it down. I refill it and see everyone around me laughing, and they're laughing *about the video.* I want to die. I keep refilling my cup and chugging more alcohol down. I walk into the living room. I see Luke, just as someone puts their phone in front of him. At first, he looks disgusted, then utter horror transforms his features as he looks up at me from the phone. I'm across the room, straight across from him. His mouth is open as he does a double-take from the video to me. His big sister. What a great role model.

He's disgusted with *me,* and rightfully so. That's why he doesn't come toward me. I stop in my tracks and look at him, just as bewildered as he is. A half-empty beer cup is in my right hand, and he sees it. I turn on my heel and run out of the room before I can see the disappointment on his face.

When I finally get out of the house, a van pulls up with a few drunk teenagers already inside and only more are piling in. I take my opportunity for escape and approach them.

"Where are you guys going?" I question. They're too drunk to recognize me.

"The Cliff. We're going to see if we can conjure up some ghosts." They all break into a fit of laughter, and a few of the guys tease the girls, making "ghost" noises. I know they're talking about Daniel, and it's like a knife to my heart.

"Can I come?" I manage to squeak out, seemingly calm.

"Sure," The driver shrugs. "Hop in."

So I do. Thankfully, there's alcohol in here. I chug everything they give me. By the time we reach the Cliff, I'm smashed. I want to fight somebody, but I keep it to myself. I keep drinking. I keep drinking. I keep drinking. I start laughing in the middle of their conversation.

"What's up with you?" One of them asks.

"It's my birthday," I say, giggling like an idiot.

"Oh, you're the girl that got Jamie in trouble. Happy birthday." He says it lightheartedly, like it was nothing, but it still cut off my laughing instantly.

They have a Ouija board and ask me if I want to play. I shake my head, because I don't trust my voice. My blood is pumping and my heart is hammering in my ears. Eventually, we reach our destination and the kids disperse into the woods to get a creepier feel. I stay back by the Cliff. I stare at the edge of it, where the Cliff meets the sky. I take out my phone and dial Luke's number. I've gotten six missed calls from him, four from Carlie, and ten texts from them both combined. *Funny how the moment I disappear, Carlie starts caring again.*

"Alex? Where are you?" He sounds so worried, it almost makes turn around and run back to him.

"Luke, listen to me," I slur. I don't think I can talk for much longer.

"Jesus, you're hammered. Where are you? I'm with Carlie; we'll come get you. Just tell us—"

"No!" I shout forcefully, swaying a bit. "Listen to me," I walk toward the edge. "I love you, Luke. You hear me? You've been the best goddamned brother I could've asked for. If anybody could've saved me, it would have been you. I'm sorry I wasn't a better sister."

My vision is going cloudy.

"Alex, you're scaring me. Please don't do anything stupid. I'm coming."

"Tell Carlie that she was a good best friend. Tell her that I know – I know she loved him too, in her own way. Tell her I'm sorry for being such a screw-up. I wish I could fix things between us, but tell her I love her anyway. Tell Mom I love her more than she could ever know. Don't let her blame herself, okay?"

"Alex, please," Luke is sobbing through the phone and I hear the rev of an engine in the background on his end. "Please don't do this. Just tell me where you are. I'll come get you and I'll take you home and we'll fix this. Don't leave me."

I squeeze my eyes together and choke back a sob. "I love you, Luke."

Then I hang up, and throw my phone into the ocean.

I stumble towards the edge of the Cliff, stumbling a few times. The edges of my vision are spotty with yellow stars, and I feel my knees giving out. I'm so close. So close to being back to him. Just a few more steps. I hear a few people shouting my name in the far distance, but I'm all alone out here. Standing on the very edge, I get a panoramic view of the ocean and the vast sky above me. My brain feels like it might explode, and the shouts are getting closer. I close my eyes. I spread my arms.

I collapse.

And my legs are free,

My arms are free,

My brain is free,

I'm free.

after

Luke is shaking me. His voice sounds underwater.

"Alex? Can you hear me? Alex, answer me," He's shouting over the music. I love this song. Somebody turns up the volume and turns down his voice. *The waves...*

"Luke," I try to say, then blink. Luke's face is gone, and Daniel is leaning over me and smirking.

"Alex," He speaks and that beautiful smile is back. He's the only who sounds real, and clear. I want to melt in his arms. I want to be with *him*. I want to be in the real world anymore.

"Alex!" I blink once more; Daniel's face has been replaced by Luke's. He's shouting and shaking me, then looks up past my head. I'm lying on the ground. When did I get on the ground? *"Carlie, go get help! She's not breathing."*

But I am breathing, I want to say. *Can't you see?*

"Alex, please wake up, please," Luke is sobbing over me and Carlie comes into my vision, kneeling beside me on the other side of Luke. She grabs my hand and squeezes, but I don't feel it. Tears stream down her face as she clenches her eyes shut.

I'M AWAKE! I want to scream, but my mouth and body won't move. Sirens blare in the near distance. There's no music. Just the waves. I can hear them crashing against the rocky bottom below us. I can't feel my body.

There's a lot of shouting, and Luke leaves my side. He's replaced by a man and a woman in scrub jumpsuits, with a Q.J.M.H. nametag and badge. They're probing around my body and I feel a sticky, thick liquid travel down my temple and drip on the stone beneath me. It tickles only slightly. I must be bleeding.

"We need you to hold on for us, honey," The woman says soothingly. I feel my eyelids shutting again.

"Her pulse is failing," The man says in a hurried voice. More paramedics cluster around me.

I want Luke back. If I could just see him, then I would be able to hold on. Where did he go? I hear him shouting to get back to me, but the paramedics keep holding him back. *No. I need him. Bring my brother back.*

"Honey, try to open your eyes. Stay with us..."

Silent snowflakes begin to fall around us. I imagine she says more, but I can't hear her because the darkness finally closes in on me and it feels oh-so-sweet.

before

Eighteen Years Old

I'm in the cemetery. My back is in the grass, and I'm staring up at the pale blue sky. It's summertime, but there's a cool breeze that blows the curls around my face and the hem of my dress around my thighs. It makes me smile. As I close my eyes and dig my toes into the soft soil, I hear music begin to play.

Someone's playing the piano. My eyes snap open, and I sit up slowly. Clair de Lune – Dad's favorite. Behind me, his gravestone. It would've freaked me out, normally, but I feel oddly serene. I stand up and look around. The breeze blows again, stirring my hair and tree branches. I follow the direction of the music.

"Dad?"

When he sees me, he smiles but continues playing. He's underneath a willow tree, his hair quietly rustling around in the wind.

"Hey, little astronaut. Come sit down."

He scoots over on the piano bench and I sit down next to him. He continues playing, even after the piece normally ends. He transitions into the chords of an Elliot Smith song.

I look around. "What are you doing here?"

He gives me a look. "I could ask you the same thing, Alexandria."

"I don't know. I just want to go home."

Dad shrugs. "So go home,"

Frowning, I say, "It's not that easy."

He stops playing and turns toward me. "Yes it is. All you have to do is let go."

"Of what?"

Dad shakes his head. "Not 'of what.' 'Of who.'"

Suddenly, I understand. "I can't. I can't let him go."

Slowly, he nods his head. "I know. But you have to. You have to let us both go." A tear slips out of my eye and he wipes it with his thumb. "Your mom and brother need you, Ally, now more than ever."

"But I miss you. I'm scared I'll forget," I sob.

"I know, honey," He smiles and hugs me. I'm stunned that I can actually feel him. It's first time I've hugged my father in four years. The keys keep moving, even after his fingers are no longer pressing them. "But you're still so young, Alex. You have so much more to accomplish, so much more beauty to see. It's important that you live." I wipe my tears silently. He nods his head behind my shoulder.

I turn around and see Daniel standing there, looking so healthy and so unbelievably handsome. His hair is pushed back out of his face; his skin color had returned to its normal tan color instead of a sickly pallor shade I remember. I stumble off the piano bench and run towards him, into his open arms.

Hugging him feels so... *real.* I've missed it so much. This doesn't feel like a crazy nightmare; it feels like a beautiful dream. I tighten my grip on him, only loosening it to pull back and kiss him. I feel his smile against my lips as he kisses me back. He cups my cheek and presses his forehead against mine.

"This is how I want to remember you," I whisper. "Not as a Blank. Not sad. Just like this."

He gives me a small smile. "I've missed you so much, Ally."

I whisper, "You destroyed who I was, Danny." But he doesn't let go, and neither do I.

"It'll stop hurting soon. I have to go now, Alex," He drops his arms and kisses me on the forehead, his soft lips brushing against my skin. "I love you."

I love you too.

after

I'm alive.

after

My name is Alexandria Lauren Sinclair. The people I love call me Ally. I am 18 years old. I am alive. I am breathing. That is enough for me.

Was it all just a dream?

after

Mom, Luke, Carlie, and Dr. Moore surround me. A machine beeps beside me, monitoring my heart rate. When I open my eyes, everything springs into action. Mom leaps to my bedside and flusters over me, asking how I feel, crying joyfully, calling for a nurse. A nurse rushes in and checks my vitals, then says things like, "You've been through quite a lot, honey." *Yeah, no shit, lady.*

"How do you feel? Are you thirsty? Hungry? Do you remember anything?" Mom bombards me with questions.

I shake my head. "Luke," I say. A cluster of doctors, nurses, and people have gathered around me, blocking Luke from my view. My voice comes out small and strained and at first I don't think anyone heard me, but then Luke shoves through them all and throws his arms around my neck.

I breathe a heavy sigh of relief as I wrap my arms under his arms. I feel the moisture from his tears against my neck, and I hold him tighter.

"I'm so sorry," I whisper in his ear. He shakes his head against my neck but doesn't say anything, just tightens his grip.

We're at an awkward angle because I'm still in bed hooked up to these machines, and he's so tall and lanky. Eventually, we have to pull away, but he stays right by my side. Carlie comes over slowly, with her arms folded across her chest. She looks scared, and her eyes are red and puffy. Her expression is the one that makes me cry the hardest. I was such a shitty best friend. She wraps her arms around my neck and I, too, feel the moisture from her tears against my shoulder.

"If you weren't hooked up to all these damn machines I would punch you in the face right now," She says quietly to me.

And I can't help it, but I actually breathe out a laugh.

"I'm sorry," I tell her as well.

"Don't ever even *think* about leaving me all alone in this shitty town again," I breathe out a laugh again. "I'm sorry I ignored you."

"It's okay. I understand."

She pulls away and stands next to Luke, right at my side. The doctors bombard me with a series of medical terms and questions. I never actually reached the edge of the Cliff; I had passed out before that could happen due to all the alcohol. Carlie and Luke found me with my legs and arms hanging off the Cliff, completely passed out. I woke up later, briefly, and they were forced to pump my stomach. I remember none of this. They said I was lucky that I fell backward and not forward. They said I was lucky to be alive. They do a few tests just to make sure my brain is still okay. They tell me I've got a black eye from hitting my head, with a nasty gash right above it.

Every day, Mom tells me how sorry she is for leaving me alone. Her guilt has nothing on mine.

Dr. Moore and I delve deeper into our therapy, and the only way the hospital will release me is if I spend a month in a live-in therapy program. Dr. Moore calls it a recovery program, but it's really a nuthouse. The night before I'm scheduled to leave, Luke sits at my bedside long after the sun has set. Mom is sleeping in the hospital recliner in the corner, and we finally convinced Carlie to go home.

"Are you ashamed of me?" I ask Luke quietly, knowing that he's still awake.

"No. I could never be ashamed of you, Alex. What happened… what they did to you… it's not your fault. It never was."

I disagree, but I don't argue with him. I say, quietly, "I thought I was dead."

"Me too."

Hearing the strain in his voice, I decide to keep the hallucinations to myself. "I'm sorry I put you through that."

Luke shrugs, then his face hardens. "Don't do ever do that to me again, Alex. Please."

Tears threaten to spill from my eyes, but they stay. I swallow thickly. "I won't."

"Promise me." His voice cracks.

"I promise." It comes out as a whisper, but I mean it.

after

The first hearing of the rape case is today, and is continuing despite my impromptu trip to the hospital. The video I saw that night is now a piece of evidence.

I sit in a wooden bench across from the closed double doors I will soon be walking through to face Jamie. The crowd inside has already gathered; all they're waiting on now is the judge, and me. For over a year, we've been preparing for this. Still, I'm not ready. But was I ever going to be? I hear my lawyer's expensive dress shoes clacking down the hallway, toward me.

He slows as he approaches me, then sits down next to me. Together, we stare at the double doors. I chew on the inside of my cheek nervously.

"I think it's time to go in, kid," My lawyer says next to me.

I nod and stand up. "Yeah,"

Slowly, I walk the few feet forward until I'm standing right in front of the closed doors. "Yeah, it's time." I whisper to myself. Taking a deep breath, I walk in.

after

Two Months Later

After picking up my diploma at the school, I decide to drive back out into the woods. I've finally graduated high school. Carlie, Mike, Luke, and I plan to go out to dinner tonight to celebrate.

As I'm driving, I roll down all the windows of my car and let the wind blow my hair around. Music blasts from my speakers, and I have to pull my hair into a ponytail to keep it from getting caught in my sunglasses. The sun shines bright today, making all the evergreens look tall and inviting as I drive along the deserted country highway through them.

These days, grief doesn't control me as it used to. I still have anxiety, but it's manageable. A few days ago, Jack, the boy from the winter formals a year ago, called me. He told me he was sorry things got so crazy at the dance, and if I'm willing, he'd love to go out with me sometime. I told him that would be wonderful.

The quaint log cabin in the middle of the woods looks exactly how I pictured it. I pull up, my tires crunching over the old gravel driveway, and cut the engine. Taking a deep breath, I get out and start to walk toward the front door. They may not even be home, but it was worth a shot. Knocking on the door, I remove my sunglasses and shove them into my back pocket. I straighten my shirt self-consciously, fidgeting. I hear laughing inside, as if there's a gathering of some sort.

Suddenly, the door opens and there she is – Penny, dressed in a casual dress with her hair braided back. Her smile fades infinitesimally when she sees me, but grows again when she registers who I am.

"Hi," I start, my voice cracking with nervousness. I clear my throat. "I hope I'm not... disturbing anything."

Penny gives me a knowing smile and shakes her head. Behind her, kids and adults flutter about, all looking related. The scent of grilled food wafts through the open door.

"I just wanted to thank you and Arthur for testifying at the trial. I know you couldn't be there for the verdict, but they all got put away. Jamie got 15 years with probation."

Penny's eyes sparkle and her smile grows.

"I'm sorry for not coming by sooner. I'm really thankful for all you and Arthur did for me. It was just really painful to come back here. I don't... I don't know what would've happened to me if you hadn't found me that day." My voice breaks a bit, but I quickly recover.

"I know, Alex," She speaks, and her voice is warm and loving. "You don't have to apologize for that. We're proud of you."

I smile at her. "Thank you."

"Mom, who's this?" A middle-aged blonde pokes her head around Penny's shoulders. She looks startlingly similar to Penny, and she looks at me with kind eyes.

"This is Alex, dear," Penny explains. "Alex, this is my daughter, Kate."

"Nice to meet you," I say, smiling shyly.

"Alex was just coming for Arthur's party, dear. You can stay, can't you, Alex?" Penny asks. It must be his birthday. They both look at me expectantly.

"Yeah," I answer quietly, shocked and warmed by her invite. "Yeah, I can stay."

Penny and Arthur's children and grandchildren are vibrant with life and unique in their own way, not surprisingly. When he sees it was me at the door, he rises from his seat at the breakfast table and takes me into a long hug.

They make up a story for how they really got to know me, saying I was a volunteer at the hospital or something. Apparently, despite being retired, Penny still volunteers there. I didn't know she was in the medical profession before. Her daughter, Kate, welcomes me and introduces me to her many kids of all ages and genders. She has a newborn baby, whom she named Penelope, after her mother.

The family shows no blatant affection towards one another. Instead, they all have a certain familiarity and closeness. They poke fun at each other and laugh freely. Arthur, being the patriarch, is the loudest and funniest of the gang.

"I'm old!" He explains to me, defending himself. "I can say whatever I want!"

Penny, Arthur, and I sit around the breakfast table, just like we did once way back when. They supply sweet tea and laughter.

"So, you're a high school graduate now, yeah?" Arthur asks.

"Yeah," I smile.

"What are your plans?"

"I'm gonna go to Boston for college. My best friend, Carlie, is going to USC, so the distance will be hard. But we'll try to see each other whenever we can. My mom's job gave her a huge promotion, so she'll be moving farther down the coast with my brother."

"What are you going to study?"

"Astronomy."

"Really? What got you into that?"

"My dad," I smile with the memory. "He was really into that stuff, and I fell in love with it."

"That's awesome, Alex," Penny says with a smile.

I grin. "Thanks."

"You'll have to send us post cards from Boston," Arthur jokes. "That's where Penny and I met."

"So, what happened to the other boys from the trial? Penny told me the ring leader got 15 years with probation, but what about the others?"

"Well, Jamie got such a long sentence because they pinned him with a bunch of other drug crimes, so that was added onto his sentence. And then another boy got 10 years with parole for rape, drug possession, assault, et cetera. The other boys weren't videotaped raping me, but they all sent it to their friends, so they got five years for child pornography."

By now, I'm used to saying it all. I've come to terms with it all. Frankly, that's the only part of the story that I'm happy telling.

"Good. They all deserve to rot there. Those boys shouldn't have even gotten parole." Arthur blurts the sentence out unabashedly.

"Arthur," Penny chastises.

"It's okay," I chuckle at her. "I feel the same way, Arthur."

"How are you doing, dear?"

"I'm..." I pause, considering the question. "Good. I'm good. I'm ready to start my life." I grin at them.

We continue to talk about my future and their past. As the sun sets and the crowd begins to disperse, I start to look at their family pictures. A new photograph of little Penelope with a bow on her head hangs on the wall proudly.

When I drive home, I sing along to the radio and beat my hands against the steering wheel in tune with the beat. I feel the music push its way through my soul and pour out of my mouth. I am happy.

Epilogue

It is my 19th birthday. I stand on Jack's apartment balcony. In my peripheral vision, I see him come up to me and wrap his arms around my waist from behind as I watch the city below. He kisses the top of my head.

Carlie couldn't make the trip from USC, but it's okay. I'm surrounded by the new friends I made my first year of college and my family. Luke is so grown up and handsome; he'll be graduating high school this year. He has a new girlfriend now – a nice one. She's here, too.

"So, is this a good birthday?" Jack asks softly in my ear. I can hear the smirk in his voice and I smile in response.

"Yes," I crane my neck to look at him behind me. "One of the best."

His grin deepens. I hear Mom approach us. "Alex?"

I turn around to look at her, but Jack keeps a hand on my back. "Yeah?"

"I have something for you. One last birthday present."

Looking over at Jack—who is clueless—I follow her over to the door of the apartment. She digs through her purse and produces a faded white envelope with my name scrawled on it. It's not her handwriting, but it's familiar.

"I was supposed to give this to you on your 18th birthday, but with everything that happened, I just didn't have time..." She trails off. "It's a letter from your dad. I thought about giving it to you over the years, but he made me promise when you were born..." Once more, her voice falters.

Utterly entranced, I stare at the envelope in her hands. Its crisp whiteness has faded into a cream color over the years. Tentatively, I grab it from her hands. Jack joins everyone else inside as I walk back out onto the patio, never taking my eyes off the letter. I sit down and carefully open it, trying to preserve the paper.

To my beautiful, radiant baby girl,

After nine months and four, painful days of waiting, you are finally with us. Healthy and happy, just as we'd imagined you to be. I swear, I thought your mother was going to pull you out herself during those last four days. We were very anxious to meet you.

When I first laid my eyes on you, I knew that instant that you were the most beautiful, precious thing I had ever seen. You opened your wide, blue eyes, looked up at me, and wrapped your impossibly-small fingers around my thumb. That moment I just knew: I'm in trouble. It's going to be a long time until you understand this, little one; but when you have children, your entire world view shifts. It no longer becomes about your needs and wants. Suddenly, you realize that your whole heart is walking around in another (albeit, tiny) human's body. The love your mother and I feel for you is unconditional, unending, boundless.

Yesterday, you were born, but I am writing this for your 18th birthday. Officially, you are an adult. You'll be going to college soon... Or not. The world is yours, angel, starting right now. Never forget that. Again, officially you're an adult, but you'll always be my baby girl. (I'm sure we'd have already bashed heads together on that one.)

Sitting here, thinking about all the memories you'll have made by then, and all the memories you have yet to make... Well, it brings tears to my eyes. Happy tears.

I hope you know it pains me, as your father, to write this paragraph. But, it must be said. One day, you're going to meet a boy with a cute smile and muscles and you're going to think you love him. Plenty of people do it, and more power to them, but try to remember that high school is not where you will find your Prince Charming. Your Prince Charming will not just have a cute smile, he will be able to make you laugh your hardest on the bad days, the worst days, the days where all you feel like doing is giving up — not just the good days. Your Prince Charming will not just have muscles; he will make you feel safe; he will make you feel warm; he will protect you against the other men who are not as kind as him. You will not just think you love him; you will know it with your whole heart, mind, and soul. Relationships take a lot of hard work, my love. If you find yourself to be only giving and not receiving, it will not matter how much you love him. You should never, ever settle for less than what you deserve. Know that it will hurt when things end. But also know that you will live. In your lifetime, you will have so many great loves and it'll feel like the world is falling apart when they come to an end. Only when you find yourself old and gray will you realize who your true love was. Remember that you were beautiful before he noticed.

Sex doesn't make you an adult. 'Nuff said.

Don't sweat the small stuff, kid. Your world will not implode if you fail a test, or if you get detention for talking in class. If you're tired, sleep. If you're hungry, eat. If you're happy, dance around your bedroom and tell the people you love that you love them. Mental health will always come before a piece of paper.

Never, ever choose a boy over your friends.

Be brave. Even if you're not, pretend to be. No one can tell the difference.

You were not made to sit quietly in the corner. You were not made to be merely "content." You were made to move mountains. You were made to experience adventure, always — whether that adventure is going on a late-night grocery run to a place you've never been with someone you enjoy, or backpacking across a different continent. Don't settle just because it's easy.

You were made to do difficult things — believe in yourself.

We have brought you into this world with so much happiness, so much love, it's hard to imagine how you could ever experience pain or sadness, but you will. You're a phoenix, and you will rise from the ashes. Eat ice cream if it makes you feel better; go dancing if it makes you feel better; scream if it makes you feel better.

Sometimes, the world is not a kind place. Sometimes, it is very, very cruel. Sometimes, life kicks you when you're down. Sometimes, bad things happen to good people with no rhyme or reason. And just when you think you can't handle anymore, just when you think you might give up, more shit gets thrown at you and you survive through that, too. You pick yourself up, and you keep fighting.

Your father or not, I am a male, and we are profoundly dumb. When I make mistakes (and I will), try to remember that I could only ever want what's best for you.

I love you, little Alex. Whatever you do in life, never forget that.

Sincerely,

Dad

Tears plop down on the pages, smudging the words etched in ink in his handwriting. I hold his letter to my chest, which the closest I can come to having him here with me.

All around me, the sun sets in brilliant colors on the Boston skyline.

About the Author

Jillian Szweda is currently a high school student in her rural, northern Indiana hometown. When she isn't writing, she enjoys making people laugh, playing golf, and hanging out with her younger brother. This is her first novel.